THE GIFT OF DEATH

By Joyce Elaine

First paperback edition November 2021

ISBN 9798762444644

Dedicated to everyone who struggles to finish something they started and to those who never turned their back on their passions.

PART ONE

Chapter 1

Sara tensed as Thomas Sharver came out of Dr. Simms's office. She never knew which Thomas she was going to get. Sometimes he was quiet, sometimes he said something crude to her, and sometimes he was pleasant. She only had to deal with the clients once their session was over. Most of the clients were okay. Their problems were just everyday problems that they needed help dealing with. Issues such as divorces, family relationship problems, and mental disorders. Some of the clients, though, like Thomas, had so many screws loose that she didn't think Dr. Simms would ever be able to help them. Thomas walked up to her desk and just smiled at her. His smile alone gave her the creeps, but something about him made her want to hide under her desk with a blanket covering her, like a child who is afraid of the bogeyman. "Good to see you again, Mr. Sharver," she lied.

"I'm sure," Thomas responded as his smile turned into a frown.

"Do you need to set up another appointment?" She wanted to get him away from her as quickly as possible.

"You know? I don't think I need therapy anymore. I think I'm healed." He chuckled.

"So no appointment then?" She didn't feel like playing his game this afternoon.

"I'd rather set up a date with you. I could make you a rich woman."

Sara rolled her eyes. She knew it was a mistake but she couldn't help it.

Thomas clenched his teeth. "Do you think I'm a joke?"

"No, sir." She answered without looking at him.

"I told you before, I'd love to hire you. All you'd have to do is please me and my coworkers and keep your mouth shut. You'd make a lot of money for doing such an easy job. That attitude of yours would have to go, though."

"And I've told you before that I'm not interested in your offer." She kept her tone quiet but stern. She refrained from clenching her teeth, so instead of her response sounding powerful it sounded more on the snotty side.

Thomas was feeling frisky today. He came around to her side of the desk. She jumped up and put herself up against the wall. She was trapped. "Sir, you're not allowed back here."

"I'm allowed to be anywhere I want." He got in her face and placed his fingers around her throat. "I'm allowed to do anything I want." He wasn't squeezing her neck but he had a good grip on her.

Sara held her breath and tried to look Thomas in the eyes. Being intimidating was not her style. Looking into his eyes made her more frightened than she already was so she looked away, over at the doctors' closed office doors. She began shaking as she hoped that one of them would come out and save her.

Krystal was sitting in the waiting room and saw everything that was taking place. She jumped up and went through the door that separated the waiting room from Sara's desk, just as Sara was about to start screaming for help.

"Is there a problem here?" Krystal asked as if she had some sort of authority.

Thomas laughed at her. He let go of Sara's throat and backed away from her. He walked past Krystal and answered her, "No problem, doll." He winked at her as he left the reception area and went out the door.

Chapter 2

Two hours later, Drew Foster headed northbound on Route 29. He had been hired to do a job, and he stole the SUV he was driving, along with the New Jersey tags, to carry it out. Even though Drew was no stranger to breaking the law – in more ways than one – he still felt nervous when he was doing something that could get him in a lot of trouble. But he kept on doing it because once he got away with something, nothing compared to the feeling of accomplishment. It was a high for him. It was better than any drugs or alcohol and almost better than getting your jollies off – almost.

This job had him the most nervous he'd ever been. There was so much to lose if something went wrong. He had to watch his speed and not drive recklessly. If he were to be stopped by the 5-0, he'd be arrested on the spot for driving a stolen car with stolen tags. Then there was the actual job itself that had his balls shriveling up into little grapes. He was to use this big SUV as a sort of weapon. The mission was to kill. Killing was nothing new to him. He'd murdered a few people over the years. After the first one, it was no big deal. You lose your soul, and once that's gone you can do anything and not feel bad about it. Killing was another form of addiction to him now. It made him feel powerful. He always performed his jobs sober. Actually, he lived his life sober. Drugs and alcohol were never on his list of favorite things and he had a rule to never touch them. He wanted to be able to complete his jobs as quickly and as easily as possible and get paid. Even more so, he *wanted* to remember the jobs. The feeling he got from hurting or killing someone and getting away with it was a feeling he wished he could feel all day and every day. He was naturally crazy. His crazy didn't come from a bottle or a pill. It came from within. He didn't even do it for the money – which was very rewarding – he'd do it for free if he didn't need money to survive. This job though…one wrong turn, literally, and he'd be dead himself. He had to plan it out very carefully.

This job really had his stomach in knots and in his twisted and sick way, he was enjoying every second of it. The guy who hired him to do the job was pretty well known in the criminal world and probably crazier than Drew. However, the boss was on a personal mission. Drew hadn't figured out the connection between his boss and the next few jobs he'd been hired to do, but he knew that it wasn't "business as usual" for his boss. Not this job anyway. His boss wouldn't tell him anything about why he needed these jobs done, and that was just fine with Drew because the less he knew, the better. He did tell him it wasn't for the business; it was for his own personal reasons. He told Drew that everything he's done for the past few years has been building up to this and it was time to give his payback on a personal matter. That was all Drew knew. That and he was getting paid enough money for this job and the three to follow for him to live comfortably and to never have to work again if he didn't want to. He knew he'd still want to "work" but he didn't want to mess these jobs up. If he did, he knew he'd be a dead guy, and being dead would not be good for him. He believed in hell and knew he was going straight there after his life was over, but he wasn't ready for it yet. He had more people to torture first. His thought was that one day, the "high" would no longer exist and he'd be able to quit without ever being caught and be able to retire on some tropical island. Sipping fruity, pansy-ass drinks and having bisexual orgies with people he'd hire just to fuck him and keep him satisfied was his plan once the "high" of killing wore off. If it ever did. He fantasized being seventy years old and still fucking like an eighteen-year-old

4

and having so many people wanting to be with him because of his money.

His cell phone rang. He glanced down at the screen; the boss was calling. He picked up the cell phone and put it to his ear – another law being broken, but talking on a cell phone while driving was no big deal compared to the other charges he'd get if this didn't go according to plan. "Hey, boss!"

"Where are you?" There were no hellos with this guy, and Drew knew that but he didn't care. He still had to show his respect and admiration for him, and man-oh-man was he a good-looking guy. Drew wouldn't mind having a few minutes alone with him. Drew totally forgot he had been asked a question, as he began fantasizing about being on that tropical island with his boss, who was down on his knees and sucking him off for a job well done.

"I asked you a mother fuckin' question! Are you there, stupid?" the boss shouted in Drew's ear, bringing him back to reality.

"Sorry, boss," Drew answered. "I had to put the phone down for a second, a cop was passing me and I didn't want to be caught." A little bit of a lie, of course. A cop had passed him but he didn't put his phone down, but lies came naturally for Drew. In fact, he was so good at lying that his boss believed him.

"Well, I'm glad you're being careful," he said, calmer now. "Whereabouts are you?"

Drew looked at the green sign he was approaching. "I'm on route twenty-nine, just now passing route thirty-two."

The boss knew exactly where he was. "Good! Perfect!" he said happily.

Music to Drew's ears.

"Listen to me carefully. The doctor is headed southbound on twenty-nine. She's about three miles away from you. I'm behind her

5

but I'm a few cars back so don't hit me. She's driving a black Toyota Camry and her tag number is DBL198. I know you're headed northbound so I'm going to need you to get over on the south side and face the wrong way. You are to be facing oncoming traffic. Do you understand this?"

"Yes, I do," Drew answered as he turned into an "emergency vehicles only" lane. "I just got onto the side of the southbound lanes and I'm facing the wrong way," he told his boss. "I just hope no cops show up before she does."

"There are no more cops in the area; I can assure you of that. The one that just passed you took the next exit. I've got my scanner on and you'll be fine if you do this fast and swiftly. As luck would have it, she's in the right lane and there's not much traffic. You must be sure that you hit her and only her. After you do, get out of the car as quickly as possible and Jack will be right there to scoop you up."

"Douche Bag? Really? You know I can't stand him!"

"I don't care!" the boss shouted. "He's the only one with balls to do this job so you'll have to deal with him. I'm behind him and I'm watching you two. Don't screw this up or I'll have you both killed within minutes."

Drew knew he meant that too. He had seen it happen before, right in front of his very own eyes. Drew couldn't understand why he wanted to off the doctor by staging a car accident. He knew the boss wanted to make it seem random but there were other ways to accomplish this. They could have mugged her while she was walking to her car from her office and just shoot her. That would have been easier and much cleaner than this. This way was dangerous and there were too many mistakes he could make. He wasn't going to screw this up though. His eyesight was twenty-twenty and he could see far distances better than most people. "I got this, boss," he said as he hung up. He felt the target coming. He

6

knew the car he was looking for was close. He could feel it rise up in the pit of his stomach and into his chest. He began shaking and sweating a little bit. It was showtime and he felt like he was going to vomit, but he loved that feeling.

Not even a minute later, Drew saw the approaching Toyota Camry. It was easy for him to spot because he himself drove a Camry. He verified the tag number, put on his seatbelt, and put the SUV in drive. He saw there was no one in front of the Camry and the two left lanes were mostly clear as well. This was going to be easier than he thought. He was reminded of the first time he ever killed someone. It was fifteen years ago, he was only twenty years old, and he didn't think he'd be able to shoot the person in the head. He did though, and it was the euphoria that he seemed to get from that first time that kept him coming back for more. It seemed that the harder the job was, the bigger the lasting effect was. So he knew this one was going to leave a resonating vibe within him for a while. He made sure his seatbelt was fastened tight, pulled the belt from his chest and released it so it would be tighter to his chest, gripped the steering wheel, and inhaled a big breath. He held it for a few seconds and slowly released it.

"All right, pretty lady. I hope you aren't paying too much attention. Don't make any sudden moves and this will be a painless and quick death," Drew said out loud to himself. After the last car that was in front of the Camry passed, Drew pulled out onto the highway so fast that his tires squealed. He had to go across the two left lanes before he reached the right lane. He swiftly pulled out in front of a car and missed it by a mere inch. The car blew its horn in an attempt to alert Drew. He laughed at them and yelled, "Whoops! Am I going the wrong way?" He laughed with a mixture of more pleasure than nervousness. His eyes became focused and fixed on the Camry. He smiled as the Camry advanced closer and closer to him. He didn't see anything or anyone else around him. It was just him and the Camry playing a game of chicken, only the Camry didn't know it was playing. His smile crept into a grin and then more laughter as it felt like his entire body was going to explode before impact even came. His right foot stomped on the accelerator and he once again held his breath.

He sped up in front of the Camry. He had reached a speed of eighty-five and was approaching ninety and braced for the impact. The lady did just what he was hoping she'd do. She swerved to the right, where there was nothing but a guardrail and no other cars, and as she did that, he hit the driver side door – right where she was sitting.

"Bull's-eye!" Drew shouted as his airbags deployed. For a quick second his mind raced to see if he had any injuries. He didn't hit his head on anything, his arms and legs were moving just fine and he was still alert and conscious. He fought off the airbag, unhooked his seatbelt, and quickly got out of the SUV. At first he thought he wouldn't be able to move his legs – they felt like rubber – but the blood started rushing through them and he realized he was fine. He was good to go! Another SUV had pulled around Dr. Simms's car and came to a quick stop. Drew hopped in and yelled, "Drive, douche bag! Drive!"

Douche Bag (aka Jack) took off with the sound of squealing tires as he looked in his rearview mirror to see a chain reaction of cars hitting one another while trying to avoid the Camry. "Holy shit!" Jack exclaimed. "We pulled it off."

"No, douche bag!" Drew said. "I pulled it off!"

Drew's cell phone rang. It was the boss and he was happy.

"You two meet me at our spot, but tell that douche bag of yours to slow down. We don't need you two getting pulled over right now. You guys have a huge payout coming your way. I couldn't have made that go any better than what it did."

Drew hung up again without saying goodbye. "What did he say?" Douche Bag asked.

"He said to fuckin' slow down! We don't need to be pulled over right now. Drive like a sane person before you draw attention to us!"

Jack did as he was told and slowed down to the speed limit as he moved over into the right lane. Knowing Drew was more powerful than him, he just mumbled, "You don't have to be such an asshole about it."

"You don't have to act like you don't have any common sense!"

"I fuckin' hate working with you," Jack replied a bit more confidently.

"Don't worry, feeling's mutual!"

"Well then maybe I should just stop the car and let you out!"

"Maybe you should just shut the fuck up! Look, we have to meet him at the spot so we can torch this car and then we have to go back to the office. He said we have a huge payout coming!"

"Great!" Jack said and then laughed. Not just because they had a big payout coming but because their little fight didn't escalate into something more. He was a bit terrified of Drew.

Drew joined in with the laughing. The high he was on right now couldn't be topped. He no longer felt like he was going to vomit. Instead, he felt like he just got away with murder. His head was way up in the clouds and nothing and no one could harsh his mellow. All he needed now was a blow job, and he was sure that the boss would have a hot blonde with big knockers waiting for him; that's how the boss rolled. That's how the boss took care of them after performing a job. Things like that were considered "bonuses" in his world.

Chapter 3

Dr. Simms had been in her car driving down Route 29 from her office in Columbia to her home in Maple Lawn. She had been a resident of Maryland her entire life. Last year, after her divorce, she had contemplated moving out of state. The only family she had left was one sister and one brother who both had left the area years ago. Her sister was in Massachusetts and her brother was in Virginia. Both were married with kids. Dr. Simms and her husband had never had kids, because they both were too focused on their careers. Her father died in a car accident when she was still in high school, and she lost her mom three years ago to cancer. She knew she could be a counselor anywhere in the world but she hadn't left Maryland yet. She couldn't leave her clients. She had too many people that relied on her to help them. Krystal, for example, was one of them. She had just had her monthly session with her. She was a good kid but her high energy got in her way sometimes. She had been working with Krystal since she was fourteen, and she was now twenty-three. She had watched her grow up. She had gotten to know her and her wonderful parents. She knew the time would come when Krystal wouldn't need her anymore, but she had a feeling that it wouldn't be any time soon. She felt a deep connection to Krystal and her parents.

She knew she could never tell anyone this. For starters, if she did, she might be told that she needed psychological help. It's a dangerous line when you are too connected to your clients. She didn't want anyone, especially her boss, thinking there was some sort of countertransference going on. Secondly, she didn't want to scare Krystal away. She firmly believed that her client relationships should be kept on a professional level and should never cross over into the "friend" category. It was still different with Krystal and her family, though. She almost felt like a long-lost relative when speaking with them. It was hard for her to stay professional with them, as her initial reaction was always to hug them and speak to them like family members. It seemed to her that she was supposed to be in their life for a reason. It was almost as if some outside force had made sure that they connected and stayed connected.

Dr. Simms was lost in all of her thoughts about Krystal and her family, and maybe that's why she didn't notice the car that was driving the wrong way. She also didn't notice that it was headed straight for her at a speed that seemed way beyond the speed limit. By the time she realized what was about to happen, it was almost too late. She screamed out loud and attempted to steer her car out of the way. Unfortunately she steered her car to the right, so the oncoming car ended up nailing her right on the driver-side door as she went toward the guardrail. She hit the guardrail, and between that impact and being hit by the SUV, her airbags deployed. The last thing Dr. Simms saw before her lights went out was a big black SUV with tinted windows. Luckily her lights would come back on, but she would have no recollection of the car that hit her.

Chapter 4

Krystal Jennings had just gotten back from her therapy appointment with Dr. Simms. She enjoyed the sessions with her. She was sometimes reckless with her decisions and did things without thinking about them first. It seemed the older she got, the worse it got, but Dr. Simms helped to keep her grounded. She pointed out how Krystal's shortcomings affected specific situations, made her explore why she did whatever it was that she did, and how she could handle similar situations that may arise in the future. She appreciated that Dr. Simms acknowledged that she didn't want to be on medication for her high energy. She worked with her to find ways to keep the energy under control. She exercised every day, took boxing classes (which really helped), and when she had time, she and her father went jogging together. He had recently gotten her to sign up for self-defense classes and she was really enjoying those as well. Her father was a lieutenant for the Maryland State Police, so he was always looking for ways to make sure his daughter was protected from the "animals" he locked up on a daily basis.

"Hey, Dad," Krystal said as she walked in the door. "Are we going jogging?"

"Just waiting for you," Paul answered as he grabbed his right leg and pulled his foot up to his butt.

"Just let me get changed really quick. Is Mom home this evening?"

"She should be here any minute. I think she said something about going out for dinner tonight."

"Can I bring Trent?"

"Of course. Go get changed, I'm ready to make you eat my dust."

Krystal laughed at her father as she ran upstairs to her room. Even though it was the summer before her last year of college, she didn't mind living with her parents. She was an only child, had her own room and her own bathroom, and paid rent every month. Of course, she and her boyfriend Trent had been talking about moving in together. They had only been together for six months but she already knew she loved him. He was the best guy she had ever dated. Not only was he easy on the eyes, but he also treated her really well. She figured she'd finish her undergraduate program earning her BA degree in psychology, and move in with Trent and begin her life as an adult. It sounded so easy and simple on paper and in her thoughts, but it wasn't. She had a rough time getting through her college classes due to not being able to stay focused. She spent a lot of her time with a tutor, who helped her study for exams. Although Krystal loved Trent, Dr. Simms cautioned her about moving too quickly with him. Many times she doubted herself and her feelings for him, but all it took was one look at him for her to forget her doubts. She often wished she could keep Dr. Simms at her side at all times to keep herself from making any mistakes. What Krystal portrayed – courage and stability – was unmatched with what was inside of her – chaos and confusion.

She texted Trent to invite him for dinner, got changed, and then ran downstairs and told her father she was ready. They went out the door and began running down their driveway. Their usual routine was to jog down to the end of the neighborhood, cross over into the next neighborhood, which was a mile-long loop, jog that twice, and then head home. Sometimes they'd race each other on the way home. They didn't know they had eyes following them today.

"So how are things going with Trent?" Paul asked her. He always loved jogging with Krystal because it gave them time to chat about life.

14

"Really good, actually. We've been talking about moving in together once I finish my classes up."

"Do you really think that's a good idea?"

"Why not? We get along really well."

"But that sometimes changes when you move in together and start splitting bills. Sometimes it causes problems."

"Dad, I know you're a little unsure of Trent, but you should know that I'm a good judge of character. He's one of the good guys."

"I do trust your judgment, but, you know, no guy will ever be good enough for my daughter."

Krystal smiled.

Paul flinched quietly to himself. He didn't like lying to Krystal. Trent seemed like a good guy but it always seemed forced to Paul. It seemed like he was being a fake nice. Paul thought that the phrase "too good to be true" described Trent perfectly. Of course, Krystal always rushed into everything, and moving so fast with Trent was another example of that.

They had just crossed into the next neighborhood when a car that had been parked on the side of the street roared into life. The windows were tinted so they were unable to see the driver.

Paul and Krystal made sure to move to the other side of the road. Just as they were getting comfortable in their new position, the car came barreling toward them. Out of instinct, Paul shoved Krystal onto the lawn of the house they were passing. Paul himself jumped out of the way at the very last second. The car came within inches of taking Paul out. It screeched tires and took off out of the neighborhood.

Paul made a mental note of the make and model of the car – a newer model yellow Ford Mustang. He squinted so he could get a good look at the license plate.

15

"What the fuck was that?" Krystal yelled as she jumped up and began chasing after the car. She didn't like being bullied, and her spitfire personality sprang into action. She tried with everything she had to catch up to the car but it was going way too fast. Paul, on the other hand, had been typing the tag number into his phone before he forgot it. He knew Krystal would never catch up with the car. It was already out of sight before she even got to her feet. He wasn't happy that she took off running like that, though. That was another example of how she was reckless at times and no matter how much Dr. Simms worked with her on it, she just didn't seem to grasp the whole "think before you react" thing.

He watched with a disapproving look as Krystal jogged back toward him. He knew she was an adult but he still felt the need to scold her for running off like that. That would have to wait for a minute, though, because he was currently calling his boss, Captain Zitzer. "Sir, I need you to run a tag for me. Some asshole just tried to run me and my daughter over."

"Are you guys okay?" Captain Zitzer asked with concern in his voice. They worked well together and were actually friends outside of work.

"We're okay. The tag number was JJK789."

"Give me one second."

Krystal was back with her father. "Are you okay, Dad?"

"I am. Are you?"

"I don't know. My wrist hurts a bit," she said as she held it out in front of her and began inspecting it. The adrenaline had taken over and she hadn't noticed at first that her left wrist was throbbing. She had a hard time moving it and there was a sharp pain that seemed to be getting worse.

Paul softly grabbed her arm with his free hand and looked at it. Had Krystal been a child, this would have been the moment that he would have kissed her boo-boo to make it better. "Shit," he said. "It might be broken, it doesn't look straight."

"Fuck!" Krystal said.

"Honey, I'm sorry. If I hadn't have pushed you, you wouldn't have hurt your wrist."

"It's okay. If you hadn't have pushed me, I'd probably be in a lot worse shape than I am now. He could have hit me. I thought for sure he was going to hit you after you took until the last second to jump out of the way. That was a close call, Dad!"

"Paul?" It was Captain Zitzer.

"Yes! What do you have for me?"

"Nothing. That car was reported stolen earlier this morning. Did you see the driver?"

"Negative. Windows tinted."

"Well, do you think it was personal or just someone goofing off?"

"I'm not sure. It felt personal. I need to get off here and call my wife. I think Krystal broke her wrist when she fell from me pushing her out of the way."

"Geezus! You take it easy. I'll see you tomorrow."

"Thank you, sir," he replied. Then he turned back to Krystal. "I'm going to call your mom so she can pick us up."

"Dad, I can walk back home. My legs aren't broken."

"That may be, but your mom's a nurse. She'll know what to do. Besides, who knows if this idiot will come back around to try again."

"I think it was just some dumb kid being stupid. I don't think they're gonna come back."

"Better safe than sorry. Speaking of which, what in the hell were you trying to prove by running after that car? What if they had a gun?"

"I was willing to take my chances. Just another reason that I think it was some dumb kid. A coward!"

"Dumb kids and cowards have guns too, you know!"

Paul called Laura, his wife, and asked her to come get them. Just as he hung up with her, they saw the yellow Ford Mustang coming back.

The car stopped right in front of them and revved the engine. Both Paul and Krystal were standing in someone's yard, out of the road. Paul suddenly felt like he was in that movie where the car comes alive and runs over people, killing them.

"Krystal, call nine-one-one," he said as he slowly started moving toward the car.

"Why? What're you going to do? You don't even have your gun on you. Please don't go toward that car, Dad!"

Paul stopped and looked at his daughter. She was clearly frightened. "I may not have my gun but I'm still a cop and my number-one job is to protect."

"Yeah, with nothing to protect yourself!"

"I got this. Back up a little more!"

"Dad, I don't think you should…"

"It's okay," Paul interrupted. "Make the call," he said as he approached the passenger side of the car. The driver was still revving the engine. He didn't want the car to leave before the cops got there. He tried to quickly open the passenger-side door but it was locked. Of course. He banged on the window, hoping the driver would roll it down or do something other than rev up the engine. The horn started blowing and it startled Paul. He jumped back and felt his heartbeat ramp up. He could hear the driver laughing. It was an evil-sounding laugh and it was very piercing. Paul quickly realized that his daughter was probably right. There wasn't anything he could do without any protection and not even having a car. He took a few steps back away from the car and placed his arm in front of Krystal, feeling that would protect her at least a little bit.

Just then, the window rolled down to a very small crack. Paul stepped back even more. The crack was too small to be able to see inside. "Hi, Lieutenant Jennings," the driver said.

It was definitely a male's voice that had a bit of authority behind it.

"Who are you?" Paul asked as he tried to peek through the crack by lowering his head.

The driver just laughed as Laura pulled up behind them. The driver of the Mustang revved its engine again and then took off. Paul opened the driver's-side door of his wife's car. "Get out!" he shouted at her.

"What?"

"I said get out! Now!"

Laura jumped out of the car as quickly as she could and Paul jumped in. He threw the car in drive and took off before his door was even closed all the way. Although the Mustang had a good start on him, he saw which way the guy had gone. He put the pedal to the metal and screeched his own tires as he made a right out of the neighborhood. He flipped on the sport mode on his wife's little Mazda CX3 in hopes of getting a little bit of a boost with the gas. Even though this helped a little, it still was not as powerful as his police cruiser. "Fuck!" he shouted out loud as he realized he had no idea where the Mustang was.

Feeling defeated, he drove back to his wife and daughter. He realized it was stupid of him to leave them alone like that. He felt like a dog with its tail between its legs. He knew his wife would not be happy with his taking off like that. Just like he was not happy about his daughter taking off in the same way only moments before. Luckily, they were still where he had left them, unharmed. Laura was looking at her daughter's wrist. A trooper had just arrived as well.

"Is it broken?" Paul asked as he stepped out of the car.

"If it's not, then it's badly sprained. I need to get her to the hospital for an X-ray. Are you done holding my car hostage?"

"Yes," Paul answered as he opened the driver's-side door for his wife and then the passenger-side door for his daughter. "I'm going to stay here with Trooper Thomas and give him my statement and hang out a bit in case the guy is stupid enough to come back."

"Sir, are you okay?" Trooper Thomas asked as Laura and Krystal drove off.

"Physically, yes. Mentally, no. This guy used my name. He knew who I was."

"Any idea who it could be?"

"Not a one."

"Have you arrested anyone recently?"

"You know I don't do much arresting as a lieutenant."

And that was true. It had been months since Paul had arrested anyone or even had to testify in court. He knew he'd be spending the rest of the day with his mind reeling at who could have been in that car and why he was targeted.

Chapter 5

Sean Craw laughed as he rolled down the windows to the Ford Mustang. He found it hilarious that Krystal tried running after him. Did she really think she could have caught up to him? He was hoping she was smarter than that, but he liked her bravery. Perhaps they did have something in common. He was feeling good, though. His right-hand man, Drew, had performed the job perfectly and he was almost certain that the doctor didn't survive that crash. He was feeling so good that he had to get out and have some fun of his own. Of course, they'd all be having a different kind of fun later, but he liked this kind of fun as well. Revenge was sweet but he really couldn't wait to deliver the gift of death. Much like sex, death brings a certain kind of euphoria that most people look for their entire lives. This was just his opinion, since he was still alive. How could he be wrong, though?

He had read up on near-death experiences. The stories were all too similar to not be true. When someone dies, they have this feeling of being light. All of their aches and pains are taken away and they feel more alive than when they were actually alive. They all describe heaven the same way too. Everything is brighter and there is no feeling other than the feeling of being loved. To him, it all sounded a lot like sex and the feelings you got after a good romp. To him, sex and death were one and the same, they were just on opposite ends of the spectrum. So when he murdered someone, he felt like he was giving them a gift. Not that he wanted to give Jennings any kind of gift, but this time it was more of a gift to himself.

He had been planning this for a very long time. He had the money to carry out all the hits but he wanted to have fun with it first. There was nothing wrong with having some fun, right? He had to make sure Dr. Simms was dead first. There was a reason and order to everything. He couldn't wait to have some fun with the Jennings family though, so while trying to take out Dr. Simms, he figured he'd have fun with them, especially Paul. Besides, after all the torture, he'd be giving them all the gift of death. Therefore, they could just deal with everything that was about to happen to them. He laughed again as he parked the Mustang next to his personal car in the mall parking lot. He got out and greeted one of his men.

"I'm glad you made it here on time," Sean said to him.

"Sir, what do you need?"

Sean pointed to the Mustang. "Torch it. Better make it quick though, the cops are on the lookout for it."

Sean laughed as he got into his car and drove away. As he drove back to the "office" he thought about how scared Paul looked as he was taunting him. It served him right after all the shit he had been through because of Paul, ever since he was a child. He would see to it that Paul would get what he had coming – and he was going to have fun doing it too!

He then called his friend Byron, who answered right away. "Doyle!" Byron answered happily. "How'd it go?"

"Perfectly! They were right where you said they would be. Your abilities amaze me sometimes!"

"I try. So did you guys get the doctor yet?"

"We're working on it."

"Doyle, I really feel a sense of urgency with this. I told you that the doctor has a friend who has the same ability as me. If you don't get the doctor out of the picture soon, she's going to ruin everything for you."

"It's been taken care of, my friend."

"Good. I've been trying to figure out just where her friend is so I can get to her. I'd love to meet her. But every time I get close to her, it's like the slate goes blank or something and I lose my connection to her. It's been very frustrating but it sure does excite me!"

Sean cackled. "Well, good luck with that. I'll keep you posted and let you know if I need anything else."

"Sure thing."

Sean hung up and continued to laugh as he drove back to the office.

Chapter 6

Paul Jennings stepped into the shower and allowed the cool water to run onto his face. He was a tall man, standing at six feet and five inches, with blonde hair and blue eyes, and very muscular. Being a police officer, he had to keep himself in shape, and having free access to the gym helped him do just that. He loved his job. There was never a dull moment and it was a good feeling at the end of a shift to know that he was doing his part in keeping the community safe. His career goal was to achieve the rank of at least a captain, but for now he was very happy being a lieutenant in the Criminal Enforcement Division for the state police. He had a great boss, great coworkers and worked in a great state.

He began wondering what in the hell had just happened. The guy driving the Mustang never came back, and they had absolutely no leads on him. It was as if the guy disappeared into thin air. Even after issuing a "be on the lookout," they were still unable to find the car. Weird. The most concerning part was that the guy used his name. It was personal – but who could it be? Sure, he probably had a lot of people that didn't care for him because he had arrested them, but he couldn't think of anyone that would want revenge so badly they would try to run him over. Was the guy trying to murder him or just scare him? The guy could have easily run him over and killed him right then and there, but he didn't. If he had a gun, he could have shot him and been done with it, but he didn't. Why? What was the deal with this guy? Who was this guy? For some reason, his mind went to an incident that had happened a little over six months ago.

He remembered the day so clearly. How could he not, after all the reports he had to fill out and the shit-ton of statements he had to give both verbally and written. It was only the third time he'd had to use his service pistol, and the first time he had actually killed someone. There was a call for a breaking and entering. The caller was a sixteen-year-old girl who was home alone after school. Her parents were still at work and someone was beating on a window. She ran upstairs and locked herself into her bedroom and called 9-1-1. Paul was the first officer to arrive on the scene. He quietly rolled up with his sirens off, just in time to see the burglar squeezing himself through a broken window. He called for backup but he knew there was no time to waste. It wasn't a big house and he figured it was only a matter of minutes, maybe seconds, before the intruder busted down the young girl's bedroom door.

He quietly let himself in through the same broken window after peering inside to make sure he wouldn't be seen. What Paul didn't know was that the burglar was just in the next room and heard Paul stepping on the broken glass. Just as Paul got to his feet and began to look around, he was met with a gun being pointed straight at his face. The guy's face was undetectable due to a black ski mask covering it. The only identifying feature was cloudy blue eyes – eyes that surely had the devil dancing inside of them. Somehow, though, they looked oddly familiar. He was only about four feet away, so Paul knew he had to act fast. Paul had quickly retrieved his service pistol and pointed it at the burglar and demanded that he drop his weapon. Before he could respond to Paul's orders, a movement on the stairs off to the side caught both of their eyes. It was the teenaged girl trying to slowly creep down the steps. The burglar immediately pointed his gun at the girl and told Paul that if he didn't let him leave, he was going to kill the girl and then Paul and then himself. Paul had told him that he couldn't let him leave and that was all the burglar had to hear. Without a second to even think about it, the burglar fired his gun at the girl. He hit her in her shoulder and she screamed, fell down, and rolled down to the bottom of the stairs. He then pointed his gun at Paul but it was too late. The second he shot the girl, Paul went into react mode and shot the burglar. He only wished he had acted before he was able to get a shot at the girl. Not even thinking about it, he aimed for his heart and hit it dead-on. The burglar was dead in an instant. The girl was seriously injured, but lived to tell her story. In fact, he had just met with her and her parents a couple of weeks ago. They wanted to thank him for saving the girl's life. Paul also got an award for saving her.

He didn't think he should have gotten an award. He could understand getting a thank-you from the family but that should have been where it stopped. Why give someone an award for killing another human being? In all honesty, he wished he had just shot the burglar in the foot or arm so he could live and rot in jail. He was put on paid leave until the case was closed and it was proven that he didn't shoot without reason. The department also made him see a psychologist for a few weeks to make sure that he was handling it okay. He was fine. He felt guilty for killing the guy but he knew he had to do it, not only to save the girl but also to keep himself safe. Talking to the psychologist did help him a great deal and he had been sleeping peacefully at night. He figured he would never forget the burglar's name though: Toby Craw. That name would haunt him for the rest of his life, probably, but he knew he'd be able to keep on keeping on.

Why in the hell are you thinking about that incident? Stop it! That has nothing to do with the maniac who just tried to run me and Krystal over! The truth was, that incident may have bothered him more than he let on and he thought about it frequently. Why, though, would he think about it in that moment? Maybe there was a reason he was thinking about it right now. Or maybe the crazy guy from today had nothing to do with his work. He didn't really have any secrets concerning his personal life. Well, that wasn't totally true.

There was one and it was a big one, but there was no way that it could have anything to do with the guy from today. Again, though, he wondered why that was popping up in his head now. He knew he needed to listen to his instincts. They were almost always right. Maybe it was time to tell his wife about his secret as well. It should have been done a long time ago, but something was telling him to tell her now.

Chapter 7

It was close to seven in the evening before Krystal was released from the hospital sporting a cast on her wrist. It was not broken, only badly sprained. She was not happy about it but was glad that she didn't need surgery. She was able to speak to her boss at the Italian restaurant where she was a server, and he suggested she take the next week off and then they'd figure out what to do from there. She rode back from the hospital with Trent, who had come quickly to the hospital after getting a call from Krystal's mother. He was concerned that someone had tried to hurt his girlfriend. He wondered what was going on and was scared of what the answer may be.

Her parents were already home waiting for her to get there. When Krystal and Trent walked into the house, her parents were sitting in the living room watching the news. There was a look of horror on their faces.

"Jesus!" Krystal said. "What's wrong with you two? I'm not dead!" She kind of laughed at her stupid joke but noticed that her mom and dad were not laughing. They weren't even looking at her as they were riveted by the scene being displayed on the television.

Krystal began to pay attention to the television and quickly realized what was wrong. The news reporter said, "Again. The victim was Dr. Janet Simms, and it's believed that she was headed home from her Columbia office when she was hit dead-on while driving southbound on route twenty-nine. Witnesses say that they saw the masked man who hit her get out of his SUV and jump into another one and they drove off. Because of this, it is believed that this was an intentional incident and the investigation is ongoing…"

"What the hell?" Krystal exclaimed. "This must have happened right after my session with her! Is Dr. Simms okay? They didn't say!"

"Sit down," Laura instructed her daughter. "You don't need to get all worked up after the day you've had. They said at the beginning of the report that she suffered a concussion and a few broken bones and some stitches but she's going to be okay."

"Yeah," Paul chimed in. "They said it's a miracle that she survived that crash."

Trent asked, "Do you think it was one of her crazy patients?"

"That's exactly where my thoughts are going," Paul replied. "But being taunted by that car today has me wondering if the two incidents aren't connected somehow."

Trent didn't say anything to that, but he wondered if they were connected and worried that they were.

"Well," Krystal said as she realized she was crying, "I hope they find who did this to her and they lock them up forever."

Trent sounded a little bit offended at her statement. "Well," he said, "it wouldn't be forever since she's not dead. They may try to get him with attempted murder but they'd have to prove it, and if he has no connections with Dr. Simms, then they'll have a hard time proving anything."

"What?" Krystal said, clearly upset. "Why are you defending the guy?"

"I'm not!" Trent replied. "I'm just stating the facts." The truth was that Trent couldn't stand Dr. Simms. He felt like she held Krystal back. He figured that Krystal would be more outgoing and more daring if she didn't have the doctor in her ear telling her that she needed to think about things before reacting to them.

"Unfortunately," Paul added, "he's right. It's just the way the law works."

"Well, fuck the law!" Krystal cried. "Dr. Simms is such a wonderful person and I don't know where I'd be if I hadn't had her helping me all these years. With my spur-of-the-moment reactions to things, I probably would've been locked up in juvy at some point. She still keeps me grounded and sane. If something happens to her, I don't know how I'd deal with things."

Laura finally spoke. "Let's not talk about this. We've got other things to worry about and we can go visit Dr. Simms tomorrow."

"This has been one weird day," Krystal said. "First some weird guy attacked Sara at Dr. Simms's office, and then we almost get run over by some weirdo, and now this. How is it that all this craziness happened within a few hours of each other?"

Paul lifted his eyebrows. "What do you mean some weird guy attacked Sara?"

"One of Dr. Simms's patients. He put Sara up against a wall and put his hand around her throat. I had to step in and say something because I really thought he was going to try to hurt her."

"You what?" Laura yelled at her daughter. "Why in the hell would you do that?"

"What was I supposed to do? Sit there and watch him hurt her?"

"Oh I don't know, call the cops maybe?"

"That might have took too long!"

"So? At least you would've been safe."

"Hey," Paul chimed in. "Krystal can handle herself. I hear she's been doing really good in her self-defense classes. She did the right thing."

"You should have never put her in that class! She thinks she's invincible now!"

"I'm just making sure she can defend herself, and obviously I have every reason to do so with all the shit that went on today!" Paul was mad, but he was trying to stay calm since they did have company. Even if it was Trent, the guy he was unsure of.

Laura bit her tongue. She had a lot more to say to her husband but not when there was company in the house. She already knew she was in hot water after speaking to her husband like that.

"Anyways," Krystal said. "I'm going to spend the night at Trent's house. I don't have to work for the next week thanks to my sprained wrist."

Paul flinched at the thought of his daughter lying in bed next to a man. He fought the image out of his head. "Maybe you should stay home tonight? These three incidents that happened today can't be a coincidence. Something is going on and I think it's something bad. I'd rather you stay home where I can keep you protected."

"Dad, I'll be fine. I'll…"

Trent cut her off. "I'll keep her safe, Mr. Jennings. Besides, if someone is after you, they may know where you live. She may be safer with me."

"He might be right," Laura chimed in.

Paul sighed. "I'm perfectly capable of keeping my daughter safe." He rolled his eyes to emphasize that he didn't agree with any of them.

"Dad, I'm sorry but I'm going to Trent's tonight. I think I'm going to take a hot bath first, though. Trent, I'll meet you at your place in a bit?"

"Sure thing," Trent said. "That'll give me time to pick up a little bit!" He hugged Krystal and gave her a quick kiss on her lips.

Paul flinched again. His daughter was an adult and he knew he had to let her go.

Laura smiled, happy that her daughter had a strong man other than her father to lean on.

Chapter 8

The evening slowly turned into night, and after Krystal left for Trent's house Laura and Paul had the house to themselves. They had retired to their bedroom around nine o'clock and were lying down together but they knew neither one of them was going to be sleeping any time soon. It was their normal routine to spend at least an hour before going to sleep having a conversation about whatever came to mind: that day's happenings, family things (mainly Krystal), television shows, anything of the sort. Tonight's conversation was sure to be tense so they downed a bottle and a half of wine between the two of them beforehand, not really saying anything. They were just drinking and zoning out at the TV. After all, there was nothing wrong with loosening up a little to help ease an unpleasant conversation. They took their usual spots in the bed and Laura rolled herself over on her right side, hoping he'd just pass out.

"Nope," he said as she did this. "We're gonna talk, so you might as well face me. I don't wanna talk to your back."

Laura lay still for a second without responding to him. *Maybe if I don't move, he'll think I already fell asleep. We did drink a good bit of wine. I know he's upset that I yelled at him like I did, but I'm upset that he thinks our daughter's behavior is okay. I'm mad too. Oh hell, why put off what needs to happen? I might as well get this over and done with.* She turned on her left side and faced her husband of twenty-five years. "Paul, I'm really sorry that I..."

Paul leaned in and kissed her, cutting off her apology. He placed his hand on her right cheek and caressed her face. Twenty-five years of marriage and he still had his moments where he surprised the hell out of her. He pulled back and looked at her and her face of confusion. He didn't say anything. Rather, he stared lovingly at his wife. Her blonde hair was pushed behind her shoulders and she looked almost childlike with her eyes that were portraying worry. He was upset with her, but looking at her he felt the urge to comfort her in the manliest way. He leaned in and kissed her again, only a little bit harder this time. He still hadn't said anything, but Laura would take kisses over fighting any day. She returned his kiss as she rolled over on top of him. She sat up and, while still straddling him, took off her silk nightgown, exposing her bare breasts and a pair of black panties. Paul groped both her breasts with both his hands. Even after twenty-five years of marriage and giving birth, Laura was still an attractive woman. She kept herself in shape and had a body to die for. He knew they'd be okay but he wasn't so sure how she would take what he had to tell her. He wasn't sure that tonight would be the right night for it. So much had already happened. He thought it might be best to wait. After all, he had kept the secret from her all of these years, what was one more night?

Laura was still surprised that he wanted to make love instead of talk about things, but all it took was one of Paul's passionate kisses to get her juices flowing. It wasn't long before they were both naked and making love. Sometimes their lovemaking was slow and passionate. Other nights, it was a bit rough and more on the wild side of things. Tonight was the latter. Of course it was, after all that wine and all the emotions that had surfaced earlier in the evening. There was hair pulling, ass slapping, and hard and deep thrusts for a good thirty minutes. Laura was screaming and moaning in delight, something she usually had to hold back with Krystal in the house. It made her feel more of a woman when she could just let it all out. Her face was tingling and her entire body was in ecstasy as she and her husband came at the same time. Sometimes they were on the same page. Sometimes. Paul pulled himself out of Laura slowly and carefully and then dropped in exhaustion back onto the bed. Laura giggled as she got up and headed to the bathroom.

When she came back to bed, she was dressed in her nightgown again but Paul was still naked. He got up and said he was going to use the bathroom but when he came back, they were going to talk. Laura felt her heart jump into her chest. She thought she had gotten out of having to talk. She had an idea though. She was ready to do anything if it meant not having to talk about things. Besides, even though Paul had just fully satisfied her, she was still horny. It was like that sometimes. She took her nightgown back off and waited for him, naked, outside the bathroom door.

Paul was pleasantly startled when he opened the bathroom door to his naked wife. She had never done this before, so he was a bit intrigued. "Well, hello," he said as he wrapped his arms around her waist and pulled her toward his naked body. Laura smiled at him as she dropped to her knees. He placed his hands on the back of her head as if she may need some help doing what she'd done so many times before. After a few minutes, Paul pulled himself out of her mouth and made her stand up. He forced her up against the wall and then went down on her. She came fairly quickly and then, once again, he was inside of her as he fucked her up against their bedroom wall. This was a new one for them. Usually, they were in the bed or even the floor but never up against the wall. *She really doesn't want to talk,* Paul thought to himself as he tried to keep himself from cumming. *Too bad, because no matter how many times she fucks me tonight, we will talk when we are finally finished.*

Paul sensed a feeling in the air. An odd feeling like they hadn't seen each other in years and they wouldn't see each other ever again after this night. They fucked like they would never get the chance to ever again. Paul suddenly wanted to feel every single bit of his wife and Laura was all but becoming one with her husband.

His touch felt like it was the first time he had ever touched her. The first time she had ever been touched at all. If she could have swallowed her husband whole at that moment, she would have. He picked her up and she wrapped her legs around his waist. They were hugging and squeezing each other so tight that it was hard to breathe. Neither one of them wanted to cum because they didn't want it to end. Paul was a strong man but after five minutes of holding his wife up, he began to grow weak. So, he walked with her wrapped around him and threw her onto their bed.

Paul was thrusting himself in and out of her so hard and so quick that he thought he might have a heart attack, but he liked the feeling. Laura was screaming in pleasure as she moved out of the position and forced herself on top of him. Straddling him once again, she began riding him as if she had no feeling of his dick inside of her. He was thrusting himself inside of her with each downward thrust coming from her. They were both moaning and groaning like two horny teenagers. Laura was starting to become exhausted but she still felt like this feeling could never end. It wasn't that she didn't want to have the conversation now. No, it was much more than that. She wanted her husband like she'd never wanted him before. Then all at once, calmness washed over them and their thrusting and pushing slowed down and became more sensual – more passionate. They kissed, and as they did, Laura could have sworn that she was on fire. They had kissed so many times before but never had any of his kisses made her feel like she was high, at least not to this extent. She was sure that she was floating at this point. She had no idea where this feeling was coming from but she wished it hadn't taken them so long to discover it.

Paul was on the same page as his wife. As she kissed him back he felt some sort of electric jolt shoot through his entire body every single second. Where had this come from all of a sudden? In

36

all the years they had been having sex it had never been like this. He wondered if the scary day and the fact he had to tell his wife something that could upset her made him want to get lost in her more than usual. He didn't want it to end. They truly became one in that moment and it was a new feeling. They loved each other very much and their sex was also satisfying but something was different about this night. Something was very different. It was almost as if they were with someone new and the excitement of not getting caught was what added to their feeling of pure bliss. There was just no other way to describe what was taking place.

The passionate and sensual lovemaking went on for what seemed like forever. There was nothing but love, admiration, and respect for one another. Finally, they looked into each other's eyes and they knew it was time to finish this. Again they came at the same time but it was the first time it had ever felt that good. After Paul came, Laura collapsed on top of his chest. Neither of them said anything as they cuddled in an attempt to hold on to the warmth that was flowing between them. Finally, Paul said, "Wow! What in the hell was in that wine?"

Laura snickered. "I was wondering the same thing. That was amazing! Where did all that come from? I thought I knew all your sides."

"I could say the same thing to you, you know!"

"Paul, I love you. You know that, right?"

"Of course I do. I love you too."

Laura smiled and now she was back to hoping that they wouldn't have that dreaded conversation. Paul killed that hope with his next sentence though.

"But you shouldn't have talked to me like that earlier. I know what's best for my daughter."

"You mean our daughter," Laura said, feeling the warmth with her husband start to dwindle away.

Paul was starting to feel disgust toward her. "I still know what's best for her."

"I know." Laura snuggled her head on his chest and gave him a little kiss on his nipple in an attempt to calm them both down. "I'm sorry I spoke to you like that, but you never even talked to me before signing her up for those classes. You know how our daughter is. You know she takes things like that and magnifies it by a thousand. She's going to get herself into more trouble now thinking that she can handle people who are bigger than her. It kind of goes against what Dr. Simms has been working on with her. Dr. Simms is trying to teach her to stop and think before acting. These classes are teaching her to react before thinking."

Paul was becoming agitated and raised his voice a little. "Krystal is an adult and can make decisions for herself. As her mother, you should know that and you should know that putting her into these self-defense classes was a good idea! You should also know that I don't have to discuss everything with you as far as she is concerned!"

"Don't you tell me what I should and shouldn't know, Paul Christopher Jennings!" She was furious now. She only used his full name like that when he really said something to upset her. "In fact, you know what you can do?" She was yelling now. "You can go fuck yourself!"

She got out of bed and ran into the bathroom. She locked the door and sat on the floor, up against the door, and began crying. That was a side of herself she hated. She hated that when she got angry at someone, she used words she hated and said things she knew she'd regret later. When she let her anger take over, it took over everything. She clenched her right hand into a fist and hit it back into the door. "Ow!" she screamed. She began crying harder. *What in the hell is his problem? Why does he have to make me feel even worse by saying I should have known better, as her mother? Who is he to say what is and isn't right? And not discuss things with me that involve Krystal? What is that? How could he be so nasty to me after the amazing sex we just had?*

Paul was lying in bed and wiping away his own tears. He wasn't crying as hard as his wife was, but he had a few tears quietly rolling down his cheeks. *Really, Paul? I sure do know how to fuck up a good time. Why did I have to be so hard on her? Who am I to belittle her like that? Oh god, I'm just like my father! That sex was amazing and I had to go and ruin it. Why in the hell did I get so angry? I'm a big asshole.*

Paul swallowed his pride and got out of bed. He went to the bathroom door and contemplated just walking in. He decided this would be best so he turned the knob. It was locked. He tapped on the door. "Laura? Can I come in?"

"I thought I told you to go fuck yourself!" Laura said through her tears.

Oh man, she's crying. He hated when she cried but hated it even more when it was him who made her cry. He still smiled a little, though, because he loved when she was sassy like this. It turned him on. "Honey, I'm sorry I yelled at you like that. It was uncalled for. Please, baby, open the door so I can apologize to your face."

"Please just leave me alone!" she cried.

Paul sat down with his back up against the bathroom door. "I'm not going to do that. I'm going to sit here until you come out."

"Suit yourself, but you might want to grab a pillow because I'm not coming out."

Paul could hear her sobbing through the door and his heart sank. "Please don't cry. I'm just a dumb asshole. Please just stop crying. It breaks my heart to hear you cry."

"How could you ruin such a wonderful evening by being a dick to me like that?"

"I don't know."

"You don't know what it's like to worry about her. You just have no care in the world and think nothing bad can ever happen to any of us. Well, today confirmed that that is not true! I worry about her. Just because you don't, doesn't mean my thoughts and feelings don't matter."

Paul listened to his wife through her tears and felt like an even bigger asshole. He began crying again. He leaned his head against the door and closed his eyes. "I'm sorry I was so mean to you, honey. I hate that I was that way with you. You know, my dad used to talk to me and Mom just like that all the time. I know how bad it hurts and how it can kill a good mood. You didn't deserve that. I think I'm just upset because my daughter could've been really hurt today. All I want is for you and Krystal to be happy. I don't want to be the cause of your grief." He was crying harder now. It was his fault that his wife was locked in their bathroom crying her eyes out.

Laura heard her husband crying through the door and now it was her heart that was sinking. She admired the love he had for their daughter. He was a great father and an even better husband – well, when he kept his anger away, anyway. She couldn't stand to hear him crying even though he kind of deserved this one. "You're not allowed to cry!"

"Why not? I feel bad and hearing you cry makes me cry."

"But it's your fault that I'm crying!"

"I know. I'm sorry. I really am."

40

The sincere apology was what she had been looking for.

"I can be really terrible sometimes," Paul continued.

Laura slowly stood up and opened the door. Paul fell halfway backward with the door opening, startled. Laura kneeled down in front of her husband and wiped his tears with her thumb as he began wiping her tears away from her cheeks. "You," she said, "are a great father! You are a wonderful husband. Don't ever feel like you cause either of us grief." She kissed his forehead and then he hugged her tight as he let his tears come out in full force. Laura squeezed him as hard as she could. "I'm so sorry," she said to him.

"No," he said, pulling back. "I'm the sorry one. I'm sorry I upset you."

"Let's just let it go," she said as she kissed him.

"Done. But there is something that I need to talk to you about."

Laura sighed. "What? Something bad?"

"Yeah. No. Well, I don't know. I think that when Dr. Simms is feeling better we should set up an appointment with her."

"It's that bad?"

"It could be."

"You know, the last time we saw her was when you were working all those crazy hours and I was convinced that you were cheating on me."

"Yeah, but your trust issues have gotten better and I never was cheating on you."

"I know that now. My point is we needed the professional help because it was getting bad between us. Are you telling me that what you have to tell me is going to be that bad?"

"I just think that the conversation will go better if we have her there to guide us through it. I mean, I can tell you now, but…"

"No! I want to know what it is but it's been an exhausting day. If it's not something that relates to what all happened today, then it can wait. I hope."

Paul thought to himself, *Well, it might relate to that.* That thought alone scared him but he didn't want her to know that. "It can wait. I love you."

"I love you too."

Before they knew what was happening, they were making love again, half of them on the bedroom floor and the other half of them on the bathroom floor. This session felt more like their usual lovemaking. When they were finished thirty minutes later, they retired to their bed, exhausted and drained in every way.

"That has to be some sort of record." Paul smirked.

"I think it is." Laura giggled. "Paul, do you think there's a connection to what happened today to you guys and to Dr. Simms?"

He sighed. "I want to say no but I just can't shake the idea that they are connected somehow. Hopefully, Dr. Simms pulls out of her injuries okay."

"Yeah. What do you make of all of this?"

"I don't know, but I intend to do some digging on the case when I get to work tomorrow. I'll get to the bottom of it."

She knew her husband would. In one way or another, he'd figure this whole fiasco out. She slowly drifted off to sleep while wondering what her husband had to tell her. Was he now cheating on her and finally felt the need to 'fess up?

Chapter 9

When Krystal got to Trent's house that evening, she walked into a surprise. When Trent opened the door for her, his lights were off and the apartment was lit up with candles. There was soft, classical music playing in the background and there were even rose petals thrown all over the living room with a trail leading into the bedroom. Krystal was delighted at the sight. "What's all this?" she asked with a little smile.

Trent took her hand and walked her over to his couch. He loved the alone time with Krystal and he was glad that she didn't stay home as her dad wanted her to. He wanted to keep Krystal as close to him as possible. "I know you had a rough day and I just want you to kick back and relax. I actually went out and bought that for you," he said, pointing to something off to the side.

Krystal followed his finger point and saw a massage table. "What? Where the hell did you find that?"

"Someone was selling it on Craigslist. I got a decent price for it. If you go into the bathroom, I set out a robe for you. Why don't you go change into it?"

"You don't have to ask me twice," she said, getting up and heading to the bathroom.

Trent watched her with a smile on his face as she walked away. He just wanted her to be happy and stress-free. He thought her parents held her back. They were always getting on about her being too destructive with things, but he felt like he needed Krystal to be destructive when it came to their relationship. He had been successful in getting her to fall in love with him so quickly. He felt some sort of forbidden type of love when he was with her. He liked it and he didn't want her parents to mess it all up. He also wasn't sure about what her parents thought of him. He felt like her mother was genuine but her father was a different story. Her father was always nice to him but at times he felt like it was a fake nice. He needed to stay on Paul's good side, so the less time he spent around him, the less chance he had of making any mistakes.

Krystal was in the bathroom for what seemed like forever, so he tapped on the door. "Everything okay in there?"

Krystal yelled back, "Yeah. This stupid cast makes things much harder. I didn't think it would be so hard but when you can't bend your wrist, it really makes things difficult."

"Do you need some help?"

"No. I'm just about done."

When she finally came out of the bathroom, Trent looked her over. She had tied her hair back into a loose ponytail. It was done in a sloppy way so there were strands of hair hanging out of the ponytail and lining the sides of her face. Trent thought it looked sexy. She was wearing her robe loosely as well. It was a little too big for her so it was almost hanging off her right shoulder. Another inch and her nipple would have been exposed. Again, Trent thought it was a sexy look for her. Even though she had had a rough day, he knew that he could have her right then and there. He knew that she needed him as much as he needed her.

"Why are you staring at me?" Krystal asked him with a little smile.

"Sorry. You're so beautiful."

Krystal laughed at him. "Please. I'm a mess."

Trent grabbed her hand and walked her over to the massage table. He helped her climb on, drop the robe, and lay on her stomach. "Do you even know what you're doing?" Krystal teased.

"Nope!" he answered matter-of-factly. "But how hard can this be? I put some lotion on you and rub."

"I should be worried, shouldn't I?"

"You have no faith, do you?" Trent said with a smirk. "I think I know how to make you feel good. Now just relax and let me do my thing."

"Okay," Krystal said as she sighed and closed her eyes. He was right, he couldn't really do anything wrong here. He squirted lotion on her back. "Ah!" she shrieked. "That's cold! You could've warned me first."

"I'm sorry," he said as he bent down and kissed her on her cheek. "Don't worry. It'll warm up in just a minute." He began to rub the lotion in and spread it over her entire back and arms. He squirted more on both her legs and spread it over her legs and butt. All that was left to do now was to rub every inch of her body, focusing on her back, neck, and shoulders where all the tension was. He was careful not to bump her injured wrist.

Krystal closed her eyes as she felt the stresses of the day slowly melting away. She was grateful to have Trent in her life. In fact, she didn't know where she would be right now if she didn't have him. She'd be stuck at home, with her parents worrying about her and hovering over her and stressing her out even more. She couldn't wait to move in with Trent and start a life with him. She couldn't wait to have some independence from her parents. She loved them both very much but she never felt like she really got to live her life the way she wanted. Trent allowed her to do that.

"How is your wrist feeling?"

"Hmmm?" Krystal asked him. She was relaxed and was in total meditation mode and barely even heard Trent when he spoke.

"Your wrist," he chuckled. "How does it feel?"

Krystal's thoughts went straight to her wrist and the focus made her realize that it was hurting. "Oh. It hurts. It's throbbing."

"Did they give you any pain meds?"

"They did, but you know how I feel about that stuff. It makes me feel weird."

"But if you're in pain, you should take it. Why make yourself suffer?"

Krystal sighed. "Do you have an aspirin? I'd rather take that instead."

Trent said, "No. I don't. I'm sorry. Did you bring your pain meds? You should just take one to help you relax more."

"I did bring them. They are in my bag in the front pocket."

Trent went to her bag that was sitting on the couch and found the pills right away. "Just one?" he asked.

"Yes."

He went over to the kitchen and got her a glass of water and brought it back to Krystal with the pill. "You're so nice," she said as she sat up and accepted the glass and pill.

She took her pill and handed the glass back to him. "Anything for you," he said, placing the glass on the table next to him. "Shall I finish the massage?" he asked her.

"How about you massage my front side?" Krystal smirked.

Trent thought about that for a split second. "What exactly is there to rub on your front side?" he teased.

"I don't know," she teased back. "Why don't you feel around and see what you find?"

Trent found many things to rub and succeeded in making her feel even more relaxed. Once he was finished, he bent down and kissed her on her lips. She returned the kiss as she sat up and rested her arm on his shoulder.

"How are you feeling?" he asked after she kissed him.

"Relaxed," she said. "Between that, um…massage and the pain pill, I feel very relaxed."

"Good." Trent smiled at her. "I'm glad to see you with a smile on your face." He moved her hair out of her eyes and caressed her face. "I'm sorry you got hurt today. I hope whatever is going on is nothing too crazy and it's over."

Krystal was starting to tear up. "I'm kind of scared, you know?"

"It's okay. I don't blame you!"

Krystal smiled as a tear fell out of her right eye. Trent wiped it away. "Okay. None of that. You're going to put the stress back on that I just took off of you."

"I'm so lucky to have you. You know that, right? I love you so much."

"I love you!" he said as he wiped another tear from her cheek. "I don't know…"

She cut him off with a kiss. He returned the kiss as he wrapped his right hand around the back of her neck. "Can we go to the bedroom?" she asked him.

"Are you sure you're feeling up to that?" he asked.

She grabbed his left hand and shoved it into her crotch. She was not only naked but wet. "What do you think?" She smirked.

"Wow! Where did all that come from?"

"You did it!" she said as she slid herself off the massage table. He picked her up and carried her into his bedroom. He placed her carefully on his bed and got undressed.

"I'd love to give you a massage," Krystal said as Trent lowered his body on top of hers. "But I don't think a one-handed massage would feel all that great. Except for here…"

She grabbed his penis, which was standing in a full, upright position, and massaged it.

"I think that's the best kind of massage for me," he joked as he leaned down and kissed her.

47

When they were finished having sex, Krystal cuddled up on Trent's chest. "Thank you for tonight," she said. "I really did need to de-stress."

Trent kissed her forehead. "You really did. I'm glad I could help."

Krystal was starting to doze off. "I'm afraid for what tomorrow may bring," she slurred as she drifted off.

"Shhh…" Trent said, moving her hair away from her face.

Before long, they fell asleep in each other's arms.

Chapter 10

It was close to four in the morning when Krystal began having a nightmare. She dreamed of the car that almost ran her and her father down. In her dream, though, the driver was Trent. She woke up screaming. Trent quickly turned on the bedside lamp and turned his attention toward Krystal. "Hey!" he said. "What's wrong?"

"Trent?!" she screamed and proceeded to punch him with her good arm.

He was able to duck out of the way just in time and grabbed her arm before it made any contact with his face. He restrained her on the bed, being careful not to hurt her wrist. His holding her down like that made her feel like the dream she'd just had had some merit behind it. She had never really been afraid of Trent before, but there were times he got a dark look in his eyes and he looked like a different person. She never said anything about it but it made her think about how her father didn't really care for Trent. She tried to not let her father cloud her feelings for Trent but sometimes it was like his voice was inside her head screaming at her to wake up and pay attention. Trent never gave her a reason to feel like that though. That dream, though – it painted Trent in a different light and it scared her.

"What are you doing?" he asked with fear in his voice.

She started crying hysterically and tried to free herself from his grip. "Get off me! Let me go!" she screamed.

Trent did loosen up his grip but did not let go. "Calm down, hun! Please just calm down."

"Please let me go," Krystal cried with clenched eyes. She wasn't even looking at him. It was as if she was too afraid to.

"Babe! Calm down! If I let you go, are you going to try to hit me?"

Krystal finally opened her eyes and looked at him. He was straddling her and looking down at her. She calmed down a bit. "What?"

"If I let you go, are you going to try to hit me again?"

Krystal was confused. Did she try to hit him? Didn't he just try to run down her and her father? How did they get in his bed? What was going on? "What?" she asked again, and started shaking. "Did you... Are we..." She couldn't form a sentence. It was as if she had just been shoved from a different universe into the middle of a scene that she couldn't get straight in her head. "What's going on?"

"Krystal, you woke up screaming and tried to punch me. I had to duck and restrain you so you wouldn't hurt me."

She began crying harder. "Please let me go. I'm not going to try to hit you. I promise. Just please, let go of me!"

Trent was sorry he was holding her down but felt like he had to just to protect himself. "Okay," he said. "I'm going to let go but please don't start swinging at me."

"I won't," she cried.

"You know I love you, right? I'd never do anything to hurt you. Right?" His tone was soft and gentle.

"Ye – yea – yes. I know that."

He slowly loosened his grip, let go of her, and fell onto the other side of the bed. "Do you mind telling me what that was about?"

"I...I...I don't know. I mean, I do but I don't know."

Trent grabbed the glass of water on the nightstand and handed it to her. "Please drink some water. Calm yourself down if you won't allow me to help you."

Krystal nervously took the glass of water as she sat up. She took a small sip followed by a large gulp and set the glass down on the nightstand next to her. She dropped her head and put it in the palm of her right hand. *What the fuck?* she thought to herself. She was still crying. *I know he wouldn't hurt me but why do I feel so scared right now? Maybe Dr. Simms is right. Maybe I am falling for him too quickly. Maybe I do jump into things without thinking about them first.* Trent stood up and walked over to her side of the bed. He slowly placed his hand on the back of her head and stroked her hair. "Krystal? You're scaring me."

His touch made Krystal cringe. "Get away from me!" she shouted at him. "Don't touch me!"

Trent pulled his hand away from her as fast as he could and took a few steps back. "Can you please tell me what I did wrong all of a sudden?"

She looked at him, feeling scared for her life. She grabbed the glass of water and threw it at his head. Water went everywhere and he ducked as it hit the wall behind him and shattered into pieces.

"Whoa!" Trent shouted. "What the hell's wrong with you, Krystal?"

"Get away from me! Get the fuck away from me!"

"Did you forget that we're in my apartment?" Trent screamed back. He walked out of the open door and slammed it shut behind him. He paced back and forth in his living room. *I should just go back in there and knock the ever-living piss out of her! Who does she think she is, throwing a glass at me like that? What in the hell has gotten into her? I've never seen this side of her before. Has all the stress of today caused this? What will happen if things get worse? I need to figure out how to handle this.*

Trent was beyond pissed off. One thing that Krystal did not know about him was that he had struggled with his anger his entire life. His ex-girlfriend could tell Krystal stories that she would never believe. His relationship with his ex had ended because he was abusive. He used to slap her, punch her, and knock her around any time she got out of line – which was quite often if you asked Trent. He never had that urge with Krystal, though. There was something about her that made him feel calm and loved. He had never loved anyone like her and that scared him. He knew it could cause trouble. In that moment, though, he wanted to knock her out for the first time ever. *Pull yourself together! Calm down! Do not go in there with a hot head! Don't fuck this up more than what you already have!*

In the bedroom, Krystal was trying to gain her composure. *What in the hell? Why did I dream that Trent was the one driving the car? I know he'd never hurt me. He loves me. I'm sure of that. Okay, this dream had to have been an off-the-wall one. Maybe I dreamed it because he was the last person I saw before I fell asleep. That has to be it…along with those stupid pain pills.…Breathe, just calm down.* Krystal began taking deep breaths in and releasing them slowly. It was time for her to find the strength inside that she knew she had. *When did you become such a pussy anyway? You're a stubborn and tough chick. You never let anyone mess with you, so why are you letting this nightmare screw you all up? According to Dr. Simms, I never seem to be afraid of anything, so why is this happening now?* Krystal looked at the broken pieces on the floor. She had made a mess and she knew she could have cut Trent or at least knocked him out with that glass. She had talked herself out of her tears and was feeling calmer. Looking at the broken glass was like looking at her broken self. She was a mess just like the shattered glass on the floor and she didn't like it. Not one bit. It was time to clean herself – the glass – up. She got up and began carefully picking up the broken pieces with her hand that was sporting the sprained wrist and placing them in her right hand. Once she had a handful, she stood up, took a deep breath, and let it out. It was time to own up to what she had done.

She tried opening the door with her sprained wrist but she couldn't get her fingers around the knob without her wrist throbbing. She thought about putting the pieces back on the floor, opening the door, and then picking them up again, but that sounded like too much work. She tapped on the door with her foot, hoping Trent would hear her and not be too afraid to open it. He did hear her. "Why are you banging on the door?"

"Can you open it, please? My right hand is full and I can't open it with my left hand. My wrist hurts too much."

"Are you going to start throwing punches?"

Krystal rolled her eyes even though he couldn't see her. "No. I promise."

"I'm not sure. Maybe I should just stay out here for the rest of the night. We can pick up the mess tomorrow when you've calmed down." He wasn't sure he should trust her yet, but he was even more unsure if he could trust himself.

"Trent, I'm calm. Just open the door. Please?"

Trent slowly opened the bedroom door.

"Thank you. I just want to throw these pieces away and grab the broom and dustpan."

She walked into the kitchen and disposed of the broken glass in the trash can. She grabbed the broom and dustpan from his hall closet and slowly returned to the bedroom to find Trent sitting on the bed and looking at what was left of the broken glass. He didn't say anything as she entered the room and moved toward the mess. She tried sweeping up the glass from the carpet but quickly realized how difficult it was with a sprained wrist to work the broom on a carpet. She couldn't use much pressure and she was having a hard time even getting one little piece into the dustpan. She was becoming annoyed but kept trying anyway. She would do anything at that point to not have to face him, even if that meant she would be there for the rest of the morning trying to get up every little bit of the broken glass.

Trent saw her struggling but he was unsure if he should try to help her. He was afraid to approach her. He saw her trying to sweep with just her right hand but she had no control over the broom and he felt bad for her. He slowly stood up without saying anything and walked over to her. He stood behind her and put his arms around her from behind and grabbed the broom. Krystal kept her hands on the broom as she let Trent do all the work. Neither of them said anything as Trent swept up the glass into the dustpan. Krystal felt safe. She had never felt so safe before with his arms wrapped around her. She didn't want to move out of that position so she kept her hands on the broom.

Once there was nothing left but little, tiny pieces of glass, Trent let the broom drop to the floor and embraced Krystal from behind. She fell backward into his arms. She let him embrace her with his strong arms and closed her eyes. The tears were trying to come back but she wouldn't let them. She was done being afraid. She rested her head on his left arm as he snuggled his head against hers. He kissed her on her cheek and still didn't say anything. Trent was a strong man. He was taller than Krystal and definitely stronger. She was vulnerable now. She knew he could have snapped her neck in that position but she wasn't worried. She knew he wouldn't do that. There was nothing but love pouring out of his body and it was seeping into hers. The tears were still trying to come but she kept holding them back. He whispered in her ear, "Are we okay now?" He began swaying back and forth with her, almost as if they were slow dancing.

"Yes," she whispered back. For some reason, whispering seemed to be the appropriate thing to do. Maybe it was to keep the calmness that they almost lost. Maybe it was so the other would know that they were safe. "I'm sorry, Trent," she said, still whispering.

Trent shook his head against hers softly. "No, don't be. It's okay. Did you have a nightmare?" Still whispering ever so softly.

She nodded yes.

"Do you want to talk about it?" he whispered in her ear.

"No," she whispered back. "Just know that I'm sorry and I never meant to hurt you. I'm sorry I threw that glass at you. I'm really sorry."

He turned her around so he could see her face. He was expecting to see tears but there were none. In fact, he was surprised to see a little bit of hope and strength behind her eyes. She really was sorry. He could tell. He kissed her, thinking how proud he was that he hadn't slapped her around. "I accept your apology," he whispered. "I know you'd never really try to hurt me."

"I wouldn't," she whispered back. "I love you."

She placed her hand on his face and used her thumb to trace his lips. She loved his lips.

"I know you do," he replied, still whispering. "I love you more than you'll ever know."

"Show me," she whispered as she slowly moved her lips closer to his.

He slowly pulled back a little and looked at her. He had to make sure this wasn't a trick of some sort.

Krystal pulled back as well and looked at him. She wasn't sure if he really forgave her.

Then their lips met as they moved back to the bed and made love once more.

Chapter 11

The next morning, Laura went into the hospital to start her shift. She purposely got there thirty minutes early so she could check in on Dr. Simms. She checked the computer to see which room the doctor was in, and was happy to see that the doctor would be one of her patients for the day. Dr. Simms was in a private room in the intensive care unit. Laura lightly tapped on the door to her room. There was no answer but it was early in the morning so there was a good chance that the doctor was still sleeping. She quietly and slowly opened the door and poked her head into the room. Dr. Simms appeared to be sleeping, but she also looked pretty bad. Her face was bandaged up on the left side and there was a cast on her left arm. She also had a brace on her left leg. From where Laura was standing, she saw multiple bruises on her face, legs, and arms. It broke Laura's heart to see such a wonderful person in that kind of shape.

Laura closed the door and pulled the chart that was hanging next to the door and looked it over. It was just as the news said. The doctor had seventy-five stitches on the left side of her face, a broken arm, and a sprained leg. She must have been in a lot of pain.

"Doesn't look very pretty, does it?"

Laura jumped at the voice that came from behind her.

"Sorry, I didn't mean to scare you, hun," Cheryl said.

Cheryl was not only another nurse but also one of Laura's closest friends at work. "Were you here when they brought her in yesterday?"

"Negative," Cheryl answered. "When I got in she had been here for a few hours. Do you know her?"

"Yes," Laura answered while putting the chart back into its place. "She's Krystal's therapist. She kind of became a friend of the

56

family in a way. I heard about the accident on the news yesterday. Do you know if they found the person who did this to her?"

"I don't know," Cheryl answered, "but you may want to ask him." Her gaze was pointed toward a trooper sitting in a chair in the waiting room. "He's been here all night. Said he's been assigned to keep an eye on her since it seemed like the crash was intentional. Do you know him?"

Laura eyed the trooper up. She didn't recognize him but thought that throwing her husband's name out there might help her get some information that he wouldn't otherwise give out.

Laura walked over to the trooper, who was flipping through a *Cosmopolitan* magazine. She smirked at this and asked, "Are you taking notes?"

The trooper looked up from the magazine without any hint of being startled. He smiled and said, "No wonder I'm single. You girls are batshit crazy."

Laura couldn't help but laugh at that statement. "Hey, not all of us," she said with the most flirtatious smile she could deliver.

"Bet me," the trooper joked.

Laura sat down next to him and put out her hand. "I'm Laura Jennings."

The trooper shook her hand. "Jennings? Any relation to Paul Jennings?"

"Yup!" she proudly answered. "That's my husband."

"Oh! It's very nice to meet you. I trained with Paul a few months ago. He's a good guy. I'm Art."

"Nice to meet you, Art."

"He mentioned that his wife was a nurse."

"I wanted to ask you if you could tell me what you know about the accident that Dr. Simms was in yesterday."

"Well, I could tell you a lot but I'm not allowed to."

"I get it, I get it, but I am the wife of a trooper and Dr. Simms is on my watch today. Any information you can give me to help keep her safe would be appreciated. Besides, she's a friend of the family so I really would like to know what's going on."

Art sighed. He was clearly contemplating how much he should tell her. "I'm still pretty new on the force. In fact, I'm still on probation, which is why I got the job to guard Dr. Simms. I don't want to get myself into any trouble by telling things I'm not supposed to."

Laura understood but that wasn't going to stop her. "Okay. Buuuuut, you could tell another trooper, right?" She pulled her cell phone out of her pants pocket.

"Oh, sure. I can talk to another trooper about the case."

Laura was just about to dial her husband's cell phone number when she heard his voice in front of her. She looked up to see him walking toward her and Art. "Hey, honey!" Art jokingly said as Paul got closer.

"I see you got the shit job," Paul said, shaking Art's hand.

"You know how us rookies have it." Art laughed. "Lovely wife you got here."

"Yeah, I know," Paul responded as he gave Laura a quick peck on her lips. He was instantly tingling as the kiss flooded his mind with the sex from last night. The look on Laura's face revealed that she was having the same flashback. "I bet she was drilling you for information."

"Yup," Art answered. "But you'll be happy to know that I didn't tell her anything!"

"Good job," Paul said as his eyes were still fixed on his wife.

"Well, I guess I'll leave you two so you can discuss police matters in private," Laura said as she walked away. She knew her husband would tell her everything he knew.

After Laura walked away, Paul sat down next to Art. "So I went to the office and read the reports on the accident. Do they really have no idea who hit her?"

"Well, there's no definite leads…"

"Buuuut?" Paul asked.

"But," Art answered, "there was a witness who called into the Waterloo barrack and said he wanted to remain anonymous. The captain took the call and he tried like hell to get this guy's name but he wouldn't give it up. They tried tracing the call but he must have been using one of those burner phones."

"What did he say?"

"He said he knew who caused the accident, but when the captain asked for a name he wouldn't give it up. The captain asked him why he was calling us then. His answer was that he wanted us to know that the doctor is in danger, and if she didn't die from the accident, she'd surely be dying some other way. He said that the guy who is responsible for the accident is out for blood."

"Jesus! Did he say why?"

"Nope. That was the entire conversation and that's why I'm here guarding her."

Paul thought about it for a minute. "There were witnesses to the accident, though. They got a tag number of the getaway car. It came back stolen, right?"

"Right."

"Okay. Has anyone contacted the owner of the other stolen car yet? The one used in the accident?"

"Not yet. Not that I know of. We still haven't located the getaway car yet. The captain was trying to get someone to investigate the case but we're all so swamped."

"I know," Paul responded. "I took the reports and left him an email telling him I'd take it. The doctor is a friend of ours so I want to get to the bottom of it."

"Well, what kind of doctor is she?"

"She's a psychologist."

"Bingo!" Art said with a smile. "I bet it's one of her crazy patients."

"Yeah, but that's almost too easy. There's got to be more to it than that."

"Maybe so, but I'd check her client roster. I bet the idiot who did this is on her list."

"Yeah, but how far back do we go? He could be someone she had years ago who just got out of jail or something. Not only that, I think this is all connected to me somehow. What are the odds that the same day someone tries to run me and my daughter down, someone also tries to take out Dr. Simms, our daughter's therapist, as well? It's too big a coincidence!"

"Krystal's therapist? But why? I mean, she's just a therapist, right?"

"She is, but she has helped Krystal out so much over the years and we have sat in on some of her sessions and she always talked to us like a friend, not a doctor, you know? We kind of view Dr. Simms as an extended family member. We've always felt connected to her somehow. It's hard to explain but this entire thing is even harder to explain."

"Sounds like you have a big project on your hands." Art smiled like he hadn't a care in the world.

Paul stood up, as did Art, and they shook hands. "I guess I better get started on it. You keep a good eye on her, okay? She's a VIP."

"I got this. I'm off duty in three hours but I'll make sure whoever they send up here gets the memo."

"Thanks. You call me if anything happens," Paul said as he walked away. He found Laura at the front desk and he told her everything he knew. He also told her to make sure that Dr. Simms stayed safe. After kissing his wife goodbye and walking away, he suddenly stopped without any warning. An eerie feeling came over him. In all the years he's been a cop, he had only gotten that feeling a handful of times before, and usually when he did it was his instincts telling him to pay attention, that something very bad was about to happen. Without really knowing why, he turned around and walked back toward his wife.

"Paul? What's wrong? Your face is really pale!"

"I don't know," he answered honestly. "I just got a really bad feeling all of a sudden. I want you to be careful today too. Keep your eyes peeled for anything that seems out of the ordinary and watch your back."

"Paul, you're scaring me. What's going on?"

"I just got a sinking feeling that what happened to Dr. Simms is connected to us and what happened yesterday. The fact that we got a call warning us that Dr. Simms is not safe, well, that may just be messing with me but I really think we're involved in this somehow too. I have no evidence of that but the feeling is there. My gut is punching me right now."

Laura didn't like that. She knew her husband had killer instincts. She suddenly didn't like that she was so easygoing about Krystal staying the night at Trent's house. She knew she had to call Krystal.

"I'm going to start working on this case. Check in with me throughout the day, okay?"

"Okay," Laura said. "I think I'm going to give Krystal a call real quick and see how she's doing. I love you."

"I love you," he said as he kissed her again and finally left.

Paul got in his police cruiser, which he had left parked in front of the main entrance. Being in a police car did have its perks. He sat there for a minute, letting his thoughts run around a bit. *Whoever tried to take out Dr. Simms is going to come back. She was purposely attacked with a car that obviously had a maniac driving. Krystal and I were taunted by a maniac driver as well. Something is seriously wrong. I know these two incidents are connected. So does that mean they are going to come after us again?* Before he turned his car on, he pulled his phone off his waist holder and called the barrack to speak to his captain.

"Captain Zitzer."

"Captain! It's Paul."

"Paul, I got your email. Thank you for taking that case. I thought I was going to have to draw straws for that one."

"Oh, it's no problem. I know that doctor, she's a family friend."

"Well then, maybe you shouldn't be the one in charge?"

"It'll be okay. I want to be in charge so I can stay on top of this. I know it may be a conflict of interest but she is just a family friend, nothing more."

"Okay. I'll give it try and see how it all goes. You'll be really dedicated to it at least."

"I will. I am. Any word on that car that tried to take me and my daughter out yesterday?"

"Nothing. We were never able to find the car. I think it's safe to say that we won't at this point. Any idea who it could've been?"

"No. None at all. I can't shake this feeling that it's connected to Dr. Simms's accident though. Captain, I have a favor to ask." At this point, Paul was glad that he and the captain got along so well. Weekend barbeques together with their families proved to have been a good move on Paul's part.

"For you? Anything!"

"I can't really explain it but I have a terrible feeling right now. Is there any way we can get someone to trail Laura?"

"Your wife? What in the world for? Has she done something wrong?"

"No, no, nothing like that. I might just be a little too worried but I'd like her to have some protection while I'm at work."

"Where's this coming from, Paul?"

"I don't know. It's just one of my gut instincts. I have nothing to base the way I'm feeling off of. I'd also like someone on Krystal too if possible."

The captain sighed. "Well, your gut instincts are almost always spot on. I'll get a rookie on both of them. I'm assuming Laura's at the hospital?"

"Yup."

"And Krystal? Where is she right now?"

"She spent the night at Trent's house so I'd assume she's still there. If not there, then she should be at home."

"Okay. I will get this worked out right now."

"Thank you so much. I owe ya a steak and a beer."

"I'll cash in on that, too!" Captain Zitzer said before hanging up.

Chapter 12

"Wake up!" Doyle shouted at Drew Foster. "Wake the fuck up!" he screamed louder as he kicked the mattress that Drew was sleeping on. Drew slowly woke up in a cloud of confusion and the taste of last night's sex in his mouth. He looked around, not seeing Doyle yet. He saw that the hot blonde Doyle gave him last night was still in his bed, completely naked and almost lying on top of him. He was naked too. He touched the blonde's head and smiled. He began to push the blonde down to his crotch hoping she'd wake up in midflight when he heard Doyle again.

"What the fuck are you doing, asshole?" Doyle shouted.

Drew jumped and quickly pushed the blonde off him and covered himself up. "Boss?! Geezus, what the fuck are you doing here?"

"This is my goddamned pad!"

"Right," Drew said, rubbing his eyes. "Stupid question." Let the ass kissing begin.

"Get the fuck outta bed and get dressed! I have no desire to ever see that sorry excuse for a cock ever again. I'll be in my office. We have a huge problem!"

Drew waited for Doyle to leave the area and sat up. The blonde had just woken up and smiled at her partner from the night before. "Good morning, lover," she said.

Drew was in no mood for her right now. The boss, the man he'd love to fuck more than anyone, had just insulted him in the worst possible way. His dick wasn't that small, was it? Seeing that he appeared to be upset, the hot blonde did the only thing she knew how to do. She slowly lowered her body down to his crotch and began sucking him off. At first Drew was going to push her away, but this was the best way to take care of some morning wood so he let her go to town. It only took him a minute before he came all over her face. She giggled in a schoolgirl way and began slithering her way up to his face. He had gotten what he wanted, though, so he backslapped her across the face and pushed her off the bed. "Get the fuck off me, whore!"

It was okay. She was used to this kind of treatment. She got paid big bucks to be one of the resident whores and even more bucks to keep her mouth shut in regard to things she saw and heard. She slowly got up and took herself to the bathroom with her head hanging low. "Don't pout!" Drew demanded. "You look like an ugly bitch when you do!" He had to find his power after the boss just insulted him so badly.

Drew got dressed rather quickly and braced himself for whatever conversation was about to happen. He didn't know why the boss was so pissed. He was in great spirits last night. They all partied like they'd never partied before. Everyone was drunk and stoned, except for Drew of course. His drug was sex. He had an orgy with two women and another man. They were all wasted and were willing to do whatever Drew wanted them to. He was probably the only one who would even remember what they had done. He kicked a pair of handcuffs to the side with his bare foot and sat down to put on his socks and boots. He didn't know if he'd have to leave quickly but thought it would be better to be prepared.

The space they were in was a one-floor studio in a warehouse type of building. The boss called it his pad. No one really lived there. It was more like a clubhouse for them to have their meetings in private and to party when they completed a job. Drew was off in a side room that had no door. It was more like an open closet. Drew called it the nook because that's where they all went to make nookie. As he made his way to the other side of the flat to the office, he took in the glorious sights. First he saw Jack, aka "the douche bag," on the leather couch, passed out with two chicks on top of him. No doubt he'd be suffering from a bad hangover this morning. They were all naked and Drew took a second to check out the douche bag's package. He confirmed that Jack would be a waste of his time and chuckled to himself.

There were beer and liquor bottles lying around that were half empty or completely empty. There were bongs and half-smoked roaches lying around, and huge bags of weed and blow sitting on the coffee table. The entire room smelled like sex, beer, liquor, and weed. Drew couldn't stand it. He looked at the flat-screen TV that was affixed to the wall and there was a porno playing with the sound all the way down. He smirked at the sight of two chicks getting it on. He reached the office and stepped in through the open door. "Shut the door," Doyle ordered.

Drew did as he was told and took his seat across from the desk. He noticed that the bedroom door in Doyle's office was closed. It always was, as it was his private room. It was off-limits to everyone. "Sorry about earlier, boss," Drew said.

"We got other matters to worry about."

"What's going on? Last night everything was hunky-dory."

Doyle was a slender man – a good-looking, slender man. Drew began thinking about knocking everything off his desk and taking him right there. He was so in love with Doyle, but he'd never tell him. Doyle was straight and would never make it with a man, especially one of his employees.

"Are you fuckin' listening to me?" Doyle shouted.

Drew shook out his personal porno and tried to refocus on work. "Sorry. Long night."

"You are one of the best guys I got, but I can't stand it when you do that zoned-out thing. What the fuck is wrong with you, anyway?"

I want to fuck your brains out, Drew thought, but rather said, "It's probably better that you don't know." He felt his face get hot. He was blushing.

"You're probably right. Did you hear anything I said?"

"No. I'm sorry. Can you repeat it?"

"I said that the fucking bitch you hit yesterday didn't die. You didn't complete the job as ordered!"

"What? That's impossible! I hit her driver side. Her airbags deployed. I saw her flopping around in the car. There's no way. I hit right into her."

"I know, but I guess her car was built better than what we were hoping for. According to the news, she's got a concussion, a few broken bones, and some stitches, but she's going to be fine."

"Fuck! Boss, I'm really sorry. I don't know how she survived that."

"It's not your fault. Well, I mean technically it is. Maybe you should've hit her harder but you did exactly what I asked of you. I wasn't expecting her to survive that shit."

"So what now?"

"Well, we have to be careful. The news reported that the authorities believe it was an intentional hit. If they follow up on that hunch, we could be fucked. Your face was covered, right?"

"Yes, sir. I wore my ski mask. Only my eyes were showing. No one could identify me, even if they saw me."

"Good. My guess is they'll start looking into the doctor's patients. Please tell me when you were seeing her that you didn't use your real name."

"Well of course I didn't. I used my Thomas Sharver ID, just like you told me to."

"Good. You need to stop using it then. I'll have another one for you later today. What address did I put on that ID?"

"Your buddy's place in Laurel, but you said he's moved since then, so there's no connection to me."

"Good. At least we're safe with all that. Now we have to find a way to kill the good doctor for real."

"I can sneak into her hospital room and finish the job."

"Nope. She's got a guard on her. Too risky."

"Well, she's gonna have to be released at some point. We'll just have to wait until then."

The boss studied Drew's face. Drew was his right-hand man, more like a brother to him, and he knew he could trust him as much as he'd allow himself to trust anyone. He also knew that Drew wanted to fuck him. He wasn't stupid. He also knew it would never happen because he was one hundred percent straight. However, the crush allowed him to get whatever he wanted from Drew, so he went on acting like he didn't know about it.

"I think you're right. We'll have to hit her when she's home. Make it look like a break-in even though the authorities will know it wasn't. I have a connection at the hospital so as soon as I hear she's been released, I'll let you know."

"You got it."

"In the meantime, it's almost time for part two of this job. I hope you're ready because there'll be no turning back once it's started."

"I was born ready, boss."

"Good. You can go back to your whore now if you want, but be ready to roll in a couple of hours. We have to keep moving forward. And no more fuck-ups! Understood?"

"Yes, boss," Drew mumbled as he stood up and walked himself back to the nook. The blonde whore wasn't in the room anymore, but he heard her taking a shower and helped himself into the tub. He always got turned on after plotting with the boss, and if he couldn't fuck him, he could at least pretend he was as he butt-fucked the whore.

Chapter 13

Paul parked his police cruiser in the parking lot of the building where Dr. Simms's office was. He knew that her secretary would be there to handle calls. He also knew that the secretary was sweet on him and she would be more than accommodating to him. It occurred to Paul that his family being so close to Dr. Simms was considered to be boundary crossing; his working on this case was technically crossing some ethical boundaries too. His using his looks to get what he wanted wasn't very honorable either. But that was the thing. They were so close that they knew they could trust each other. They each knew how the other operated and what they were capable of achieving, so it really wasn't a big deal. To an outsider, though, it probably looked like a huge deal.

"Mr. Jennings!" Sara excitedly greeted him as he entered the office. "What a pleasant surprise!"

Paul gave her one of his award-winning smiles. "Sara. How are you doing?"

"Me? Oh, I'm okay. I'm just trying to handle all these calls and cancellations. I guess you heard what happened."

"I did. That's why I'm here."

"You are in uniform, aren't you?" Sara asked, biting her lower lip. She began fanning herself with a piece of paper that she had in her hands. "Your wife is one lucky woman."

Paul just kept smiling. "I'm the lucky one, actually." He winked at Sara.

"So, um…what can I do for you?" Sara asked as she broke eye contact with him. "You know Dr. Simms isn't here."

"I know. I was hoping you could help me." Smiling was still happening.

"Me? Help you? I don't see how, but I'd love to."

"Well, I'm not sure how much you've heard, but we believe that the accident was not really an accident."

"Come again?"

"We think someone planned that crash. We think someone wants Dr. Simms dead."

"That's what they said on the news. She's such an awesome person. Who would want to do such a thing?"

"That's where you come in. We were thinking that since she's a psychologist, it may be one of her patients or former patients."

"Oh. I see where you're going with this."

"Could I maybe take a look at her client list for the past few years?"

"No," Sara answered quickly. "All patient files are to be kept private. We're not allowed, by law, to give any information out."

"I know that," Paul said, smiling a bit bigger. "This will be off the record, of course. It'll stay between you and me."

"I don't know," Sara said. She was swooning over Paul's smile but still holding her ground. "I could get into a lot of trouble if someone found out."

Paul thought for a second. "Well, can you maybe tell me if there are or were any clients of hers that seemed off or gave you the creeps?"

Sara nervously laughed. "Maybe a few of them!"

Paul laughed a little. "Do any of them stand out in your mind."

Sara was quiet for a minute as she sat there staring off into the wall. She was thinking about Thomas Sharver, but she wasn't sure how much she should say. She liked her job and wanted to keep it, but she'd do anything to help Dr. Simms. She finally looked at Paul with eyes that clearly told him she knew someone.

Paul, trying to get the information, said, "This is for Dr. Simms. Someone is trying to hurt her and you may be able to help us capture him…or her."

"But if I tell you and it is the guy, how are you going to cover up that I was the one who gave you the lead? I can't get in trouble here, Paul."

Paul flashed his smile at her. "Well, if you should happen to go to the bathroom with his file sitting on your desk, it wouldn't be your fault if I took a peek inside the file. Would it?"

"It wouldn't cause me to lose my job, at least," Sara answered as she stood up and went to the filing cabinet. She was glad that there were no cameras in the office. She pulled a file out of the second drawer and dropped it on her desk. "This guy, he has the look of death in his eyes, like he has no soul. He gives me the creeps. If it was anyone…" She stopped midsentence and changed her thought. "It was really nice seeing you, Mr. Jennings, but I just can't help you with this. If you'll excuse me, I have to use the little girls' room. You know your way out."

Paul gave her another wink before she turned around and left the office. He waited for her to be totally gone and opened the file. There was a name and address and some background information as well as notebook pages full of notes. Paul took a picture of each page and realized that the last time this guy saw the doctor was just yesterday. After he got pictures of every page in the file, he put the papers back in the file, left them on the desk, and showed himself out.

He went to his car and looked through the photos. The guy's name was Thomas Sharver and he lived in Laurel. He began reading the notes that the doctor had taken during their sessions. He read various things, such as "patient has reactive detachment disorder." "Patient is showing signs of bipolar disorder as well as severe depression." "Patient may be a bit narcissistic." "Patient refuses to use medication." It appeared that Dr. Simms had worked with this guy for close to six months. Paul's next stop would be the address of Thomas Sharver. He punched the address into his GPS system.

He pulled up to a small house in Laurel. It looked to be pretty old and not very well kept. He also noticed a moving truck sitting in the driveway with Texas tags. This could be bad. Paul got out of his cruiser and walked to the door. He was about to knock when the door came open. The woman who opened the door jumped at the sight of Paul. "Oh my!" the woman exclaimed. "You startled me. I didn't know someone was here, let alone a police officer."

"Sorry about that, ma'am," Paul replied. "I'm looking for Thomas Sharver. Is he here?"

"I'm sorry, Officer, but I just moved in here yesterday. There's no Thomas Sharver here. It's just me and my husband Cliff."

Paul took his notebook out of his shirt breast pocket. "And your name is?"

"Am I in some sort of trouble?" the woman asked.

Paul smiled. "I don't believe so, unless you're running from the law for some reason?"

"Well, no, of course not. I'm sorry. My name's Shelly Cord."

"Thank you, Mrs. Cord. You said you just moved here yesterday? Do you know who lived here before you?"

"I have his name and new address written down in the kitchen but I'm sure it wasn't no Thomas Sharver."

"Can you tell me the name and forwarding address?"

"Sure. Please come in."

Paul followed Shelly Cord into the kitchen of the house. There were boxes everywhere but the kitchen seemed to be pretty well put together.

"Sorry about the mess," Shelly said. "The kitchen is the only room that is totally ready. We thought it was the most important."

"No worries."

Shelly pulled a pad off the refrigerator. "It was just one guy that lived here, from what I understand. His name was Carl Eck. What a last name, Eck."

Something soared through Paul's blood. He had heard that last name before, Eck. He knew that name from somewhere but wasn't sure. He wrote down the name and forwarding address, which was somewhere in Virginia. "You said no one else lived here with Mr. Eck?"

"Not that I know of," she answered. "Mr. Eck was the only one that our realtor dealt with. Maybe you can talk to some of the neighbors? They would know better than me, I think."

"You read my mind." Paul smiled. "Thank you for your time. I'll let you get back to your unpacking. Good luck with your new home."

"Thank you, Officer," Shelly replied as she led him to the front door.

There were plenty of neighbors to ask, so he went to the house on the left first and rang the doorbell. No one answered. It was in the middle of the afternoon, so most people were probably working. He tried the house on the right and got the same result. Finally, he walked to the house across the street and someone opened the door after he knocked. It was an older lady, probably in her seventies. "Good afternoon, ma'am. I wonder if I might have a minute of your time?" Paul greeted her.

"Is something wrong? What has my son done now?"

"Pardon me?"

"You are here about my son, Chuck, right?"

"No," Paul answered. "I wanted to ask you about the neighbor across the street that recently moved. Mr. Eck?"

"Eck!" the old woman said while sticking her tongue out. "That name suited him perfectly! I was glad to see him move. He got my Chucky in a lot of trouble over the years."

"Can you tell me more about Mr. Eck?"

"I'll tell you everything I know." The old lady smiled.

Paul spent the next hour and a half sitting in the old woman's living room and hearing story after story about Carl Eck. He found out that the man was in the drug dealing business and he had people coming in and out of his house at all hours of the day and night. The old lady's son was one of his dealers and had done jail time but recently got out. He also found out that no one named Thomas Sharver had ever lived there. The old lady was very sure of that. She said she was a master snooper and she could point out every person that had ever visited that house across the street. She said no one ever lived there other than Mr. Eck. Sometimes people would stay for a night or two, but nothing more than that. She said that her son told her that Mr. Eck moved because he was ready to get out of the drug business and start a more honest life, and the only way he could do that was to sell the house and move. The old lady wasn't sure how true that was, though.

When Paul got back to his cruiser, he checked the time. It was already two o'clock. He called Laura and Krystal to check in on them, and then decided to pay a visit to the owner of the stolen vehicle that was used in the crash. The New Jersey plates were reported stolen months ago and did not fit the SUV that had been stolen. They had to go by the VIN in order to find the owners. The owners of the stolen plates were unable to be located for questioning. The owners of the SUV still didn't know that their car had been involved in the accident. They lived right there in Laurel – right down the street, in fact.

Luckily, the owners were home. Mr. and Mrs. Waller had the day off together and Paul had interrupted their afternoon movie. They didn't mind, though. "Did you guys find our car?" Mr. Waller asked.

"Well, yes, but you can't have it back just yet," Paul answered.

"Then why are you even here?" Mrs. Waller asked, clearly annoyed.

"Honey, calm down," Mr. Waller said to his wife. "I apologize for her. She's a bit upset, as it was her car that was stolen. She hates having to drive my car."

"It's okay. It's understandable," Paul said.

"So why can't we have it back yet?" Mr. Waller asked.

"Well, your vehicle was involved in a pretty bad accident yesterday," Paul informed them.

"What?" Mrs. Waller screeched. "Is it totaled? We just bought that damned car."

"It's badly damaged. It'll be up to your insurance company to determine if it's totaled or not. Just be glad you weren't in the car when it was stolen."

"So where is it? I guess we should send an adjuster out to check it out," Mr. Waller said.

"It's in our impound lot right now. I'd hold off on sending anyone out just yet. We have to check the car for any DNA evidence. We believe that the accident was intentional. The woman that got hit was hurt pretty badly. It's a miracle that she survived the crash."

"Wow," Mrs. Waller said, a little calmer now. "I'm glad she's okay."

"Me too," Paul said. "I was wondering if you can tell me more about when it was stolen. The report said you woke up in the morning and realized it was gone. Did you see or hear anything that night or maybe previously in the evening?"

"No," Mr. Waller answered. "We were at my mother's house all evening. When we got home around nine o'clock, the car was still in the driveway. We didn't hear anything all night but when we got up in the morning, it was gone."

"So no ideas of who could've taken it?" Paul asked.

"None," Mr. Waller answered. "I'm sorry."

"Oh my god!" Mrs. Waller shouted, startling both Paul and her husband.

"Ma'am?" Paul asked.

"I'm sorry. I just remembered about the camera."

"Camera?" Paul asked her.

"That's right!" Mr. Waller added. "We let our babysitter use that car while she's watching our daughter. We decided to put a hidden camera in the car so we'd know that the babysitter was a safe driver and was putting our daughter in the car seat properly. We're new parents so I guess we're a little overprotective."

"Wait," Paul said excitedly. "Are you telling me that this camera is in your vehicle and you never thought to tell us that you may have video footage of your car being stolen?"

"Honestly," Mr. Waller answered, "I guess we forgot all about it. It's been a few months and we watched the video from time to time for the first couple of weeks and then just forgot about it because everything looked fine."

"Does it record all the time?" Paul asked.

"Only when the car is on. It stops recording when the car is turned off," Mr. Waller answered.

"How do we check out the videos?" Paul questioned.

"That's simple," Mrs. Waller answered. "We just have to get online and pick what date and time we want to watch."

Paul was very happy to hear this. It meant quite possibly having a face for the crime. "Do you have time to do this right now? If not, I'd have to get a warrant. It would be much easier to do it now."

"Sure, we don't mind," Mr. Waller answered. "I can even email the video link to you or copy it onto a flash drive if you'd like."

"That would be great," Paul said as he followed them inside their house. They led Paul upstairs to a spare bedroom that had been set up as an office. He took his flash drive off of his key ring and handed it to Mr. Waller. "If you don't mind copying it onto my flash drive, I'd really appreciate it."

"Not a problem," Mr. Waller replied, accepting the flash drive.

It only took a minute for Mr. Waller to log on to the website and click on the date that their car was stolen. Just like a well-oiled machine, there was a link for 11:34 that night. They had a video! All three of them waited in anticipation for the video to load. Once it started playing, they were disappointed.

"Of course he'd cover his face when he's stealing a car," Mrs. Waller said. "Maybe he'll take it off, though, once he gets moving in it."

As they watched the car thief quickly slide himself into the driver seat, they were astonished at how fast he was able to hotwire the car. They watched him put the car in drive and take off swiftly, but quietly. A minute of him driving went by before he finally pulled off his ski mask. "Pause it!" Paul ordered.

Mr. Waller did as he was told and they all three studied the man on the video. He had light brown hair, a thick mustache and goatee, a very round but rugged face, and brown, dull, beady eyes that reflected a troubled soul.

"Is he anyone you guys know?" Paul asked.

"No, I don't think so," Mrs. Waller answered.

"Not familiar at all," Mr. Waller answered. "I'll do a screen capture and put the picture on your flash drive as well."

He finished playing the video. It went on for another twenty minutes until the thief stopped somewhere and turned the car off. The camera only faced toward the inside of the car, so it was difficult to see where it stopped.

"Any chance you have some sort of GPS in that car?" Paul asked them.

"We do, but only because it's linked in with the video camera." Mr. Waller answered. "I'll give you the coordinates as well."

"This is wonderful," Paul said. He was glad he had a face now. That would be all he'd need to find this guy. Sometimes, the news channels were good for something. They'd also be able to run his face through their face recognition system. They'd find him one way or the other for sure. "Can we click on yesterday's link as well, real quick? I'd like to see if he had his face covered up for the accident."

"Sure thing," Mr. Waller answered.

They watched as the thief got in the car without a mask on. It was daylight now, so his face was even clearer. They watched him answer his phone. "Does the camera pick up sound as well?" Paul asked.

"Duh," Mr. Waller said, rolling his eyes at himself. "I forgot to turn up the volume."

They listened while the thief had a conversation with someone on his cell phone that they couldn't hear. Then they watched him put the phone down, pull the car over, put on a mask and wait for a minute, and then they watched him take off. They heard him talking out loud and they heard him yell "bull's-eye" right after the collision.

"This was definitely planned," Paul said out loud.

"How awful," Mrs. Waller said. "I hope you all catch this guy and not just because he stole our car. How could anyone do that to another human being?"

"It's the world we live in," Paul responded. "I want to thank you two for being so helpful with this. I'm relieved and ecstatic that you had a camera in your car. It will help us catch this guy much faster."

"If you blast his face on the news," Mr. Waller said, "can you guys refrain from using our name? I don't want our name and our privacy to be violated. I don't want to be in more danger than we already are."

"You don't think the guy will retaliate against us since we handed over the videos, do you?" Mrs. Waller asked in a worried tone of voice.

"I don't think he will," Paul answered. "This was someone with a mission and you guys were just the ones who got caught in the middle. I'll make sure your name isn't released to the media. If you'd like, once this has gone public, we can keep a trooper outside your house for a few days to keep an eye on you."

"I'd like that," Mrs. Waller replied.

"Okay," Paul said while collecting his things. "Me or someone from my department will be in touch. We'll be sure to let you know when this is going to go public. If I have anything to say about it, it will be on tonight's news."

"That soon?" Mrs. Waller asked with a touch of nervousness in her voice. "I don't think I'm ready for that."

"It'll be okay," Paul said as nicely as he could. "We won't use your names."

"But obviously they know where we live!" Mrs. Waller shrieked. "They don't need our names to come find us!"

Paul sighed. "You're right. We can also report that we got the video by obtaining a warrant. I assure you that you guys will be okay."

Mr. Waller put his arm around his wife. "A trooper will be here, right?"

"I promise you that."

"Okay. Well, we'll just take things as they come, I guess," Mr. Waller said while rubbing his wife's shoulder, perhaps trying to convince himself that they were going to be okay.

Paul smiled. He understood their concern but believed they would be just fine. "Thank you for your time and cooperation."

"You're welcome," Mr. Waller replied as he led Paul back to the front door.

Paul quickly drove back to the barrack. He couldn't wait to tell the captain what he had found out and to get in touch with their media department so that they could get the picture of the thief out. The captain was just as excited to see him. "We think we found the getaway car from the accident," the captain said.

"Really?" Paul questioned with very little enthusiasm.

"Yes, except it was burned to a crisp. Any DNA evidence is gone. It was another stolen car, of course."

"Well, what would you say if I told you that I have a picture of the thief?"

"I'd say there's no fucking way!"

Paul smirked as he took his flash drive off his key ring. "Put this bad boy in your computer." The captain did so and Paul told him where to click. Within seconds, they were watching the videos.

"This is amazing!" the captain said. He looked like a child on Christmas morning. "I didn't even know this technology was out there. I'm making a copy of this and sending it over to media. We'll have this guy's face plastered on every news channel and media outlet by this evening! Someone has to know who this joker is."

"Can we run it through the face recognition system first?"

"Duh, why didn't I think of that? Let's go see Diana."

They walked up to the second floor where Diana Strick was clacking away at her computer keyboard. She ran multiple databases and the face recognition system was one of them.

"I don't see you two up here too often. What's up?"

Paul handed her his flash drive. "We need you to run this idiot's face and see if he pops up in anything."

It only took a couple of seconds for the picture to be scanned but it took a few minutes for the database to search through its thousands of records. No one said anything as they waited. Finally, a box popped up on the monitor that read, "No records found."

"Sorry, guys," Diana said as she handed the flash drive back to Paul. "Either he's never been in trouble with the law, or the system just couldn't match his face. It's happened before."

Paul sighed in defeat. "I'm going to print out a picture of him and go over to the hospital and see if the doctor recognizes him. It could be one of her patients."

Suddenly, Paul had that bad feeling come over him again. He felt uneasy. Feeling thankful for technology, he whipped out his cell phone and called the trooper that was on Krystal. He reassured Paul that she was fine. He hung up with that trooper and still had a sinking feeling in the pit of his stomach. He called the rookie cop who was assigned to protect his wife. There was no answer. Without saying anything to the captain, Paul ran out to his patrol car. With lights and sirens activated, he peeled out of the parking lot, tires squealing, as his captain ran out behind him, confused. Paul was headed to the hospital to make sure that Laura was all right.

Chapter 14

Drew Foster was entering foreplay mode. He and Douche Bag were on their way to the hospital too, and as he carefully and very lawfully drove to the hospital, his mental picture was exciting him more than the foursome he had had the night before. He was planning his move inside his head. He always did this on his way to a hit. It not only prepared him for the mission but also excited him and threw him into a level of ecstasy like nothing else ever could. He was on cloud nine as he studied the picture that was taped to the center of the dashboard.

"You are one fine-looking lady, Mrs. Jennings," Drew said out loud, forgetting that he wasn't alone in the car. "I hope there is time for me to ravage you before I beat you to a pulp." Drew laughed as he envisioned throwing Laura against the concrete wall in the parking garage of the hospital and having his way with her. He thought of her screaming and squirming to try to get away from him, and that excited him more. He was only a couple of minutes away from completing the second hit of this monstrous job.

The douche bag just rolled his eyes and said, "You have got to be one of the sickest people I know." He didn't understand how Drew could be thinking about sex right before he was supposed to kill someone. He felt like he didn't have his priorities straight.

Drew laughed. "Thank you! You just better be ready to put the pedal to the metal when I come out of the hospital. If you fuck this up, then I'm gonna fuck you up."

The douche bag just rolled his eyes and gave no response.

A minute after Laura walked out of the hospital to leave for the day, Dr. Simms had just gotten off the phone with her good friend, Mimi Calt, who was a legit psychic. She wasn't one of the looney ones who were just looking to swindle a buck out of someone. She was the real deal. She could sense things that most people couldn't, and Dr. Simms had used her a few times to help out some of her patients.

Dr. Simms immediately pressed the button for the nurse, hoping that Laura would be there. It wasn't Laura, though; it was a new nurse. "Where's Nurse Jennings?" Dr. Simms asked.

"Her shift is over. She wanted to say goodbye, but she said she had plans with her family and to tell you she'll see you tomorrow."

Dr. Simms felt sick. She asked the nurse for the trash can and the nurse got it to her just in time for her to upchuck her lunch that she had consumed a few hours ago. She wiped her mouth and looked up at the new nurse who asked, "Are you okay?"

"I need that cop outside to come here, immediately."

"What? But...why? I can..."

"Now!" Dr. Simms shouted as she grimaced at the pain that the yelling caused her.

The nurse realized that Dr. Simms wasn't playing around and dashed out of the room. The trooper ran into the room in a panic. The name on his nameplate read "Carpenter." "What's wrong, Doc?"

"It's Laura. Jennings. She's in trouble," Dr. Simms said through heavy breaths.

"Laura? She just left. How do you know? What happened?"

Dr. Simms was very agitated at this point. Through clenched teeth, she said, "Listen to me! I don't have time to explain how I know! You have to catch up to her. She's going to be in trouble."

The rookie cop showed no concern and no worries. "She has a trooper tailing her. She'll be okay."

"No, she doesn't," Dr. Simms said, getting madder by the minute. "Please, just go after her!"

"I'll have to call it in. I can't leave you."

"I'm telling you there is no time!" She was shouting now. "Forget about me! Go find Laura before it's too late. Go now!"

The rookie knew he didn't take orders from her, but there was something in her face that read this was serious. As he dashed toward the parking garage, he called for backup.

As Laura got on the elevator and turned around to face the doors, she was surprised to see that her trooper was not behind her. She felt a quick panic and almost got back out of the elevator, but it was too late. The doors closed. She pushed the button for the parking garage and as the elevator started moving down, she dug her Mace out of her purse. She wasn't sure why she did, but something told her to grab it and have it ready – just in case. Her husband's warning from earlier was still on her mind.

As the elevator came to a stop on the garage level, the doors dinged open and Laura's legs felt like rubber. She couldn't move and she thought for sure her legs were going to collapse underneath her. She looked out at the garage without moving from the safety that the elevator seemed to be providing. It was eerily quiet and there wasn't another person in sight. The elevator dinged again as the doors closed. She was now just standing in the elevator, not moving. The elevator wasn't moving either. Didn't anyone else need to use it?

Just as she was about to press the button to send her back up to the fourth floor, the elevator dinged again and the doors swung open. Laura backed up into the back corner of the elevator. She gripped the Mace in her right hand. At first, she thought it must be a dream. There was no way that a masked man was standing there in front of the elevator. She thought about pressing the button to close the doors, but that would only mean she'd have to step closer to the masked man. She held her breath as she looked him dead in his eyes – his brown, beady eyes that looked like they had the devil dancing in them. She felt like she needed to scream but she was in too much shock and couldn't believe this was really happening. She figured if she tried to scream that nothing would come out – just like when you try to scream in a dream.

The masked man didn't say anything until he stepped inside the elevator with Laura. "Nurse Jennings! It's such a privilege to meet you."

Although Laura felt light-headed, she finally managed to scream and point the Mace at the masked man. She pushed down on the pumper and showed no mercy as she sprayed him in the only part of his face that was showing.

Drew Foster dropped to his knees as his eyes burned in pain. He usually welcomed most kinds of pain with a smile and open arms, but this pain caught him off guard, and he couldn't see a damned thing.

Without wasting any time, Laura began kicking him in the side of his stomach while the sight of those brown eyes lingered in her mind. The doors had shut by this time and Laura frantically pushed the button to open the doors. She was thankful that the elevator hadn't started moving to a different level. Being trapped in the elevator with him while it was moving would have sent her into an even bigger panic. The elevator doors swung open yet again. Laura kicked him one more time before she attempted to step over him. Drew grabbed her leg right after she stepped over him and made her fall on her face. The elevator dinged as the doors tried to close but they were unable to. They hit Laura's legs and then opened back up. Drew was trying to climb on top of her. She squirmed and thrashed her body back and forth to try to keep him from getting power over her. She thought for sure this was going to be her last few seconds alive. As she screamed she had images in her mind of her and Paul the previous night. No wonder the sex was the way it was. It was the last time she would ever be able to even kiss her husband, she was sure of it. She screamed again and pushed down on the Mace trigger once again as it sprayed in his face.

Drew screamed and threw his hands up to his eyes.

Laura was finally able to stand up and kicked him one more time, in the face, and that gave her just enough time to start running. She took off toward her car but was stopped within a second by Paul, who had just come flying into the garage with his sirens and lights activated.

She quickly opened the passenger door and threw herself into the bucket seat.

"Honey!" Paul exclaimed. "What's wrong? What happened?"

"Some guy tried to attack me in the elevator!" She was crying now. "I Maced him and kicked him to get away. Get me out of here, please!"

"Where is he now?" Paul wanted to go after him.

"I don't know. I guess he's still in the elevator. Please just get out of here. He was after me personally. He said my name!"

"Shit. I knew something was wrong." He picked up his radio to find out where the other troopers were. "I'm sorry," he said to Laura, "but I'm not leaving. You're safe now. We have to try to find this guy before he gets away."

Trooper Carpenter came out of the stairwell area at that moment, looking all around.

Paul parked his car and told Laura to stay put. He locked the doors as he got out. He ran over to Trooper Carpenter. "Where the fuck is Taylor?"

"I don't know. I thought he was on your wife but Dr. Simms put the fear of death in me. She told me your wife wasn't safe."

"She wasn't. She was attacked. We have to find the guy. He might be in the elevator still," Paul said, storing away the fact that Dr. Simms knew something was wrong.

"The elevator was taking forever," Trooper Carpenter stated. "That's why I took the stairs."

They took off toward the elevator as they heard sirens approaching the parking garage. The elevator light was lit up on Level 5 and was slowly going down. "Let's just wait and see where it goes," Paul said.

It stopped on the garage level. Both Paul and Trooper Carpenter unhooked their holsters and kept their hand on their gun. The doors swung open. A doctor walked out. He looked sickened.

"Was there anyone in the elevator?" Paul asked him.

"No. No...but...but...we found one of your officers in our utility closet. He's dead. Isn't that why you're here? I came out here to escort you up."

"What? No!" Paul answered. "My wife, Nurse Jennings, was attacked in the elevator. One of my guys is dead? What the fuck!"

"Nurse Jennings?" the doctor asked frantically. "Is she okay?"

"She's shook up but she's okay. Can you lock down the hospital? Our guy could be hiding in the building somewhere."

The doctor nodded yes and pulled out his cell phone. He was speaking to someone and informed them the hospital needed to be locked down. There were a total of ten troopers and a K-9 looking for the masked attacker. They never found him, and in a couple more hours, the hospital was up and running again as if nothing had ever happened.

Chapter 15

Drew Foster had no idea how he was going to tell his boss that he fucked up so badly. His plan had started off perfectly. He was able to get their connection from the hospital, a badly paid janitor that Doyle knew somehow, to lure the trooper into the utility closet, where Drew was waiting behind the door, in the dark. Drew quietly stepped up behind him and used his knife to slit the trooper's throat. He killed him so quickly that the trooper probably had no idea what even hit him. It was almost too easy. He should have known that the rest of the plan wouldn't go so smoothly. He should have been more on his game. He should have been prepared for anything, but he wasn't.

After he slit the throat of the trooper, he put on some scrubs that he had been given by their connection and slithered quietly out of the utility closet. No one noticed him and if they did, they didn't notice anything weird about him. Right away, he had seen Laura getting on the elevator with her purse and keys in her hand. He ran down the stairs and waited for her outside the elevator. It was just pure dumb luck that no one else was in the parking garage at that time. Otherwise, there would have been more dead bodies. He got down to the garage with enough time to put on his mask.

When the elevator doors opened, he was already on cloud nine as adrenaline flowed all through him. Maybe that's why the Mace caught him off guard. He wasn't expecting that. *How did that bitch know I was going to be there? I'm just lucky that she and her husband were distracted with each other. Otherwise, they may have seen me running out of the elevator. I'm even more lucky that Douche Bag was waiting for me in the car right outside of the garage. We drove by all those cops! The fucking idiots!*

Drew was also lucky that he had water in the car. Flushing his eyes out felt better than sex.

Drew and the douche bag had just pulled up to the warehouse where Doyle was. "I'm not going in there," Douche Bag said. "I'm going home. You're on your own."

"Thanks a lot," Drew said as he got out of the car. Then as he shut the car door, he mumbled, "Worthless piece of shit!"

Drew felt like he was doing the walk of shame as he very slowly dragged himself up to Doyle's office. "There you fucking are!" Doyle screamed. "What the fuck happened? I just heard on the news that the nurse had no injuries! How did you fuck *this* one up?"

Drew swallowed his pride as he told Doyle exactly what occurred. "I'm really sorry, man. I don't know how she knew I was gonna be there."

"Oh come off of it! If she knew you were going to be there, then she wouldn't have put herself in that spot. She probably had a hunch or something. Women have great instincts, you know." He was calmer now.

"Boss, I'm really sorry. I never screw up like this."

"I know you *usually* don't. But this is twice in a row now! I'm sure we'll have more chances, somehow."

"How? Now that they know that someone is after her, her hubby isn't gonna let her out of his sight."

"They don't know shit! You could've been a junkie trying to mug her for money."

Drew swallowed hard. "Except I'm not…and they know that."

"How would they know that?"

"Because. I said hi to her and I used her name when I did."

"You what?" He was angry now. "Why would you do that?"

"You said you wanted to terrorize her. Hurt her. Beat her so much that she wouldn't be able to remember the attack. I figured it would creep her out more if she knew that I was targeting her specifically in that moment. I didn't think ahead. I kind of got off on it."

"I thought I was a sick fuck."

Drew looked at the boss with eyes of gratitude. The fact that Doyle said he was sicker than him was a compliment in Drew's book.

There was a moment of silence. Drew was trying to compose himself, as he had good and bad feelings running through his head.

"Okay," Doyle finally said. "We can still pull this off. We just have to let a few days go by and let things calm down. Our connection at the hospital is going to be our biggest asset. I'm going to sweeten the pot for him so he'll keep helping us. In the meantime, I need you to be ready at a moment's notice. The doctor still needs to be offed first."

"No disrespect, boss, but why does it matter which order we kill them?"

"You don't need to know that right now. Play your cards right and complete this task and I'll tell you everything. Until then, don't ask me any fuckin' questions."

Drew hung his head like a child who just got caught stealing a cookie right before dinner. "Sorry, sir."

"In the meantime…" Doyle froze. He was looking at his computer screen with a stunned look on his face.

"Boss? What's wrong?"

"Holy shit," he answered.

Drew swallowed hard. He could tell by the look on his face that whatever it was, it was bad.

"We've now got a bigger problem." He turned the computer screen around so Drew could see it. "You fucking idiot!"

Drew's mouth dropped open. There on the screen was a big picture of Drew himself with a headline that he was wanted for car theft and attempted murder. His heart leaped up into his throat. "Oh fuck! Where did they get that picture from? How did they know?"

Doyle read through the article. "Evidently, that car you stole had a fucking video camera in it. You were recorded every time you were driving. It even says that they heard your conversation with me. Thank god we don't use real names."

Drew felt his face get hot with anger. "Are you fucking kidding me?!" he shouted. "A fucking camera?"

"Don't I always tell you to check for cameras? What the fuck, Drew?"

"You do! And I did! I didn't see any cameras anywhere!"

"Maybe you should have looked harder! You're better than this. What the fuck is going on?"

Drew didn't bother to answer his questions. He was too wrapped up in what was going to happen to him. "What the fuck am I gonna do now? Are you going to drop me now?"

Doyle didn't answer right away. His mind was working overtime. He needed to figure this out. There was no way he wanted to get rid of Drew, he knew too much – but now that his face was out there, he was useless. He contemplated killing him. That would be hard to do because he was his best guy. Suddenly, an idea popped into his head. He loved how his mind worked sometimes. "You can handle pain, right?"

"Boss?" Drew asked as if he wanted him to repeat himself. "What are you going to do to me?" Drew stood up and began backing away from him.

"Relax. Sit down. I'm not gonna hurt you, but I have an idea."

"That involves pain?"

"A bit. What about plastic surgery? We could give you a whole new look, change the color of your hair, give you contacts to change your eye color."

"Do we have time for all of that?"

Doyle smirked. "When you're me you do. You know I know people in almost every place and field and job that you can think of. Most of them are on retainer and will help me at the drop of a hat. It just so happens that I have a close friend, kind of like a cousin, who does plastic surgery."

"Can we trust him, though? I mean, if he knows that I'm a wanted man, would he still do the job?"

"First of all, it's a she, and yes, she will. I funded her schooling and helped her start her own practice. She owes me and let's just say that her and I, well, we're apples that fell from the same tree. She's helped me out before. Money talks."

Drew didn't answer him right away. He wasn't sure how he felt about getting plastic surgery. He rather liked his face the way it was. It was the only one he'd had his entire life. How could he look in the mirror and see someone that wasn't him? He found his answer quickly. If he didn't, he would more than likely end up in jail.

"Well, I guess I'm down to do it. I always wanted to look like Brad Pitt."

"Then you shall."

Drew felt relieved as he let a little smile cross his face. "Thanks, boss, for not killing me or dropping me for this."

"You're my best man. You've been having a streak of bad luck lately, though. Maybe a new look will give you some new luck?" He then began laughing hysterically. It was an evil laugh –

94

one that said he was happy to have come up with a solution – but there was also a hint of nervousness in that laugh. His plan was going to shit and having to think fast was never a good thing. He really needed to watch how they carried out the next few tasks.

Drew laughed along with him. He was happy he was going to live to see another day, get a makeover (maybe his new look would turn the boss on), and he was ecstatic that he was still on the job that would allow him to live comfortably for the rest of his life, but he didn't like the bad luck he had been having. The good forces were fighting with the bad forces for sure and he knew the good always won. That's why he always fought it. It was his goal to make sure that evil would be the winner at least once.

Doyle calmed down and said, "I'm going to call her right now. In the meantime, call the boys, get the whores here, and get ready for the party of your life. Tonight we celebrate the end of your ugly mug."

Drew forced a smile. *Ugly? Does he really think I'm ugly?* He was crushed. He stood up and walked out without saying another word to his boss.

Chapter 16

Laura threw herself into the couch. After hours of being questioned by troopers other than her husband and having to relive the scare, she was exhausted. Paul sat down next to her and wrapped his arm around her. She accepted his embrace and rested her head on his shoulder. "I'm sorry you had to go through all that today. How ya feeling?"

"Exhausted. Scared. What if this guy comes back to try and finish the job?"

"He won't. I'm not gonna let him."

"Just like you wouldn't let him get me at the hospital?"

"That's not fair."

"I'm sorry, but this guy was able to nab the trooper you put on me and slit his throat. He obviously knows what he's doing."

"He'd be stupid to try again. Surely he knows that we're on high alert now. Only a fool would try again."

"Soon. Only a fool would try again soon. He could wait it out for a while, couldn't he?"

"I don't know," Paul answered, and kissed his wife on the top of her head. He really didn't know. He didn't know how this guy got away so easily today, let alone how he was able to achieve what he did.

"Do we tell Krystal?"

"I think we should. She needs to know what's going on. I think we all are in danger."

Laura started crying. She was still shaken up from the attack and couldn't get the vision of the guy out of her head. "What if I wasn't able to fight him off? What would have happened to me then?"

"That's not what happened, though. You can't harp on that. You're okay now. You're safe."

"I don't feel safe. I close my eyes and all I see is that covered face and those brown, beady eyes. I swear those eyes had no soul in them."

His wife's description immediately made him think of the guy who stole the Wallers' car. Could it be the same guy? He pulled out a printed picture from the stolen car's camera from his back pocket. He unfolded it and held it up to Laura. "Did they look like this?"

Laura took the picture from him and held it in front of her face. She wiped tears from her eyes and blinked so that she could see the picture more clearly. She looked at his eyes and there was no doubt in her mind that they were the same eyes that were looking out of the ski mask hours before. "Wh…where did you get this?"

"Is it the same guy, you think?"

"It's hard to say, since all I saw of his face were his eyes."

Paul opened his cell phone and pulled up the other pictures he had saved. One was of the guy with just his face showing. "Does this help?" he asked as he handed his phone to her.

She stared into the eyes in the new picture as the attack flashed in her head. They were the same eyes, all right. She was certain. She shoved the phone back at Paul and asked, "Why in the hell are you showing me this? I don't want to ever see those eyes again."

"So you think it's the same guy?"

"If it's not, then it's his doppelganger. It even looks like the same ski mask. Where did you get that picture? Who is that?"

"The car that was used to crash into Dr. Simms's car? It was stolen but it had a camera in it that automatically records when the

97

car is moving. This is the guy who stole the car and tried to use it as a murder weapon."

Laura's mind started racing. "Wait. What? Are you saying the guy that tried to kill Dr. Simms is the same guy who attacked me today? Why? Why is he trying to hurt us? Who is he?"

"I'm not really sure yet but I have a couple of leads I'm going to follow up on. His face is going to be on the six o'clock news this evening. It's already been put onto social media. He's not gonna be able to hide from us now, and he's not gonna be able to show his face. I'll make sure that his face gets plastered everywhere. This motherfucker isn't going to fuck with my family and get away with it. I bet this is the same guy who taunted me and Krystal as well. It has to be the same person."

"I'm just confused. Who is this guy and why does he wanna hurt us?"

Chapter 17

Krystal and Trent walked into her parents' house about an hour later and found her mom sitting on the couch in silence. "Mom?" Krystal asked as she sat down next to her. "Are you okay?"

Laura looked at her daughter, wishing she didn't have to tell her what had happened and wishing she could protect her only child from all the craziness. "I'm okay now."

"What do you mean, now?" Krystal asked her.

"I think we should wait until your dad comes back downstairs. He's talking to his boss right now."

"Did something happen?" Krystal asked as she glanced over at Trent, who had just sat down in the recliner chair next to the couch.

"Mrs. J.?" Trent asked. "Can I get you some water or anything?"

Laura smiled at Trent, hoping that someday he would be her son-in-law. "Thank you, but I'm okay."

"Okay," Trent said. "I think I'm going to go see if Mr. J. needs anything."

Trent got up and showed himself toward the steps to go upstairs. Once he was out of sight of Krystal and Laura, he slowed down and made sure to step lightly. He didn't want Paul to hear him coming. He counted the eleven steps up, making sure not to step on the spots that creaked. He knew that the third step had a squeaky spot right in the middle, so he put his foot on the right side. He also knew that the seventh step was squeaky on the entire surface so he skipped it altogether. Once he got to the top, he stopped and stood still as he tried to find the sound of Paul's voice. He heard it coming from the office room. He tiptoed toward the door, making sure to glance behind him every once in a while. He walked past Laura and

Paul's bedroom – the door was shut. Krystal's door was open so he peeked inside as he walked by. Then he stopped. He went into Krystal's room and crept over to her laundry basket, which was overflowing in her closet. It only took him a second to find what he was looking for – a dirty pair of her underwear. It was a black bikini pair and as he slid his fingers across the crotch area he pictured them on Krystal and got aroused. He then brought the fabric up to his nose and inhaled the scent of the worn underwear. He felt like a rabid dog who was just about to sink his teeth into the perfect chunk of meat. His hard-on was now standing at full attention. He crept into Krystal's bathroom, with the underwear still smashed up against his nose, and dropped his pants. He jerked off into the toilet, smelled the underwear one last time, and placed them back into the laundry basket.

What Trent failed to realize was that Paul had finished his phone and he walked by Krystal's room just as Trent was smelling the underwear while walking into Krystal's bathroom. He had stopped dead in his tracks, trying to process what he had just seen. Did he really just see that? Was what he was hearing now the unmistakable sound of a guy jerking off? He was certain it was, and as he heard the toilet flush only a few seconds later, he quickly turned around and walked back to his office. He quietly shut the office door and got madder by the second, replaying what he just saw in his mind's eye. *That son of a bitch! That little piece of shit! I knew something was wrong with that guy but I never would have pegged him for a panty sniffer. Does Krystal know he does that shit? Should I tell her? No, I better keep this one to myself for now.* Paul took a couple of deep breaths as he tried to calm himself down. He took one last deep breath in and let it out with a huge sigh as he opened the office door. There was Trent, right in front of him, and his cheeks looked a little flushed. *He was just jerking off,*

Paul quickly thought to himself. Paul jumped back and out of habit, reached for his service pistol, even though he wasn't in uniform and didn't have his pistol on his hip.

Trent seemed startled as well as he jumped and put his hand on his chest and breathed heavily to calm himself down. "Mr. J.! I'm sorry! I didn't mean to scare the crap out of both of us like that."

Paul swallowed his pride. "You sure were quiet. I had no idea you were even up here. What's up?"

"Well, Mrs. J. said something happened today. She seemed rather upset, so I came up here to find you to see if you were okay or if you needed anything."

Paul wanted to punch him right in the nose. He wanted to break it so he'd never be able to smell again. Instead, he said, "That's nice of you to be concerned. Something bad did happen today. We were waiting for Krystal to get home so we could speak to her about it. Let's go downstairs." Paul led Trent down the steps as he thought that he had to keep Krystal away from him somehow.

When they got downstairs, Paul was sure to sit next to Krystal and Laura on the couch so Trent would have to sit alone on the loveseat. He really didn't even want him there.

"So, what's going on?" Krystal asked.

Laura began crying. She was still shaken up.

Krystal looked at her father, asking for answers with her confused look.

"Krystal, your mother was attacked today when she was leaving the hospital."

"What?" Krystal shouted. "What happened? You're okay, right?"

Paul answered for Laura. "She's okay physically. She was attacked in the garage as she was trying to get out of the elevator. Luckily, your mom sensed something and had her Mace ready. That helped her to be able to get away. We weren't able to find the guy but your mom is sure it's the same guy who crashed into Dr. Simms. I also think it might be the same guy who taunted us the other day."

Krystal began shaking. "What in the hell is going on? Who is doing this to us?"

"I don't know," Paul answered. He really just wanted to take his wife and his daughter into his arms and comfort them and keep them safe.

"I'm really sorry, Mr. and Mrs. J.," Trent piped in. "If there's anything I can do to help you guys, please just let me know."

Paul looked at Trent. Was he smirking? Paul swallowed hard and said, "I appreciate that, Trent, but I have my guys on this. We're going to find out who's doing this and they're gonna pay." He said this to Trent as if Trent were the guilty party.

"I'm sure you will," Trent said, not feeling the least bit of Paul's anger. "Krystal, why don't you crash with me again tonight? I'd feel better if you were with me so I can keep you safe."

Laura wiped her tears. "That might be a good idea," she said.

"No!" Paul said quickly. "Trent, if you don't mind, I'd like to just be alone with my wife and daughter tonight. I got a trooper outside keeping watch while we sleep. My family really just needs to go through this on our own."

"Dad!" Krystal said, shocked. "Trent is just trying to help and keep me safe."

"I know," Paul said, swallowing his pride, "and I appreciate that, but I just want my family close to me right now."

"I understand," Trent said, looking down at his feet. He really didn't. "Krystal, it's okay. Your dad is right. You should just stay here tonight. You're probably safer with your dad, who's a cop, than just me."

"Fine," Krystal said. "At least stay a while? Have some dinner with us?"

Trent was about to say sure, but Paul cut him off. "No. Krystal, your mother really needs to rest this evening and I'd feel better if it's just us three for right now."

Krystal was about to protest but Trent stood up before she could say anything. He knew when he wasn't wanted. "It's okay. I'm gonna go. Krystal, I'll call you later tonight and check in on you."

"Okay," Krystal said, feeling defeated. "I'll walk out with you."

Laura looked at Paul with some confusion. "What in the world? It was okay if he stayed for dinner. I don't mind."

"I do," Paul said.

Later that night, Laura tried to go to sleep but she just tossed and turned. Every time she closed her eyes, all she saw were those ugly brown eyes taunting her. Paul held on to her tight, wishing he could figure out who was tormenting him and his family. He was also trying to figure out how to convince both Krystal and Laura that Krystal needed to stay away from Trent. Now that he had an actual reason to not like Trent, other than just his instincts, he knew he needed to be a bit more firm about this. There was too much weirdness going on, and Trent didn't help the stress that Paul was currently dealing with. He only made things worse.

Chapter 18

The next morning, Laura and Paul were in their bedroom waking up. They were both scared and unsure of what was going on. Paul thought for sure this all circled back to him somehow but he wasn't sure how. He had stayed up half the night trying to rack his brain and couldn't come up with anything. The guy in the picture was not familiar to him. The only thing that had even sounded somewhat familiar during his investigations was the name Carl Eck – the guy who used to live at the house that he stopped at yesterday. He spent the other half of the night trying to figure out why that name sounded so familiar. Also circling around in his mind was that he still needed to tell his wife his little secret. Of course, what he witnessed Trent doing did not help his state of mind any.

He had a lot on his plate today. He was going to run the name Carl Eck and see what came up. Maybe he had arrested him in the past. He was going to go see Dr. Simms, as well as her secretary, and run the picture by them. Also, he was going to go visit the old lady that gave him an earful about Mr. Eck and see if she recognized the photo. Maybe one of them could tell him more about this guy and that could help them find him.

There was one other thing that he had to check into. The camera in the stolen car also came with a GPS. The Wallers added the coordinates on his flash drive but he hadn't had time to check them out. That could lead him straight to this guy. He knew that the guy was probably going to get scared and try to come back sooner rather than later. Of course, Paul had no idea that the next few weeks were going to be fairly quiet and uneventful, as Drew Foster was getting plastic surgery and changing his entire look.

Paul got out of bed behind his wife and they showered together. After they were finished in the shower and were getting dressed, Laura asked Paul, "You know, I meant to ask you, why exactly did you ask Trent to leave last night?"

Paul quickly had the vision of Trent sniffing his daughter's underwear flash in his mind. He tensed up and made a gagging noise. "It's probably better that you don't know," he answered.

"Oh really? With everything going on now, I think I have a right to know."

Paul considered this for a second and he knew that his wife was right. She was always right. "Okay, but you may want to sit down."

Laura just finished putting on her shirt and sat down on the bed with her shoes in her hand. "I'm sitting down."

Paul sat down next to her. "Well, yesterday, when he was here, I saw something disturbing."

"Such as?"

"Well, you wouldn't believe what I saw him doing yesterday in Krystal's bedroom when you and her were downstairs."

"What?"

"He had a pair of our daughter's underwear and he was sniffing them as he was walking into the bathroom."

Laura slowly processed what her husband was saying to her.

"And then I heard him jerking off in her bathroom."

"Are you sure?"

"Look, I know you like the guy, but you know I've never really cared all that much for him. I heard the unmistakable sound of someone jerking off. It only took him a few seconds and then I heard the toilet flush, so I quickly went back to the office. I calmed myself down because you know I wanted to pound the shit out of him after seeing that. After I was composed enough, I opened the door and there he was, standing right in front of me."

"Well, he knew something was going on and that's why he went upstairs. He said he wanted to check in on you and see if you needed anything."

"Well, he took a pit stop along the way."

"Okay. So he's got a weird fetish. Does that make him such a bad guy?"

"Are you seriously defending him right now? How do you think Krystal would feel if she knew about this?"

"I hate to tell you this but our daughter is an adult. I'm sure they're having sex, so maybe she knows."

Paul looked at his wife, surprised by her response. "I really doubt she knows about this."

"Well, we can't exactly ask her, now can we?"

"I'm not going to, that's for sure! The guy has always given me the creeps and this just reinforced it. Something isn't right about him."

"He was sniffing his girlfriend's underwear. We should be glad that you didn't catch him sniffing the neighbor's underwear, or even worse, my underwear."

"I would've killed him then!"

"He's in love with Krystal, so is sniffing her underwear and getting excited by it so weird? I mean, I've seen you smell my underwear before." She gave her husband a flirtatious smile.

"But that's different! I do it in front of you! You know about it. Wouldn't you feel weird if you walked in on me smelling them when you weren't there?"

"Nope! You're my husband and it would flatter me that I still turn you on. We should be glad that he's so in love with our daughter."

Paul looked at his wife in surprised bewilderment. "I will never understand the way you think sometimes."

"It's probably better that way," Laura said, giggling. "It's animalistic if you think about. It's kind of like a monkey throwing shit at someone."

Paul chuckled. "I don't see humans throwing shit at people though."

"Of course not, because we've evolved. Well, most of us have. I'm sure someone who is messed up on something throws their shit at people. No matter how much we evolve, people are still going to have animalistic desires, especially men."

"It's still creepy, though. For him to do that behind her back with all of us in the house? To do it in secret? There's something not right there."

"I think you're overthinking it. Just try not to snub him anymore. I'm sure Krystal is freaked out enough right now with everything that's been going on. We don't need her being upset because her father won't let her see her boyfriend."

"How can I not snub him after seeing that? I don't want him anywhere around her. With everything that's going on, I want to keep Krystal safe and I don't think she's safe being with him. Especially after seeing that."

"Well, why don't you run his name at work? See if he's got anything on record? I'm surprised you haven't already done that."

"Oh believe me, I would love to, but I can't just run a name because he's dating our daughter. He needs to be involved in an actual investigation."

"Well, even though I disagree, you said it's weird that he was sniffing Krystal's underwear. Is that enough for an investigation?"

"Hardly."

Laura placed her hand on Paul's shoulder and looked him in the eye. "I think it's a bad idea to ask Krystal to stay away from him, especially right now with everything going on. You think she's not safe with him, right?"

"Right."

"And if you tell her to stay away from him or forbid her to see him, what do you think she'll do?"

"Run straight to him."

"Right. So will you please just try to let it go for now? Will you please do it, for me? I'd like a little bit of peace around here."

Paul knew he couldn't tell her no. He sighed. "I guess I can try, but I can't make any promises."

"That's all I ask. I love you," she said before kissing him on his cheek.

Chapter 19

At the same time that the Paul and Laura were having their conversation about Trent, he was throwing his cell phone across his bedroom. He went to bed in a bad mood from not knowing why he was asked to leave Krystal's house. He woke up in a bad mood because someone had been blowing up his cell phone. The only person that would have gotten a pass from doing that would have been Krystal but she hadn't called him since he left her house last night. The person blowing up his phone was his boss. He didn't want to hear his bullshit today so he ignored the calls and finally, after the fifth call, he threw the phone against the wall. He knew it would be okay, this wasn't the first time he had thrown that damned phone against the wall. He made good money working for this guy under the table, but he wasn't sure he could continue on with the job. It was starting to get personal, and even though everyone had told him his entire life to not let business get personal, it had crept up on him this time.

As he walked out of his bedroom, he heard someone banging on his door. His apartment was equipped with a doorbell and most normal and sane people used it. That's how he knew it was his boss banging on the door. That's how he always made his presence known, by making the greatest amount of noise possible. Of course, he was the quietest person there ever was if he didn't want to be detected. Trent had no desire to talk to his boss right now but he knew he'd know he was there. He knew where all his employees were at all times.

Trent walked over to the door and peeked through the peephole. It was his boss, just as he figured, but he had his hoodie tied up around his face. It made him stand out, since it was warm outside, and Trent wondered why he was trying to conceal his face.

Trent put on his angry face, then unlocked the door and swung it open in one quick motion. "What the fuck do you want?" he asked the man staring just as angrily back at him.

"That's no way to fucking talk to me. Are you gonna let me in or do you wanna talk right here where your neighbors can hear?"

Trent slowly backed away so the man could come in. He shut the door behind him and locked it back up. "I asked you a question," Trent said as he walked into the kitchen to start some coffee.

"I've been calling you all morning."

"I know. I didn't wanna talk to you."

"Trent, you need to stop. You're headed down the wrong road."

"You got this wrong. This job is all wrong."

"All wrong for you maybe, but not for my boss. I don't know the fucking story and I don't want to know it. I take my orders from him just like you take orders from me. I'm just the middleman. If you want to protest this job, then you need to go to the big guy. I wouldn't suggest doing that, though. He's gung ho on this job and you're pissing him off. I wouldn't piss him off anymore if I were you."

"But you aren't me! I've never even met this guy. I've only spoken to him on the phone. What am I supposed to do, call him and tell him I quit? How in the fuck am I supposed to protest this job to him?"

"You don't, nimrod! You knew what this job entailed from the very beginning. We let you in because you had proven yourself already with the past two jobs. You're going to make a shit-ton of money at the end of this one. You could retire, you fucking idiot. My advice is to not fuck this up!"

"Please! You only let me in on this one because my age was right. Otherwise, you would've went on to do it without me. I wish I never agreed to do this shit. The other jobs were easy, I was just a hired hand. The role I'm playing in this job is such a head fuck! It was a mistake taking this job!"

At that moment, Trent's guest was mad. He grabbed Trent by the collar of his T-shirt and shoved him up against the kitchen wall. He got in his face, so close they could have kissed. "Listen to me, you little piece of shit! If you know what's good for you, you'll get your priorities straight. Things have already gone wrong that were out of our hands. I'm not gonna let you fuck this up any more than what it already is. If you want out, then you know what will happen to you. You better think about that before you do anything stupid." He loosened his grip on Trent's T-shirt and took a half step backward. He smoothed out Trent's T-shirt with his left hand, then swung his right hand down to Trent's ball sack. He slid his fingers along Trent's member and began stroking it back and forth.

Trent began thinking back to when he first got involved with these guys. He had received a call out of the blue from Doyle, who said he got his name from a mutual friend. He never told him who the mutual friend was, but Trent never harped on it because the job he wanted to hire him to do was going to pay a lot of money. More money than Trent had ever seen in his life, and all he had to do was kill some dude who had stabbed Doyle in the back. It was over and done with before Trent even had a chance to back out of it. Then he was hired for a couple more similar jobs after that. Then the day came when Doyle called and talked to him for almost two hours straight about the current job. Doyle sure did talk it up, telling him it was not only going to pay more money than Trent could imagine but Trent would be able to have fun with it too. He made it sound so easy and fun that he couldn't turn him down. But now here he was, with a grown man fondling his genitals and creeping him out. This wasn't easy or fun.

In a very quiet yet creepy tone, his boss said, "You know, there is one way I'd let you out of this job."

Trent swallowed hard. "Ho-how-how's that?"

The man laughed and backed away from Trent. "You couldn't handle it. You are in this whether you want to be or not. Straighten up and give us what we need, or you won't be able to do anything but try to run from the hot fires of hell. Capisce?"

Trent wanted to tell him to get lost and tell him that he was out, but he wasn't ready to die yet. He'd figure a way out of this. "Fine. Whatever you say."

"Good. Now come with me."

"What?" Trent asked, confused.

"Did I stutter? Come with me. The boss wants to meet you!"

"Are you fucking kidding me? I thought I wasn't allowed to meet him."

"Yeah, well, he's worried that you're going to stray from us. He wants to make sure that you know what will happen if you do. He just wants to do a little job observation on you."

Trent thought for sure this was going to be his last day on earth.

Chapter 20

Krystal tapped the hang-up button on her cell phone. Trent's phone went straight to voicemail so she didn't bother leaving a message. She stepped into her bathroom and started the warm water in the bathtub. She wiggled out of her pajamas and then turned the shower on. She put her plastic cover over her arm and then stepped into the steaming hot shower. She stood face first in the stream of water and closed her eyes. Her head was throbbing but not as much as her wrist was. As the bathroom filled up with steam and she inhaled the warmth of the moisture, she suddenly felt like a huge burden had been lifted off her shoulders. At a time when she and the rest of her family should be on high alert, she felt like there was nothing to worry about. It was as if someone or something told her it was all over. Had this Thomas Sharver guy finally given up? Maybe he was going to flee now that his face was out there. She wasn't sure if she really believed that theory, but something was telling her it was okay now. They were all going to be safe.

Her thoughts went back to Trent. It was odd that his phone went straight to voicemail. He always kept it on. Always! If he did miss her call, he always immediately called her back. It worried her that his phone seemed to be turned off. He was always there when she needed him. This was the first time that he wasn't. She got herself out of the shower and put on her robe. She grabbed her pain pills and downed two. She had hardly slept last night and all she wanted to do right now was sleep. She was feeling good and strong. She wasn't feeling afraid, so sleeping seemed like a good idea. She took a third pain pill and lay down on her bed. She knew taking three pills would knock her out good and quick and keep her knocked out for a long time. As she closed her eyes, her mind drifted to her nightmare from the night before. The dream she had about Trent seemed so real, and she wondered if her father's doubts about Trent were now creeping into her mind. She thought about the few times that Trent seemed to be somewhere else when they were talking and his eyes looked like some sort of evil had taken over for just a second. She knew it was just her crazy mind working overtime but since she had that dream about him, she wasn't too sure. Her thoughts about Trent started to fade as she finally fell asleep.

A noise woke her up about an hour later. Both her parents were at work, so she knew she was home alone. She was sure she had heard something. She wasn't sure what it was, though. She didn't make a move as she listened closely to see if she heard anything else. She felt groggy and her eyes were heavy. She wanted to go back to sleep. Just as she was dozing off, her bedroom window started to slowly come open.

Krystal sat straight up in her bed, eyes opened wide, and looked at the gloved hands that were wrapped around the bottom of her window and pushing it up. How could this be? How could anyone get in their house right now with a trooper on watch outside? How is this person even opening her window when her bedroom is on the second floor? She tried to get out of bed but she felt heavy and ended up falling on the floor. She felt like she was drunk. As she cursed herself for taking three pain pills, she used the side of her bed to pull herself up to her feet. By then, the intruder was standing in front of her. He wasn't even wearing a mask. How bold was this guy! Who was this guy? It wasn't Thomas Sharver. She knew that by the picture.

"Hello, Krystal," the man said.

He was slender and very good-looking. His shoulder-length hair was slicked back. The bare face revealed light blue eyes. They kind of looked familiar. As she stared into his eyes, she realized that his right eye looked warm and inviting but his left eye, well, his left eye looked cold and evil. Krystal blinked, sure that her eyes were playing tricks on her. The man was wearing a shiny suit that appeared to be very expensive. It made him look important. He was wearing a bracelet that seemed to glimmer and a cross around his neck.

"Who are you? Why are you in my room?" She couldn't move.

"I just wanted to stop in and say hello. Is there something wrong with that?"

Krystal closed her eyes, hoping that when she opened them back up, the man would be gone. Surely, she was just tripping on the pain pills. Unfortunately, he was still there when her eyes slowly opened.

"Get out!" she shouted.

The man laughed. It was a piercing evil laugh and she recalled the laugh of the man in the car who tried to hit her and her father. It was eerily similar. He walked over to her. He smiled. It must be how the devil looked when he smiled. Krystal tried to take a step back but she was frozen. The man slowly raised his right hand and caressed her cheek. "You're so beautiful. It's too bad things weren't different. You're probably a really cool person. One I would've gotten along with. Too late for all that, though."

"What? Wha...what are you talking about?"

He continued to stroke her face. "I just wanted to lay eyes on you in person before...well, while I still can. I wanted to give you a message too, before your world crumbles around you."

Krystal was physically shaking.

The man chuckled. "I could have taught you a lot but I never got the chance. I just wanted to be sure that I taught you one lesson. Are you listening?"

Krystal slowly nodded yes but couldn't find the words.

"Good." He then grabbed Krystal's right hand and placed his other hand on top of it. "Krystal, did you know that death and sex are pretty much the same thing?"

Krystal shook her head no.

The man smiled at her as if he were a caring father trying to teach his daughter the most important lesson in life. "Oh, they are. You see, when you die, you are suddenly relieved of all of your aches and pain, both physically and mentally. Did you know that when someone who has been blind their entire life dies, they can all of a sudden see?"

Krystal just looked at him. Was this a dream?

He lightly squeezed her hand to get her attention and looked at her sternly as if she'd better answer him right now.

She just shook her head no again.

"It's true!" He seemed really happy to be telling her this. "Imagine the best orgasm you've ever had. It probably felt really good, huh? Well, they say death feels even better than that! Can you imagine that! To feel that way for an eternity! So you see, death and sex are the same thing. They're just on opposite ends of the spectrum. So, when I kill someone, I consider it to be a gift. Krystal, I'm going to be giving your family the gift of death."

Krystal began trembling. She took a deep breath in and as she slowly let it out, it came out in shaky little rasps. She then began breathing heavier as she tried to keep herself from totally losing it.

"There's no need to thank me. I'm only giving you the gift because I think you'd appreciate it more than if I let you live. When the day comes, and it's going to be very soon, I promise, don't fight it. Okay? Just know that I'm doing it because I want you to be happy and feel that euphoria forever. Only you and your mom, though. Your father, well, he'll be getting the gift of death but it will be hell for him first. I have to have some fun first, so forgive me for the impending wreckage. I can't give myself the gift of death, so I have to have fun in other ways."

Krystal just looked at him. What the fuck was this guy talking about? Was she high or was he? He let go of her hand. "I have to go now, honeybee. I'll be seeing you soon, though." He kissed her on her cheek and she immediately stepped back away from him, falling down onto her bed.

He laughed and went back to the window. She watched him climb out of the window and slowly descend.

It took her a second to come back to reality. When she did, she ran over to the window to see this man jump off a ladder and take off running. She wasn't dreaming this. It really did just happen. She screamed. She picked up her phone and called her father. He was there within minutes to comfort her and give the trooper outside the house hell. He hadn't been watching the back of the house where Krystal's bedroom window was located. He was sitting in front of the house and saw nothing and no one suspicious. Krystal lay back in her bed and cuddled on her father. She told him the whole story and then cried until she finally fell back to sleep.

Chapter 21

Once Paul got Krystal calmed down she went into a nice, deep sleep. After a second trooper was parked outside his house, Paul got in his car to make his way to the hospital. He stopped by the office first to run the Eck guy, but their computers were down. Go figure. So he decided to go to the hospital to let Laura know what had just happened. He knew he should have put up those outside cameras last year like he wanted to. Laura was against it though. She said no one would ever break into a cop's house. Ha! He was also going to see Dr. Simms while he was at the hospital. Maybe she'd be up to looking at the photo. He also wanted to run it by her secretary, Sara.

Laura was at the front desk when he walked in. He didn't want to tell her what had happened, but he had to. Someone was after his family and it was his job to keep them protected. It seemed he was failing at that, though. "Hey, honey," he said as he looked at her with dread.

"Paul? What now?"

Paul lowered his voice. "Someone broke into Krystal's bedroom while she was sleeping."

"What?" she shouted. It seemed everyone dropped what they were doing to stare at them.

"Sssh," Paul ordered. "Keep your voice down, please. She's all right. He put a ladder up to her window and came on in. The damn trooper outside our house didn't even see him."

"Is she okay?" Laura whispered. She began shaking a bit, and felt like she was going to throw up.

"She's okay. The guy just said some really weird shit to her and then left."

"What kind of weird shit?"

118

"She's fuzzy on everything. She said she took three pain pills, but according to her, he was going on about death and sex being the same thing."

"What?"

"Yeah. I know. That sounds weird. She also said he told her that she's gonna die soon, that all of us were."

Laura started crying. "Paul, I don't like this. What's going on? Was it the same guy that attacked me and Dr. Simms?"

"I don't think so. This guy didn't even cover his face, but she's having a hard time remembering what he looked like. She was certain that it wasn't the same guy, though. I'm hoping that when she wakes up, she will remember more. She did say that the laugh sounded like the guy in the car that tried to hit us."

"So you're telling me that there's two different guys doing this?"

"I'm starting to think that."

"Krystal's home alone?"

"Yes, but I put another trooper outside our house. She was fast asleep when I left. I think she'll be okay. I'm gonna have the alarm company come over and update our system. I never thought I'd have to put alarms on the upstairs windows but I guess I do."

"I agree. We should do that as soon as possible. I don't want Krystal to be home alone when she wakes up. I'm gonna get the rest of my shift covered and get home as soon as possible."

"That's a good idea. I'm gonna go talk to Dr. Simms if she's up. I love you."

"Love you too," she responded as she gave him a quick kiss.

When Paul poked his head into Dr. Simms's room, he was overjoyed to see that Sara was there visiting. He could kill two birds with one stone. He was also relieved to see that there was a trooper

119

outside of the doctor's room as well as one keeping an eye on his wife.

When Paul walked into the room, Sara's eyes lit up. "Paul!" she exclaimed. "What a pleasant surprise!"

"Likewise," Paul replied with his award-winning smile. "Doctor, how are you feeling?"

"All things considered, I'm feeling okay. I was scared out of my mind yesterday. I'm glad you and your wife are okay."

"How did you know that someone was coming after my wife?" Paul questioned her.

"Well, I had just got a call from my friend Mimi. She can sense things like this and she called me to tell me that something bad was about to happen with my nurse friend. That was all I needed to hear to know to get the trooper on her as quickly as possible."

"Well," Paul said, "you will have to thank your friend for us. Maybe we should keep her around us from now on." He wasn't really being serious, as he thought it might have just been a lucky guess. He wasn't so sure that people could actually see things like that.

The doctor giggled. "She said the same thing, but she said she had a couple of weeks before she'd have to be here. She wouldn't tell me what that meant though."

"It's nice to see you again, Mr. Jennings," Sara said to him with her flirtatious smile.

The doctor rolled her eyes at her. "Would you stop flirting? He's a married man!"

Sara blushed and looked away.

"I'm really glad to see some color back in your face," Paul said, trying to change the subject. "I'm also glad you're here," he said to Sara. "I have a picture here that I'd like you both to look at. I wonder if you happen to know him."

120

He produced the picture out of his back pocket and unfolded it. Sara gasped. "He's one of my clients," Dr. Simms said. "Where did that picture come from?"

Paul sat down in the chair beside the bed. "Well, the car that was stolen and ran into you? It had a camera in it. He's the guy that was driving the car that almost killed you."

Dr. Simms was quiet for a few seconds. She was trying to process what she had just been told. "Are you sure, Paul?" she asked.

"One hundred percent sure."

Sara said nothing. She only looked down at her feet.

"I'm just surprised. He had his issues, of course, but he was a nice guy for the most part. We had a bit of a breakthrough during his last session and he even thanked me for all the work I've done with him. Why would he do this to me?"

"Well, he might've been putting on an act when he was with you. I don't know why he did this but we're gonna figure that out. I'm going to need any information that you guys can give me on him. His name, his address, any reasons you may think he'd do this, and anyone he talked about that may be able to tell us where he could be if we can't find him at his residence."

"Well," Dr. Simms sighed, "I'd need to see his folder to jog my memory and pull up his personal information. Maybe you can fetch it from the office and bring it to me?" she asked Sara.

"S-s-sure," she stuttered. "Paul, can I walk out with you?"

"Of course you can."

As Paul walked out with Sara, he knew that she wanted to talk to him about the photo, and that was okay because he wanted to talk to her too. "Paul," she said. "The guy in that photo is the same guy that I was thinking of the other day when you came to visit me."

121

"That's what I was wanting to know, but I didn't want to say anything in front of the doctor. I went to the address that was in your file and whoever lived there just moved out. I spoke to the neighbor and she told me that the guy that lived there before was a Mr. Eck. I'm gonna go see her next to see if the picture is this Mr. Eck but I have a feeling that it isn't. I think the guy who lived there was just an associate or something. The phone number listed in his file is no longer in service. No shock there. Is there anything you can tell me about him that might be of help?" Paul made sure that his eyes were smiling at her.

"He always gave me the creeps, looked at me like he was undressing me with his eyes, and you'd never know if he was going to be nice or mean. He even called me a bitch one day for no reason at all. I don't know if Krystal told you, but I had a scary run-in with him the other day. Krystal came to my rescue."

"Wait! This is the same guy that put you up against the wall?" His heart jumped in his chest.

"That's him. I never told Dr. Simms, for some reason. He's a creep, Paul."

"He's also the one that tried to attack Laura. Can you think of anything else I need to know about him?"

"That's really all I can say about him."

"Could I send our forensic team down to your office to dust for fingerprints?"

"You could, but it would be no use. I cleaned the office today from top to bottom and scrubbed everything. I was just really bored. You won't get any prints. I'm sorry. I wasn't thinking."

"It's okay, no need to apologize. You didn't know. We've put his face out on the news but so far no one has come forward to say they know him. But anyway, if you think of anything else at all, please give me a call."

122

Chapter 22

Trent was in his car, following his boss to their "office." He knew these guys meant business, but they were expecting him to do something that he just didn't want to do. The two previous jobs he completed were easy. He didn't care about those people that he harmed and helped put six feet under. Those people didn't mean anything to him. Krystal, though, she meant everything to him. He was even madder at himself for letting his feelings get involved in a job. What did they expect, though? They threw one of the most beautiful girls he had ever seen in his entire life in front of his face and told him, "Go!" How could he not have fallen for her? She was gorgeous, had great taste in music, and her friends were loyal and dedicated. He had never met people like that before. Her family really loved one another. He never realized how much he missed that in his own life. And on top of all that, Krystal's personality was killer. She wasn't like most girls that had to be put in their place. She never flirted with other men, she was always there for him no matter how bad his attitude was, and she was fun. Fun! He loved being with her, spending time with her, and just straight up loving her. He had never felt this way in his entire life before, and now he's being told to stop? He didn't know how he was going to get out of this one. He had been in some pretty bad situations in his lifetime but this was by far the worst because his emotions were involved. He hadn't even known he had emotions. Not to mention that his life was literally on the line as well.

He grew up in and out of foster homes until he turned eighteen, when he was finally set free to be on his own. Each foster family gave the same reason for returning him. "His anger is too much for us to handle. We can't help him, much less take care of him." Sure, he may have pushed one of his foster sisters down the stairs, but the little snotty kid had gotten into his Halloween candy. He was only six, how was he supposed to know that she'd get hurt so badly? The next foster family after that one was abusive. He was stuck with them until he was thirteen and the only reason he got "returned" was because he fought back at his foster father one night and bludgeoned him with a hammer. He wasn't sorry, either. That fucker deserved that and more. Had he had a bit more strength, he would have killed that guy. He still had scars on his back from the many beatings he got with the leather belt. Even to this day, he still couldn't wear a belt, or even look at one.

Being thirteen made it a bit harder for the state to find him a foster family. They did find one for him though, right after his fifteenth birthday. He was pretty sure they only took him for the money, and planned to kick him out when he turned eighteen. He was sure of it. That's why he thought nothing of fucking their fourteen-year-old daughter. She was his first and he was her first. He popped her cherry one night while the parents were sleeping in the next room. They were quiet and were able to continue the nightly fuckings for the next six months. As their sexual relationship evolved, it turned into something that Trent couldn't explain at the time. He could now, but then, he was still figuring out why he did the things he did. He began tying her up and blindfolding her and fucking her until she couldn't stand it. Most nights she was into it but sometimes she would try to scream to make him stop but he always quieted her with a slap across her face. One night, things got way out of hand. She was able to get out of the ropes that he had her bound with, and she threw herself off the bed. He got on top of her and began choking her. She was pounding her fist on the floor so hard and so loud that her parents heard and came running into the room. If they hadn't gotten there when they did, he probably would have choked her to death. Because he was a minor and had a history

124

of being passed off from foster home to foster home, the state decided to keep him in a state-run facility until he turned eighteen. No more foster families for Trent.

What did they expect? He was taken away from his parents when he was five because they were heroin addicts who were trying to sell Trent for money. When no one would buy him, they began letting grown men and women rape him for money. Some of the people who paid for that also physically abused him. That didn't mean anything to Trent, though, as his father beat him nightly to get him to go to sleep. How was he supposed to know that what was happening to him wasn't "normal"? He thought that all the anger he felt was normal until he reached his early twenties. He had met a girl named Stacey and she was the first girl he ever really loved. He abused her at least once a week because she was constantly pissing him off. She took the abuse for a while, as he promised he'd stop, but it eventually got to be too much. She told him that their relationship wasn't healthy and the way he treated her was disrespectful and she deserved better. He spent two years with her, and when she told him she was leaving he had never felt so much anger. He beat her up good, almost killed her. She was too scared to press charges against him so she moved away, disappeared, and he never saw her again. Two years later he met his boss and then met Krystal.

He was never told exactly what the job was. All he knew was that he was to get close to Krystal and her family so they would have an "in" later on down the road. Doyle also told him that he would be allowed to do whatever he wanted with Krystal at the end of it. He thought he'd have some fun with her and then pull one of his old tricks and bloody her to death. Something happened, though. Something inside of him changed and he didn't want to hurt Krystal. Quite the opposite, actually. He wanted to protect her. Not just from

125

his boss and his "coworkers" but from anything bad ever happening to her. Something about Krystal soothed him and calmed him down. Her eyes were so bright and loving and her touch made him feel love that he had never felt in his entire life. He even started seeing a therapist a few months ago because he wanted to make himself better, for Krystal. No one knew he was talking to a head shrink and the head shrink didn't know *everything* about his life. He wanted to be with Krystal for the rest of his life. The therapist wanted to put him on medicine but he refused. He was determined to do this on his own. He was already doing well before seeing a therapist and now he was doing really good...until this morning.

The anger that he had been trying so hard to keep at the wayside was back in full force and he didn't know if he could keep it under control. He was afraid that this was going to be his last day on earth. Was this what his life was for? To be abused, to abuse, only to die? He knew he was going to have to fight with his boss and his coworkers, but how bad was it going to get? His anger was bad right now.

Little did he know that all the anger and abuse that he had learned was wrong and had fought to keep away had only turned into obsession. He wasn't in love with Krystal, because he didn't even know what it meant to be in love with someone. He was obsessed with her, and that was just as dangerous as the anger that he had been fighting so he could stay with her. He would kill for Krystal, for his obsession, but he knew he wouldn't kill her. He had been doing his job really well by keeping his true self a secret. He wasn't too sure how he was doing it, but he figured he must really love Krystal if he was so easily able to bury the anger inside of him deep down. If only she knew how much he loved her. She'd never know of the fight that was about to take place because it was probably

126

going to kill him. He pulled into the parking lot of the "office" and shut off his car.

"Here goes nothing," he said out loud to no one.

His boss was already parked and met him at the door of his car. Trent played it cool. He had become very good at keeping just how angry he was hidden from other people. "The boss is waiting for you," he was told by the guy that had his hoodie smothering his face. "There's one thing you need to know before I take you in there. You refer to him as 'sir' and nothing more. Got it?"

Trent gave his boss, Drew Foster, a look that said "Whatever" as he rolled his eyes.

Drew smacked him on the back of the head. "I asked you a question! Don't make him mad! Do you got it?"

Trent, not looking at Drew but looking straight ahead, answered, "I got it. You forget that I have talked to him on the phone plenty of times!"

They went to the third floor of the warehouse and the elevators opened up to their clubhouse. Trent used to love coming here. The parties were some of the best he had ever been to, but since his relationship had grown with Krystal, he'd stopped coming. He walked in and was immediately welcomed with open arms by two of the blonde whores. "Trent, baby!" one of them said as she ran into his arms. "Where have you been, love? I've missed you so much."

Trent loved the whores but not as much as he loved Krystal. He winked at his admirer and said, "I've been busy, hun. Ya know, working."

The whore pulled out of the hug and looked at him. "You look different, Trent." She ran her fingers through his long hair. "Oh, honey…" she said, studying his eyes. She had been in the business for a long time. "You didn't…" She trailed off as she let her hand fall to her side. She knew what was coming. It would be fun for her but probably not for him. She always thought he was the most handsome one out of the bunch and even had a little crush on him. She missed spending nights with him, but it came with the job. People came and went, but when they came back, like Trent, it only meant one of two things. If he walked out of there alive, he would be the old person that she knew. She was hoping for that because the other option was that she'd never see him again.

"There'll be time for catching up later," Drew said. "Well, maybe. The boss is waiting for you. Follow me."

Trent was nervous. He had partied many times here but had never had the "pleasure" of meeting the boss. He only let a couple of people know his identity. Any time he was there partying, either the boss wasn't there, or he stayed in his office the entire time without being seen. No one really knew what the boss did in his office alone while the rest of them partied, but there was speculation that he just sat back and watched them all on camera. There were rumors that he got off on watching people partying and fucking. He was sicker than all of them put together, but he kept it hidden for the most part.

The rumors were true. He did get off on watching their festivities. He jerked off many times in his office while watching the live feed, but what none of them knew was that he had an entrance and exit in his office. There was a hidden elevator behind the wall behind his desk. He had so many whores in there with him on a nightly basis that he couldn't keep track of them. They were his whores, though; they were not for sharing. He liked his to be committed to him and only him. He had his own private party in his office when the rest were partying. If his workers knew of the orgies that took place in his office, they would have been jealous. He was always the only man and most nights he had at least three women in there with him performing sex acts that would make the biggest porn

128

stars blush. Sometimes he just sat back and watched them go at each other, but most nights, he was the center of their attention. The ecstasy that he got from those nights was like none other. He paralleled the feeling with death. Sex and death were the same things – they were just on opposite ends of the spectrum. At least, that's how he saw things. He was in love with both of them just the same, but he had a feeling that death was a bigger gift than sex. After all, you only got the gift of death once in your life. Sex was also about to play a big part in Trent's life if things went the way he was hoping.

Drew knocked on the office door and they quickly heard, "It's open!" yelled from the other side. Drew pushed Trent through the doorway after he opened it and walked himself in behind him. He not only shut the door behind him but locked it. The office was clean, organized, and tidy. The desk was a big shiny oak desk with two computer monitors on it. Trent also noticed three flat-screen televisions on the walls around the desk. There was a door off to the side but it was shut. The boss was definitely a neat freak. Nothing on his desk was crooked. In fact, it was picture perfect, as if no one ever sat there.

But there was someone sitting there. As Trent finished scanning the room, he allowed his eyes to look over the boss – the man calling the shots. He was a handsome, blond-haired, blue-eyed man. He looked important. He was wearing a shiny suit that appeared to be very expensive. His hair was slicked back and he wore a bracelet that glimmered and a cross necklace around his neck. He also looked very familiar. Trent scrunched his eyebrows down and tilted his head to the right as he looked closer at this man.

The boss studied Trent. He was just as he remembered him. Good-looking but a little unraveled at the same time. "Hello, Trent." He didn't get up. He smiled and gestured for Trent to sit down on one of the chairs opposite his desk. Trent kept his eyes on this guy as he walked over to the chair and sat down. Drew followed and began to sit down but the boss held his hand up to Drew. "Please, Drew. Can you give us some privacy?"

This pissed Drew off. "Are you sure? I'm not so sure…"

"I'm sure," the boss answered. "I'll call for you when I'm ready to continue this with Trent."

Drew gave Trent a threatening look and excused himself from the office. Trent waited until the door was shut. "What the fuck?" he shouted as he stood up and leaned on the desk so he could be closer to the boss.

The boss sat back in his chair and smirked at Trent. "Hey, old friend."

"I know you!" Trent shouted. "Where do I know you from?" He was shaking and felt like his legs were going out from under him.

"Please, calm down." The boss sat back up in the chair and a bit more firmly said, "And sit down!"

Trent contemplated what he should do at that moment but quickly decided he had better sit down until he figured out how he knew this guy.

"You do know me, Trent."

"I know you look familiar but I can't place you." He was calming down as he found himself getting lost in studying the man sitting across from him.

"Well, it has been over ten years."

Trent looked at this man who appeared to be close to his age. Suddenly, it all came rushing back to him. He knew this guy from one of his foster homes. It was the same house where the father beat him with a belt. This guy was a foster kid as well. "Sean?"

"In the flesh!" He smiled and sat back again and began rocking in his chair.

"What…how…where…" Trent sighed. Memories came flooding back to the front of Trent's mind. Sean would sometimes take the attention off Trent when he was about to get beaten and take the beating himself. He was like a brother until Trent got taken away. He left but Sean stayed. He always wondered what happened to him. "You're the boss?"

"I am. And no one around here knows me as Sean. They call me Doyle, and I'd appreciate it if you'd do the same. No one knows my past or where I came from and I'd like to keep it that way…if you know what's good for you."

"Fine, whatever." Trent felt like he didn't have any need to be afraid anymore. After all, this was his brother, in a sense. He wouldn't hurt him. They were family. "How…I mean, what…"

Sean raised his hand to cut off Trent. "Please. Let me explain. After you were taken away, Rich – you know, our foster father – got even worse. He beat me more the week after you left than the entire time I had lived with them. I never fought him back like you did, though. My mind always did work differently than yours. I was there until I turned eighteen. The day I turned eighteen, I had Rich arrested for abuse. I sued his ass. Did you know that motherfucker was rich? No wonder his name was Rich! Him and Mommy Dearest were good with money and had made many great investments. They only adopted us foster kids to make themselves look good. I ended up suing them for everything they had. It made me rich and I learned from their investments, only I was better than them so I quadrupled my settlement. They both went to jail, where they both died…thanks to me. I saw to that. Drew scouting you out was no accident. I never forgot about you over the years. I knew where you were, how you were doing, the trouble you were getting in to. I pulled you in so I could give you a better life. Besides, I remembered that rage you had and that was just the type of person I was in need of. Drew is great and I'll never find anyone as perfect as him. I'll never admit to saying this, but you have given him a run for his money. The last two jobs you helped with – you were golden. That's why I put you on this job. I knew between you and Drew, I'd be able to succeed."

Trent remained speechless even though his anger wasn't getting any better. He only stared a hole through Sean as he remembered the times they had spent together. Before he got taken away from the house, the last thing Sean said to him was, "I'll never forget you. I'll make this better." The dude stood by his word.

"Are you still with me, Trent?"

"Yes," Trent answered quickly. "Excuse me for not being talkative. Seeing you is bringing back some pretty fucked-up memories. No offense!"

"None taken. You and I suffered a lot at the hands of those people. They paid up and that's what I'm doing now with you. I'm paying up."

Trent was getting even angrier. He couldn't hold it in anymore. "You're paying up?" Trent shouted. "I was abused just as much as you were until I beat the shit out of him and got myself removed. You get a nice payout and instead of giving me some cash for my suffering, you make me work for it? What gives you the right?"

Sean didn't like being shouted at, but he actually admired the anger that Trent was able to project. He only smiled at Trent until he finally shut up. "Trent," Sean began. "First of all, don't ever yell at me like that again. Second of all, if I just gave you a wad of cash, you wouldn't have appreciated it. You would've blew it on fast cars and lavish trips. It would've been gone as fast as you got it. I wanted you to work for the money to appreciate it. I'm always looking out for you. You should remember that from before."

Trent was still mad but he didn't know what to say. He just kept staring into the eyes that flooded his brain with horrible memories.

"I've been watching you, Trent. You've changed over the past few months. I'm not saying that's a bad thing. It's good that you are seeking professional help for your anger issues." He smirked after saying this, almost as if he were making fun of Trent.

"How did you know that? I haven't told anyone about that." He wasn't shouting but he was still talking angrily with a raised voice.

"I told you, I've been watching you. I see everything. I know everything. I even know that you called the cops and left a tip that the doctor was in trouble."

Trent looked down at his shoes. He thought he had gotten away with that move even though he felt guilty after doing it.

"The problem is, Trent, your anger is what made me want you on my team. Now, though, you are going soft on me. I'm afraid that you're losing sight of the job. In fact, I know you are."

Trent was searching for words. He had already been starting to think of ways to mess up the plans. Calling in the tip about Dr. Simms was just the beginning. He was trying to plan on what else he could do to stop the job he was hired to do. He wasn't able to say anything as Sean continued on.

"I brought you here to remind you of your task at hand. I want to remind you that Krystal is the enemy and you know what the outcome of this project is to be."

"No, I don't. I have an idea but I have no idea what you're planning. As far as my therapy, you told me that I had to make Krystal fall in love with me. If I didn't get therapy to help with my anger issues, this would've never have worked out. I don't even understand why you are after Krystal and her family." Trent stopped talking for a second as he contemplated saying what he was about to say. He figured he was already in hot water so why stop now. "They are good people."

"See! That! That right there," Sean said, shaking his pointer finger at Trent. "That's what I mean. They are not good people and I don't have to explain myself to you. All I will tell you is that I have reasons, good reasons, for doing what I'm doing. I don't have to tell you why. You were hired to do a fucking job and I see that you are starting to fail."

"So you brought me here to shake your finger in my face?" Trent's stare was cold and hollow.

Sean didn't like it. He was even a little frightened of it. He was glad, though. He opened his mouth and let out the loudest laugh that Trent had ever heard. He was pretty sure that people ten miles away heard that laugh. It only pissed Trent off even more. "Trent, you were like my little brother, but shaking my finger in your face is not how I get my point across."

"So, what then? Are you going to end me?" Trent stood up, ready for a fight. "Because if that's what you're going to do, I won't go down without a fight. I don't care how many men you have on me."

Sean stood up and leaned across his desk so that he would be face-to-face with Trent. "I think you need to mind your fucking manners and sit back down." Now Sean's blue eyes looked cold.

"And if I don't?"

"Then this will be a trillion times worse for you."

Trent picked up his chair, threw it across the room and watched it bounce off the wall. "Oh, really? Is that a promise, Mr. Hotshot? Because I don't take too kindly to fucking threats." He began walking around to the side of the desk that Sean was standing at. Sean met him halfway.

Sean got in his face, not backing down. "It's a threat and a promise. How do you like that answer, asshole?" He shoved Trent up against the wall. He put his right hand around Trent's throat. "Shut your fucking face and listen to me. I'm not going to kill you. I brought you here to remind you of who you are and why you are here and the job you have to do. But if you don't start to mind your fucking manners, I'm going to have to hurt you. Have I made myself clear yet?" His eyes were fixated on Trent's and there was no bluff for miles. He meant what he had just said.

Trent was still pissed off and he tried to calm himself down before he got himself killed, but he couldn't. He just couldn't. He pushed back toward Sean and overtook him. He shoved Sean pretty hard but Sean didn't go down. "There you go!" Sean screamed at him. "Hit me, motherfucker! Hit me!"

Trent didn't have to be told to hit him – he was already getting ready to. He pulled back his arm and landed one right below Sean's right eye. It felt good to Trent. He then punched him again and again. Sean began to fight back and before long they were both getting blows in. It was a fair match and there was no winner in sight. After beating on each other for a good five minutes, they both fell over on the floor, panting but wanting to continue. "I know you enjoyed that," Sean said through breaths.

Trent only looked at Sean, wishing he had a gun on him to finish the job. All the time and hard work that Trent had put in to work through his anger issues were washed away with that one fight. In fact, the anger raging through him right now was worse than he had ever felt in his entire life. It was as if his body and mind had taken all the controlled anger and stored it away for this very moment, only to unleash it with the energy of a million young men. "Fuck you!" was all Trent could say.

Sean laughed.

Trent sat there, watching his old "brother" laugh with blood running down his chin. Wasn't that a funny picture? He was blacked, bruised, and bloody but he was still laughing. This guy was crazier than he was. That thought alone tickled his funny bone and before he could even explain it, he was laughing too. The two men laughed together and it ended in an embrace.

"Welcome back to us," Sean said as he pulled out of the hug.

Trent understood now why he was brought there. He had to be beaten back to his senses.

"How about we sit back down and finish this conversation," Sean said as he used his desk to help pull himself to his feet. He then extended his left hand (the right one was far too sore from punching Trent) to help Trent up. Trent refused his hand and got up on his own. Sean took his place back at his desk and pulled a few tissues out of the box and offered the box to Trent. Trent retrieved a few for himself as well. "I need you," Sean said as he patted the blood off his lower lip, "to refocus. You are too close to Krystal and her family."

"Wasn't that what I was supposed to be doing?"

"Of course, but you are letting your emotions get involved. You know it as well as I do."

Trent looked down at his lap. Sean was right. "How do you even know that?"

"I have a guy who, well, he can see things that I can't see. He keeps me informed. You work for me, you are on my team. I can't be worried that you are going to protect Krystal when it's time to finish this."

Trent continued to look down.

"Has the cat got your tongue?"

Trent knew he had to pick his words wisely here. "I just…" He trailed off.

"You just what? Spit it out!"

"When you put me on this job, I thought it was going to be an easy money-maker. You failed to mention to me how beautiful Krystal was…and how awesome…and down-to-earth…"

"Trent, I hired you for this job because you did so well with the last two and confirmed that I can trust you. Regardless of the type of person Krystal is or how she looks, she's still just another job. You need to remember that."

Trent didn't like what he was hearing. "That's easier said than done. She's like the perfect woman. I'm not sure I can live without her."

Sean was not surprised by what he was hearing. "I already knew you were struggling with this…with her." He picked up his phone and called Drew. "Drew, I need you to fetch Candy and bring her to me."

Drew was walking through the door with Candy (the blonde whore who greeted Trent when he walked in) within ten seconds. He took one look at Sean's beautiful face and reached for the gun that he had concealed in the back of the waistband of his pants. Sean quickly raised his hand at Drew. "I'm okay. It's okay. We're okay."

Drew confusedly dropped his hand to his side. "You two look awful."

"We had some things to…work out," Sean replied. "We're okay now, though. Right, Trent?"

Trent only lowered his head. He had a feeling he knew what was coming.

"I fixed one problem that our buddy is struggling with," Sean said, "but I can't fix the other one. You two know what to do."

With that, Drew and Candy walked over to Trent and each grabbed an arm. "I need you to come with us," Drew said as they pulled Trent out of the chair.

Trent gave one last look at Sean, wishing he had killed him, as he allowed himself to be dragged out the door.

After they left the office, Drew said to Trent, "You look like hell. I'm going to have to ask you to go clean up. Take a shower, even." He pushed Trent into the bathroom and said, "You have fifteen minutes." Drew and Candy left the bathroom so Trent could shower alone.

Trent took a look at himself in the mirror. Both of his eyes were blackened, his upper lip was busted on the left side, and his nose had a pretty good knot on the bridge. It wasn't broken, but the pain was still just as bad. He stared at himself in the mirror, into his own eyes. He didn't know who he was anymore. He was ashamed of the fury that he had just unleashed, but he was even more ashamed at the fact that he enjoyed it. Maybe being "normal" just wasn't in his cards. He undressed and started the water in the shower. As he let the hot water hit his face, he wasn't sure what he was going to do now. He contemplated trying to run out but he knew it would be no use. They would find him eventually. In all the time he had been with Krystal, he could honestly say he had never cheated on her, and he didn't want to start now. The very thought of it made him want to vomit. Even though he had allowed his anger to resurface, he still didn't want to hurt Krystal. He'd much rather take another beating than let what was about to happen take place. He drifted off into his own thoughts as the water soothed his sore body.

It felt like only ten seconds had gone by when he heard the bathroom door being opened. He heard clicks on the floor, the unmistakable sound of high heels. The shower curtain was slowly pushed open to reveal a naked whore in nothing but her red stilettos. This wasn't Candy, though. It was another whore that was almost as hot as Candy. Trent knew Candy was there, though....She was probably a little tied up. He looked at this whore with eyes that probably said, "Please don't do this." She was hot, and no man in his right mind would turn someone like her away, but he wasn't in his right mind. Trent turned the water off and faced the whore. "Please," he began. "You don't have to do this. It's okay."

She placed her left index finger on his lips, lightly so as not to hurt his busted lip, and simply shook her head no. He stood there in the tub, naked before her, and watched her lower herself down to his crotch. She began kissing and licking his limp penis. He tried to push her off him but Drew was right there, watching, and told him to allow it. As she began sucking him off, he was getting angry. Not only because he was being forced to do this, but also because he was getting hard. The anger only made him get harder, faster. Anger turned him on. As his penis was extended out as far as it could go, he finally gave in to temptation and placed his hands on the back of the whore's head – just in case she needed help. A few more minutes of this and he would be cumming all over her tits.

He wasn't allowed to do that, though. Drew told her to stop. She did as she was told, stood up, wiped her mouth off, and then grabbed Trent's hand. She led him to the nook where Candy was, naked and tied up by her wrists and ankles. She also had a handkerchief tied over her mouth so she could not speak. Trent didn't think his penis could get any harder, but it did. She really was a beautiful lady and seeing her all naked and tied up brought back some good memories for him. He was turned on but still felt a little ashamed because of it. The other whore sat Trent down in a chair and told him not to move. Drew sat in the doorway of the nook. He only got to enjoy the show. Trent and Drew watched as the whore crawled on top of Candy and pulled down her handkerchief. She began kissing her and rubbing her pussy. Candy moaned and squirmed her arms and legs that were not able to move very much. The whore then sat on Candy's face and began riding her mouth. Before long, she was moaning as well. The whore then turned herself around into the "sixty-nine" position so they could eat each other out at the same time. Trent was still hard and was fighting the urge to join in. Drew had already pulled down his pants and was jerking himself off. Trent looked down at his bare feet and tried to bring Krystal's beautiful face to his mind's eye. He was trying so hard to remember how much he loved her so that he could maybe fight this.

The whore finally got off of Candy and walked over to Trent. She grabbed both of his hands with hers and helped him stand up. She then shoved him onto the bed. Trent only sat there at first, looking down at the floor. He really didn't want to do this but his penis was saying otherwise. The whore slapped him across his face, which stung more than it should have considering the beating it had taken moments before. This pissed Trent off. He stood back up and put his left hand around the whore's throat. He shoved her against the wall and told her to never lay a hand on him like that again. She only smirked at him. He pushed his naked body up against hers and the genital contact turned him on in a way he hadn't felt in a really long time. His head and his penis were fighting back and forth but his penis was winning. He kissed the whore as hard as he could, his hand still wrapped around her throat. He then shoved his penis inside her loose and open vagina and pounded into it as hard as he could. She screamed a scream that was hard to distinguish if it was pleasure or pain. This turned Trent on even more.

After a few pumps, he looked over at Candy who was still lying naked on the bed, all tied up. That view was much better than his current one, so he shoved the whore aside and went over to the bed. He crawled on top of Candy and began kissing her. Her lips, although not touched by him for months, felt so familiar and

140

so comfortable on his. He shoved his tongue in her throat as far as he could and she retaliated with hers. He stopped for a second to pull back and look at her. Memories of their drunken nights together came back to him front and center. Almost all of his thoughts about Krystal were gone. They'd be totally gone by the time this escapade was over. Sean sat at his desk watching the entire thing, and smiled.

Chapter 23

It was a twenty-minute drive from the hospital in Columbia to the house in Laurel. Paul got there in ten minutes with the help of his sirens and lights. He was feeling a bit impatient today as that last name – Eck – kept running through his mind. He couldn't wait to show the old lady the picture. Her door swung open as he was about to push the doorbell. "Lieutenant! So nice to see you again! Please come in." She stood back and allowed Paul to walk in. She led him to the kitchen and poured them both a cup of coffee without even asking Paul if he wanted any. "Please, sit down, Lieutenant Jennings. I'm surprised to see you here again. I'm pretty sure I told you everything I know about my old piece of you-know-what neighbor."

Paul sat down and thanked her for the coffee. He took a sip and said, "Well, I have a picture I wanted to show you. I'm wondering if it's Mr. Eck."

"Let's see it!" the old lady said. She was more excited than a junkie scoring their daily drugs.

Paul pulled the picture out of his notebook pad and showed it to the old lady. "Is this Mr. Eck?"

The lady only needed half a second to look at it. "Nope! That's not him. Mr. Eck is a tad bit older than that and he has no hair. This guy is kind of handsome. I always did think he was easy on the eyes."

"So you know him?"

"Well, I don't *know him* know him, but he was one of the guys who was always around."

"Can you tell me anything about him? A name or where he may be now?"

142

"I think his name was Thomas but I hadn't seen him for a few weeks before Mr. Eck moved out. I'm pretty sure he's one of his dealers or at least was. But there was something else about Thomas. One day he'd be just so sweet to me and the next, he'd damn near bite my head off just for looking at him. He had an anger problem, that's for sure. I think him and Mr. Eck got in a really bad fight, because the last time he was here, he left out of here squealing tires."

"Interesting," Paul said, racking his brain. "Anything else you can tell me about this Thomas guy?"

"Nothing really. There was one day he was here with some guy who had these bright blue eyes but they had a dark shade of gray in them. Just looking at this guy scared the hell out of me. I could tell he was bad news."

"Any idea of who that was?"

"Nope. I shut my door and minded my own business that day. First time for everything," she said before chuckling to herself.

Paul's mind was working in overdrive now but he was coming up empty. "Is there anything else that you haven't told me already that you can think of? Anything that may be important or something you may think is worth mentioning? Even the smallest thing?"

The old lady pushed her eyes up and to the right as she tried to rack her brain for anything she could tell him. Just as Paul was about to tell her to call him if anything came to mind, she said, "Well, there was the one day when he yelled at some guy who was there with them."

"What was he yelling about?"

"Oh, he was mad! I heard everything! This guy, I think his name was Trent…"

Everything stopped in Paul's mind. He was no longer hearing what the old lady was saying. All that was echoing in his head was the name Trent. Could it be Krystal's Trent? It couldn't be. Could it? How many Trents could there be in the area? He then realized that the old lady was snapping her fingers in front of his face.

"Are you with me, Lieutenant?"

He shook his head and came out of his thoughts. "I'm sorry. I got hung up on that name, Trent. It's not a very common name. I didn't hear anything you said after that."

The old woman giggled. "That's okay. I'm sure you got a lot going on up in that noggin of yours. I was saying that he was yelling at this Trent kid for calling him Drew instead of Thomas. Thomas was mad because he was outside working on his car and Trent opened the door and yelled for him but he didn't yell for Thomas. He yelled for Drew. Thomas responded to him and laid into him. I thought for sure they were gonna fight, but they both went inside the house and slammed the door behind them. Maybe they fought inside. I don't know."

"So you think Thomas is not a real name, then?"

"I think it's a made-up name. I even heard them call him Foster sometimes."

Paul scribbled the names Drew and Foster on his notepad but didn't give it any thought. He was still thinking about Trent. "I just have one more question for you," he said before taking the final sip from his coffee cup. "This Trent guy you mentioned, can you describe him to me?"

"Oh, of course I can! He's got the blond hair thing going on and it's long. He's in really good shape. I saw him once without a shirt on and, well…let's just say I had a reaction that I haven't had in a very long time. He usually has a guitar strapped to his back but I haven't seen him around here in a very long time."

Paul was frozen in his thoughts. She had just described Trent to a T. He was speechless.

"Lieutenant Jennings? Are you still with me?"

Paul heard the old lady and somewhere in his mind processed that she was snapping her fingers in front of his face again, but he was somewhere else altogether. He started thinking about what he caught Trent doing the other day in Krystal's room, how he had always had a funny feeling about Trent but always ignored it because he came off as if he were a good kid, and how many times he had been in his house and what's worse – how many times Krystal had spent the night with Trent, alone, in his apartment. He was becoming more and more furious as his thoughts raced.

"Lieutenant?"

Paul snapped out of it. "I'm sorry. Can I show you another picture?"

"Of course you can."

Paul retrieved his personal phone from the case that was hooked on his belt. He had a picture of him, Krystal, Laura, and Trent when they all went hiking in western Maryland a few months back. He swiped through his photo gallery until he found it, enlarged it, and showed it to the old lady. "Is this the Trent you know?"

"Oh yes, that's him, all right!" she answered. "Is that your family, Lieutenant? Do you know Trent?"

Paul didn't want to answer her, but he felt like if he didn't tell someone, he would bust. "Yes, he's dating my daughter and has been for about six months now."

"Well," she began as she searched for the right words to say, "I can tell you it's been a very long time since he had been here before Mr. Eck left. Maybe he got out of the mess and is trying to make his life better. People can change."

"Yeah," Paul replied. His mind was trying to process how Krystal was going to handle this news, or if he should even tell her. Knowing that Trent may be a part of this entire ordeal meant that he could quite possibly have a solid lead now. It also meant he didn't want his daughter anywhere near him.

Chapter 24

Paul was sitting in his cruiser outside of the old lady's house. He was still in a bit of shock over the fact that Trent was involved with the entire mess in one way or another – or at least had been. He knew he needed to talk to Trent, but he wasn't sure if there would be any point. He figured Trent would just deny it all. *Do I tell Krystal? What about Laura? She'd be pissed if I didn't tell her about this. At least now I have a reason to look Trent up in the system and see if he has anything on his record. That is, if Trent is even his real name. None of this is making any sense. I have to be missing something! I'm going to follow the coordinates from the GPS tracker from the stolen car. Maybe that will give me more answers.*

Paul called the troopers who were protecting Krystal and Laura, and was reassured that both were at home and okay. With that done, Paul started up his cruiser and flipped on the lights and sirens. He was feeling very impatient today. The coordinates led him to a sketchy area in Jessup only fifteen minutes away. It was a huge warehouse that appeared to be full of business-type places. There was a replacement window shop, a car stereo system dealer, a kitchen cabinet maker, and even a place that appeared to be a space for bands to practice in. There were other businesses as well, and the warehouse was four stories tall. Who knew what else was in this building. He figured the best place to look first would be the band practice site. Trent did play music and that was all he had to go on.

Just as he was about to turn off his car, he saw someone coming out of a door on the far right. For once, he wished he weren't in his police cruiser. He managed to back up the cruiser in his spot so that only the front of his car could be seen, the rest of it concealed by the big SUV he was parked next to. He slumped down a little as he looked through his passenger-side window and through the

SUV's windows at a man that looked very familiar to him. As his eyes focused on the man, he realized it was Trent, but he looked to be in bad shape. He was walking really slowly and it looked like he had two black eyes. The other problem was that he didn't come out of the band practice space.

What in the hell? Paul thought. He suddenly wished his captain was there with him, because Zitzer always knew what to do in situations like this. Trent got in his car and drove out of the entrance that was farther away from where Paul was. He waited for Trent's car to be out of sight and shut off his engine. He got out and began walking toward the band practice space but he wasn't sure why. Obviously, that's not where Trent was coming from, but the fact that this was where the GPS coordinates led him to told him that Trent was involved with this whole mess somehow – and that Krystal was in more danger than he and his wife. As he began walking toward the loud music that sounded like nails being dragged down a chalkboard, he came upon a door that stated it was the warehouse's main office. He changed his course of travel and went through that door. Inside, there was a pretty blonde receptionist sitting at the desk facing the entrance. She looked about thirty years old and Paul knew he could use that to his advantage. The woman looked up from her computer screen and was clearly startled to see a trooper standing before her. "Hello, ma'am," Paul said, giving her his award-winning smile.

"Officer? May I help you?"

Paul flashed his badge even though his uniform confirmed that he was official. "I'm Lieutenant Jennings and I just have a few questions that I was hoping you could help me with." His flirtatious eyes looked her over from head to toe as he winked at her.

The woman was not impressed, not one single bit.

"I'll do my best," she replied, hardly looking away from the computer screen.

"Can you possibly tell me all the businesses that are housed in this warehouse?"

"No," she answered simply, with no explanation.

"No?"

"No." She was still looking at her computer screen.

"Why not? It's public knowledge, isn't it?"

The woman finally looked away from the computer screen and at Paul. "Well now," she said in a rather stuck-up tone of voice, "if it was public knowledge, then you'd know all the businesses, wouldn't you?" She stared a hole through him.

Paul didn't like the tone that she was using with him. "With all due respect, ma'am, I can get a warrant to search every single nook and cranny in this warehouse, so you might as well just give me a list of businesses."

"You might as well just leave," she responded without missing a beat.

Paul tried to intimidate her with a look before he finally turned to leave.

She returned to her computer screen and didn't give him a second glance.

Paul kept his head held up high as he turned and walked out. The second the door closed behind him, the pretty blonde picked up her phone and dialed four numbers. "Sir?" she said as there was an answer on the receiving end. "I just thought you'd like to know that there was a Lieutenant Jennings here asking about the businesses in the building. I didn't give him any information but he did threaten to get a search warrant...yes, sir. No problem."

She hung up.

Paul, on the other hand, was hauling ass back to the office. He had to run everything by the captain and get an approval for a search warrant. He wasn't really sure if he could get a search warrant on an entire warehouse, but he was going to try his hardest. Luckily, the captain was in his office. "Paul! How's it going? Have a seat."

Paul sat down with a sigh as he stared down at the floor, not sure where to start.

"Bad day?"

Paul looked up at the captain – his boss, his mentor, his friend. "I don't even know where to start, but you need to know what all I've uncovered. Things are not looking good for me personally."

Paul told the captain everything he had found out, seen, and heard. He even told him about Trent sniffing Krystal's underwear.

The captain sat back after Paul was finished and let his thoughts run around before he opened his mouth.

"I'm taking you off this case, Paul."

"What? No! You can't do that!"

"I can. I don't want to, but surely you understand why I have to. If Trent is involved with this whole mess somewhere, you could make it personal."

"I won't! I can't sit back and let another trooper take over this case. I won't rest and I won't be able to just hand it all over. This is my family that's involved. I will not let anyone else take this case!"

"Paul, you know I'm only looking out for you."

"I know that and I appreciate that, but you know I can handle this."

The captain thought he could maybe handle it by himself, but at the same time, he wasn't really sure. "Okay. Even though I should have taken you off the case a long time ago, I'll keep you on. From now on, though, I'm on it with you. You don't go anywhere or do anything without me. I need to be with you every step of the way, Paul. That's the only way I'm going to keep you on this case."

"I can live with that," Paul replied. "Thank you."

The captain waved his "thank you" away. "I guess we better get this search warrant as fast as possible. It sounds to me like that receptionist might not be an innocent worker."

"Great minds think alike!"

"I don't know if the judge will grant a search warrant on the entire warehouse, though. We need to know which space needs to be searched."

"I don't know what all is in there, though. The GPS coordinates didn't tell me all that!"

"You said you saw Trent coming out of one of the entrances, right?"

"Yes. The entrance on the far right."

"That may be all we need, then. We can get a warrant to search all four floors on the right-hand side of the warehouse. It's worth a shot, anyway."

"Well, let's get on this," Paul said. "I don't want to waste any more time."

"Okay, but there's one more thing."

"What?"

"When Krystal started dating Trent, did you ever run any kind of background check on him?"

"You know I couldn't have done that."

"I know you're not supposed to, but you could've done it."

"But I didn't."

"Okay, then we will now. Also, given these new details, I think we should bring Trent in for questioning."

"I'd definitely need you to sit in on that with me to make sure I don't kill him."

"Agreed."

"Just give me one second," Paul said as he pulled out his cell phone and called his wife. She answered right away. "Laura, is Krystal still at home?"

"Yes, she's still sleeping."

"Good. Can you make sure that she doesn't meet up with Trent at all today?"

"Okay, but why?"

"There are things that I need to let her know about that involve Trent."

"Are you still on the 'I hate Trent' train?"

"I never got off it," Paul answered. "And when I tell you what I've found out, you will be getting on the train with me."

"I doubt that."

"Well, we know that Trent is or was mixed up with some pretty bad people. The GPS coordinates from that stolen SUV led us to a warehouse, and guess who I saw coming out of there?"

"Trent?"

"Yes! So, throw him sniffing Krystal's panties in the mix and I'm officially driving the train. We plan to bring him in for questioning very soon."

"Okay. But like I said before, if we tell her not to see him anymore, that will just push her toward him even more."

"We have to take that chance, because after what I've discovered today, I know she is not safe with him."

"I'll make sure she doesn't."

"Good. I love you."

"Love you too."

The captain got on his computer, typed in Trent's name, and waited for the database to give him results. Paul was standing behind him and looking over his shoulder. Finally, a box popped up that said "one result found."

"Only one?" Paul questioned, clearly shocked.

The captain clicked on the link. "It's only a speeding ticket from a few months ago."

"I can't believe that's all there is."

"Could he be using a fake name, you think?"

"Anything is possible."

Chapter 25

Krystal woke up with a violent and startled reaction. She sat upright in bed and frantically looked around. The memory of the weird man that broke into her room flooded her mind. How long had she been sleeping? The alarm clock glowed 5:08. *What?* Krystal thought to herself. She looked out the window to see it was still daylight out. *There's no way I slept all day. Right? That time can't be right.* She looked at her cell phone, which confirmed the time. She also realized that she had no missed calls from Trent or text messages. *Nothing from Trent? Why have I not heard from him all day? He should be worried about me right now. Am I in a different world or something? Maybe I am dead.* She wasn't dead. She had a text message from her mom that was sent around noon, telling her that Dr. Simms was going home today and she was on her way home to be with her.

Krystal stood up and stretched. *Man, no more pain meds for me. That shit knocked me out all day long! I do feel well rested, even though I'm rattled more than just a little bit. I'm going to give Trent a call and see what he's been up to all day. Maybe he just got really busy at work.* She picked up her phone and called Trent. It went straight to voicemail. *What the fuck?*

Trent had made it back to his apartment, sore but feeling renewed. He took a shower and then lay down for a while. He couldn't believe what had just happened to him – what he had allowed to happen to him. All his therapy for anger management had been thrown out the window. If that weren't bad enough, he had cheated on Krystal – and he liked it. Isn't that what Sean wanted, though? To bring him back to his old ways, to brainwash him, in a sense, to get him to come back to his job at hand. And Trent allowed him to do it. He was weak. Then Trent's mind wandered to Candy.

He really enjoyed the time he had with her. He hadn't realized how much he missed that kind of rough sex. It was always sweet and innocent with Krystal. That was going to change, though, if he had anything to say about it!

He realized he hadn't talked to Krystal all day, and he was sure she had probably left a shit-ton of messages on his phone. His phone was still on the floor where he had thrown it. He wasn't sure if he really wanted to check it. He knew he needed to, at least for work, but what was he going to say to Krystal? What was he going to say about all of his bruises? Without thinking, he picked up his phone and turned it on. He was surprised (and angered) that he had only two missed calls from Krystal, which were from this morning and just a little while ago. Hadn't she been worrying about him? Didn't she care? He also had a text message from Drew: "Welcome back" was all it read. Trent didn't know if he should smile at that text or be pissed off. He decided to feel no emotion from it and told himself he needed to get a separate phone so he'd have one for work and one for Krystal. Upon that thought, he found himself calling Krystal.

"Hey!" she answered on the second ring.

"Hey?" he asked. He was angry. "I haven't heard from you all day and that's all I get? A hey?!"

Trent had never spoken to her that way. "What? I called you this morning and just a little bit ago but your cell went straight to voicemail both times."

"You didn't think about calling me back again?"

"I mean, you didn't answer. I took a shower this morning and then went back to sleep. I just woke up."

"It's five o'clock in the evening and you *just* woke up?" He was on the verge of shouting.

Krystal, who had never had to defend herself with Trent before, was confused by how upset he was but felt she needed to go into defense mode herself. "Yes! That's right! I took three pain pills and passed the fuck out. I needed sleep. Things haven't been exactly normal lately. But, hey, the phone goes both ways and I didn't get a call or text from you, so what in the hell is your excuse?" She was getting fired up now.

Trent finally started yelling. "What's my excuse?! I was mugged this morning and beat to a fucking pulp! I just got out of the emergency room!" The lies came naturally to him.

Krystal's heart sank. She didn't know what to say.

"Hello?" Trent shouted into his phone.

"I'm sorry, Trent," Krystal said through tears. "I didn't know. Are you okay?"

Trent liked that she was upset so he calmed his voice down. "I'm pretty bruised up but nothing is broken. I'm really sore though."

"I'm coming over," Krystal said, and hung up before he could even say anything back to her. She got dressed and ran downstairs to find her mom sitting in the kitchen, drinking a cup of coffee and reading a book. "Hey, Mom."

"You're finally up. How are you doing?"

"Okay, I guess. Mom, Trent was mugged today so I'm going to head over to his place to see him."

"No."

"Huh?" Krystal asked, caught off guard.

"You can't go over there. Your dad wants you to stay away from Trent right now and I think it's a good idea."

"What? Why?"

"He has found evidence that Trent is somehow wrapped up in everything that's been happening. Plus, we'd both feel better if you stayed home with us."

"I'm not doing that, Mom!"

Laura raised her voice. "Yes you are!"

"Mom!" Krystal said, raising her voice back. "I'm an adult. You can't tell me what to do!"

Laura sighed and more calmly said, "Okay. Then I am asking you to please stay home."

"Mom, I want to go see Trent and I'm going to go see him!"

"If you walk out that door, I'll have the cop out there restrain you."

"Seriously, Mom!"

"I'm sorry, but that's just the way it is right now."

Krystal didn't say anything. She just turned around and stomped back up to her bedroom. She called her best friend Brittany because she just needed someone to talk to. After she told her everything that had been going on, Brittany said, "Well, I think maybe you should listen to your parents. I don't think they'd forbid you from seeing Trent if they didn't have a really good reason."

"Oh please! My dad has never really liked Trent. My mom does for the most part, but she won't fight my dad on this or anything. Even if she did, she'd lose. My dad always gets his way."

"Well, looking at it from the outside, I'd say your parents are just being careful."

"Maybe, but you know what? If Trent is wrapped up in this, then I'd like to stay close to him to keep an eye on him."

"That's just too dangerous."

"I don't care. Hey, can I come over in a little while? I'm sure they won't mind if I come hang out with you at least."

"Yes. I'd love that!"

"Okay. I'll text you when I'm on my way."

Krystal hung up her phone and sat down on her bed. *That just sounded ridiculous, saying that my parents won't mind if I go hang out with Brittany. I'm an adult, not a child! I love Trent way too much to just walk away from him like that. I need him in my life, especially right now. Of course, if Dr. Simms were here, she'd tell me that I'm doing it again, that I'm reacting before thinking and putting myself in a dangerous situation. But Trent and I have been together for six months now. I'd think that if he was going to hurt me, he would've done it by now. I'm going to keep seeing him, I just won't tell Mom and Dad!*

Krystal sat in her room for another thirty minutes to calm herself down and then went back downstairs.

"Mom?"

"Are you still mad at me?"

"No. I guess I can understand where you and Dad are coming from. I don't agree with it because I really don't think Trent would ever hurt me and Dad must be wrong about what he found, but I know you are only doing it because you care about me."

"That's all it is." Laura smiled.

"So I called Brittany. It's no big deal if I go see her, right?"

Laura sighed. She didn't want to make the wrong decision here. She didn't want Paul mad at her but she didn't want Krystal mad at her either. "Only under one condition."

"Okay?"

"You text me when you get to her place so that I know you are safe."

"I can do that."

Krystal got in her car and headed to Trent's house thinking that was way too easy.

Chapter 26

Trent wanted to throw his phone again but refrained. Yelling with Krystal like that turned him on again. She was on her way over and he knew it only took around ten minutes for her to get to his apartment. That would be just enough time to set things up. Krystal was about to see a side of him she had never seen before, like it or not. As he finished getting the rope tied to the rails on the head of his bed frame, he heard his doorbell ring. He slowly walked to the door. The pain was getting worse but he knew he could handle it. He slowly opened the door and peeked his head around it as he pulled it open all the way. It was Krystal, of course, and her mouth dropped the second she saw him. He backed up so she could come in. "Trent! Oh my god!" she said through tears. He shut the door and didn't say anything. He only looked at her. She ran her fingers over his bruised face. "Does it hurt really bad?"

"It's pretty sore, but the doctor said nothing was broken. I'll be fine in a few days as the bruising goes down."

Her hand was still on his face. "I'm so sorry I was out of it all day. What exactly happened?"

Trent could have come up with a great story on the spot but he had no desire to. Instead, he said, "I don't want to talk about it. The guy didn't get anything from me. All he did was beat me up. He wasn't expecting me to hit back, I guess."

Krystal sat down on the couch in the living room as Trent followed her. "How about you? Are you okay? Sleeping all day is not something you usually do."

"Not really. I just wanted to get some sleep so I took those pain pills to help me do that. But…" Krystal began crying.

"What?" Trent asked. He really didn't care but he knew he should at least ask. He had no idea that Sean had gone to see Krystal.

"Someone broke into my room," she sobbed.

"What do you mean?"

"I mean, some guy crawled up a ladder, opened my bedroom window, and came in while I was sleeping. It woke me up."

"What? What did he do? Are you okay?" Trent was upset and angered by this.

"I guess I'm okay. It was weird. It's all a little fuzzy because of those stupid pills. All I really remember is him telling me sex and death were the same thing and he was going to give me and my family the gift of death. It was spooky and confusing and didn't make any sense. He didn't try to hurt me. He just left after saying he'd be back soon."

Trent was confused himself. Sean never said anything to him about doing this to Krystal. "What did this asshole look like?"

"It's hard for me to remember but he was not the same guy that attacked Dr. Simms and my mom. This guy was different. I remember him looking really important, like he had some kind of authority. For some reason, I remember a cross necklace that he was wearing."

Trent knew right away that it was Sean. He tried to keep himself calm.

"It's weird, because I had a strange feeling that everything was going to be okay and we didn't need to worry anymore, but then this happens."

"Why didn't you fucking call me?"

"What? I called my dad first since, you know, he's a cop. I was really upset and scared, Trent. My mom said she tried to call you but you didn't answer so it didn't really matter."

"It didn't matter? Some creep broke into your room and I'm just now hearing about it?"

"Why are you yelling at me?" Krystal's tears were quickly drying up.

"Because. I'm worried about you! I want to be here for you and you act like what happened to you today is no big deal!"

"It is a big deal! I'm scared out of my fucking mind! But really, what could you have done?"

Trent didn't like Krystal yelling at him like that. "I could have been there for you to comfort you or whatever!"

Krystal took a few deep breaths before saying anything else.

Trent got up and paced around the room, trying to blow off steam.

"I'm sorry, Trent. I did call you right when I woke up and you didn't answer. I'm here now."

"You should have kept calling me. I need to know what's going on with you while all this crazy shit is going on. I really wish you'd just stay here with me so I can keep a closer eye on you."

Trent sat back down next to her. "I'm sorry for getting so angry. I guess we both just had a bad day."

"I guess so."

Trent began kissing her neck.

Krystal was surprised. "What are you doing? Aren't you in pain? Aren't you mad?"

"I am in pain," Trent answered her through his kisses, "and I am mad but I'm also really turned on right now. Pain turns me on. The anger turns me on."

Krystal was shocked. She scooted away from Trent. "What? Are you feeling okay?"

"I'm feeling just great," Trent said as he scooted closer to her again. "I could be feeling better though."

Krystal didn't know if she should run away or be intrigued. She stood up as she contemplated what exactly was going on. "Did they put you on some sort of meds at the hospital? Are you drunk or something right now? You're acting really weird."

Trent stood up in front of her. "No. I'm not on meds, I'm not drunk, and I'm not high. I'm just turned on!"

"You said you were turned on from the pain and anger. That's not you." Krystal was starting to feel a little frightened as the thoughts of her dream about him started drawing conclusions in her mind.

"You *think* that's not me," Trent said as he shoved her onto the couch. He straddled her lap and got in her face. "We've been together for a while now and it's time for you to meet the real me."

"What do you mean, the real you?" Krystal asked as she tried to push him off of her with her one good arm.

"I mean," he said, putting his hand around her throat, "the real me." He kissed her really hard and even bit her bottom lip while he was at it.

Krystal kissed back but just barely. She was starting to feel scared and she didn't like it. It reminded her of the weird guy that broke into her bedroom. She kissed him back out of fear as she tried to think about what he meant about not knowing the real him.

Trent loosened his grip around her neck and began squeezing her left tit while kissing her on the right side of her neck. "Just feel how hard I am," he told her as he lifted himself up a bit so he could shove her good hand onto his crotch. He was hard as a rock. He looked at her and smirked and finally got off of her. He grabbed her hand and told her to come with him. Not sure what to do, she found herself standing up and letting him lead her to the bedroom. He sat her on the bed and told her to look as he pointed at the rope that was attached to the frame.

"What? What's that for?" she asked him innocently. She began thinking she should have listened to her mother.

"I want to tie you up."

"Why?"

"Because I like it and it really turns me on. I like to be in control of you."

There was a part of Krystal that was intrigued but she also had a really bad feeling come over her. "I don't know..."

"What do you mean, you don't know?" he asked her. He was starting to get mad. "Don't you trust me?"

"Of course I trust you, but..."

"But what?"

"Well, how can you tie me up when I have one of my arms in a cast?"

Trent calmed down and sat beside her. "That's not a big deal. It will not be tied up, of course. You still can't use it so it's kind of like it's tied up." He began kissing her neck again but his kisses were still rough. They weren't the kisses she was used to receiving from him.

"I just don't know if I'm okay with it."

He stopped kissing her but remained frozen with his face shoved in her neck. She held her breath. He was holding his too, as it allowed his anger to build up. He slowly pulled back from her so he could look her in the face. "What did you say?"

"I said," she replied, getting even more scared, "I don't know if I'm okay with it."

"Oh really?" He stood up and immediately slapped her across her face.

"Trent!" she shouted at him. "What the fuck is your problem?" She placed her hand on her stinging face.

"You're gonna have to find out the hard way if you're okay with it or not."

"The fuck I am!" Krystal shouted as she stood up and faced him again.

He shoved her back onto the bed. It felt good. It felt good to him to be himself again. He didn't even feel sorry for hitting her or scaring her. It was time for her to accept him for who he really was. "You are going to let me tie you up!"

She scooted over to the other side of the bed, where the doorway was, and ran for it.

He chased her and grabbed her by the back of her hair and pulled her down. She landed on her sprained wrist. "Ahhh!" she yelled in pain. "What's wrong with you?"

"I told you," he answered as he squatted down and got in her face, "it's time you met the real me. Now get up."

She slowly got up and began holding her wrist even though it was already in a cast. "Please, Trent. Stop and let's talk about this, please."

"Now, see?" He smirked. "I love to hear you begging like that. Keep doing that, babe."

Krystal really looked at him for the first time since she got there. Underneath the bruises and cuts, he looked even more awful than she had first realized. He looked like he hadn't slept in days and his eyes had a hint of crazy in them. Those were not the eyes she had been lovingly staring into for the last six months. She didn't know those eyes, and she didn't think she wanted to. "You're scaring me, Trent." She started backing away from him.

He laughed. "Good! Now get back to my bed. Now!"

"No!" she said as she turned around and headed for the door.

He grabbed her good arm and spun her around. He slapped her again and then punched her hard enough to knock her back into the door – the door that would let her out of this insanity. She was still on her feet, though, and that's all that mattered. She felt like she was back in the dream where he was driving the car that was trying to run her and her father over. As he walked toward her with hate in his eyes, she didn't think twice about raising her leg and kicking him swiftly in his nuts. As he bent over in pain, she slapped him with her good hand and he began to stand up. She then punched him in the stomach, which caused him to double over again. She then elbowed him in his back and he went down like a falling domino. Those self-defense classes were paying off.

"You fucking bitch!" he yelled through his pain.

She was finally able to get out the door and run to her car. She took off without even putting her seat belt on. The tears were streaming down her face as she shook uncontrollably. She pulled over into a parking lot of a grocery store to gather herself. She took her phone out of her pocket and pulled up the number for Brittany, who answered right away. "Hey, girl! Are you on your way?"

The tears started coming even harder now that she heard a familiar and friendly voice.

"Krystal? What's wrong?"

"I…" She didn't know what to say. "Yeah, I'm coming over now."

"Okay, but are you okay?"

"No. I'll be there in a few minutes."

"Okay, just be careful."

Krystal hung up. She wiped the tears away with the back of her good hand and was startled when she heard someone knocking on her window. Thinking it was Trent she screamed as she turned her head to look out the window. It was a trooper. She let out a deep breath and rolled down her window.

"Krystal, are you okay?"

165

"Yeah, I'm okay," she lied as she fought tears. "What are you doing here?"

"I'm on your protection detail. Your father's orders."

"I didn't know he did that. I'm okay. I'm headed to my friend's house."

"Can I ask you why you have a black eye?"

"I, um, I ran into the door. I'm clumsy, ya know?"

"Are you sure you're okay?" He didn't really believe her.

"Sure I'm sure."

"Are you? Because if Trent did that to you, just say the word and I can have him arrested."

"No! He didn't do this. We did have a fight but he didn't do this. I was mad and turned around to leave and that's when I ran into the door."

"Okay, well, I'm sorry but I still have to follow you."

"Can you not tell my dad I was here? I'm not supposed to be here."

The trooper didn't even think about it. "I'm sorry but I can't do that."

"That's fine," Krystal said, rolling her eyes. She had no desire for another fight. "I appreciate you."

She rolled up her window and pulled out of the parking lot. Brittany lived just down the street.

Trent lay on his living room floor in even more pain. *Well, you really fucked up this time. It was only a matter of time before you ruined something that could have been wonderful.*

But I had to let her see the real me.

Well, now you won't have the in they need you to have when the time comes.

Who gives a shit? Sounds like Sean has other plans of his own. Besides, that bitch just beat me up. I can't let her get away with that!

You need to calm down and figure out a way to fix this.

No! I like this hate and anger. God, it feels good! I've been missing this.

Hey, stupid! You just lost the girl of your dreams!

Fuck!

Trent fell asleep on the floor where Krystal had left him. When he woke up, it was nine o'clock and it was dark in his apartment. He got up, in even more pain than he had been in before, and turned on the lights. He grabbed his cell phone and fell into the couch. He was upset to see that there were no calls or texts from Krystal. He wasn't surprised, but he was still upset. He sat there for a minute, staring at the cell phone, hoping she'd call him. He didn't know what he was going to do now. He may have just fucked everything up. He finally decided to call her. When her phone went straight to voicemail, the anger rose up in him within a second. "That bitch!" he yelled out loud before he threw his cell phone across the room. It smashed into the wall, yet again. He was so pissed off that he had to release the anger. He stood up and walked to the wall and punched two big holes into it. He stood there, staring at the wall, waiting and looking at it as if it were going to fight back. He breathed heavy and kept his fists ready to be swung at any second. He suddenly remembered how it felt to be so angry, to let all of your energy be consumed by something that was not healthy in any way whatsoever. The feeling disgusted him, it made him feel tired, but he knew he couldn't do anything to fix it. It was back and it was here to stay. He grabbed his car keys, ran out to his car, and took off for the "office." He needed to see Candy again.

Chapter 27

"How in the fuck could that judge deny the warrant for the warehouse?" Paul shouted into the warm summer air. He and the captain had just walked out of the courthouse.

"That judge is an asshole. I knew he'd deny it. He hates me and that's the only reason he denied it."

"Well, what are we going to do now? Just start walking through the warehouse?"

"How about we put a follow on your little son-in-law before bringing him in for questioning?"

"He is not my son-in-law! Not now and not ever, so bite your tongue!"

The captain laughed. "I'm just trying to get a rise out of you! Seriously, what do you think of the idea?"

"I guess it's a start. Who should we put on him? We need one of the good ones on him."

"I think we should get Hill on the detail. He's one of our best."

"I agree with you."

"I'll make the call," the captain said, taking his cell phone off his belt.

Paul's phone started ringing. He took it out of its case and saw it was the trooper that was assigned to Krystal. "Bringman? Is Krystal okay?" he asked as he answered.

"Sir, she just left Trent's house and she had a black eye."

"What? She's not supposed to even be there!"

"She told me that, sir."

"Did he hit her?"

"I asked her that but she swore he didn't do it to her. She said they did get into a fight and she was so mad that when she turned around to leave, she ran into the door."

"Do you believe her?"

"I don't know her well enough to say if I do or not."

"Where is she now? Did she go back home?"

"No. She said she was headed to a friend's house. We didn't go too far away from where Trent's house was."

"She went to Brittany's house, probably. Thanks for letting me know and be sure to keep an eye on her."

"You got it!"

Paul called Laura to let her know what was going on, then he and the captain got in the car and headed back to the office. It was time for Paul to look up this Eck guy while he let Laura deal with Krystal.

Paul quickly punched in the name "Carl Eck" once he got seated behind his office computer. His picture popped up first. The man had long hair, a thin face, and eyes that made him look lost and soulless. He didn't look familiar to Paul at all. That name Eck was still bugging him, though. He read up on Carl Eck and learned he had a rap sheet a mile long. Most of it was drug-related charges. Paul went all the way back to his record from when the guy was eighteen years old, to his first charge as an adult. It was for intent to distribute, but the name of the person who bailed him out of jail is what made the hair on his arm stand up. Shannon Eck. It all started coming together in his mind. Shannon Eck was the mother of Maddy Eck. Carl Eck was Maddy's cousin. Maddy Eck. That was a name that Paul hadn't thought about in years. He sat back as his mind threw him back to when he was only eighteen years old.

He had just graduated from high school and had no idea what he wanted to do with himself. His parents had a good chunk of

169

money saved up for him for college, but he didn't feel like college was the thing for him. His parents agreed to let him take the money and use it for traveling. The only problem was that he didn't have a car. He had always used his parents' car whenever he had to go somewhere. He could have used the money to buy a car, but then there would have been none left to use to travel. So, he started out on the ultimate adventure and hitchhiked his way west. He grew up on the East Coast, so he wanted to see what the West Coast had to offer.

Hitchhiking in those days was relatively safe. He had a nice pocketknife on him for protection, but he never had to use it. He had enough money to keep food in his belly and shelter over his head. It was the actual traveling that was the hard part. Many truck drivers would pull over and let him ride along. Most of them admired what Paul was doing. A few of them laughed in his face, though. This night, in particular, it was around nine and it was raining. He had an umbrella but no jacket. It was mid-June so it was a little chilly in the night air. He was on a road somewhere in Missouri. He had been hoping to find a hotel but he hadn't found one in the last six miles he had walked. It was the worst night so far. The truck driver that dropped him off said he had to unload and then head back east, so he could take him no farther. The guy pretty much dumped him off in the middle of nowhere.

Just as he was about to just lie down on the side of the road in the rain, he saw headlights approaching from behind him so he put out his thumb. The car slowed down and pulled over to the side of the road. The driver rolled down their window and Paul was relieved to see that it was a woman for once. The first woman to pull over so far. She was cute too. A skinny little blonde with her tits all but hanging out. As Paul climbed into the passenger seat, he introduced himself. "I'm Paul Jennings."

"Nice to meet you, Paul. I'm Maddy Eck. What's a young boy like you doing out in the middle of nowhere at night and in the rain?"

Paul was a flirt even at an early age. "Young boy?" he had questioned her. "If I'm a young boy, then you are a young girl."

The woman laughed. "I'm twenty-five, so I am pretty young myself. How old are you, Paul?"

Paul said that he was only eighteen, and told her why he was out there in the middle of nowhere and what he was doing. "So how far do you think you can take me?"

"Oh," Maddy replied, "I can't take you very far. I was just concerned about you being out in the rain. There's a hotel about five more miles down the road. I can take you there."

"Well, that's good enough for me. I really do appreciate it. May I offer you money for gas?"

Maddy laughed. "That won't be necessary, handsome. I was going this way anyway. I do have something else in mind."

Paul saw the look in her eyes. He didn't have to ask but he did anyway. He just loved to flirt. "Oh yeah? Like what?" He gave her his award-winning smile.

She smiled back at him and licked her lips. "Let's just get you checked in and then we'll figure it out from there."

Paul only smiled at her. He could have been reading her wrong, but he was pretty sure he was about to get laid. Considering he was still a virgin, he thought he should be a little nervous, but he was ready. He had been ready for years but had never had the chance. His girlfriend of the past two years wouldn't give it up, saying she just wasn't ready. When he left for his little trip, she dumped him. She couldn't stand to be away from him all summer. He was a free man.

When she pulled up to a hotel that was a lot nicer than the ones he had been staying at, he knew he had to keep his mouth shut about the price. He wasn't going to ruin this. "Well, thank you, Ms. Eck, for getting me to shelter. I really appreciate it."

"Ms. Eck? My mom, Shannon, goes by Ms. Eck. Do I look like a mother to you?"

Paul smiled hard. "No. I was just trying to be respectful."

Maddy smiled. "It's not every day you meet a guy your age that's respectful like that. Are you sure you're eighteen years old?"

"That's what my parents tell me, so unless they're lying to me..." He let his words trail off as he realized that Maddy had begun unbuttoning the first few buttons on her shirt, revealing her tits even more. Paul didn't think he had ever seen a pair so big.

Maddy smiled at him and shrugged a little bit as if to say she didn't mean to undo those buttons. "Well, you're still fairly young so I want to make sure you get checked into your room okay, if you're cool with that."

"I'm more than cool with that," Paul told her tits.

They got out of the car and back into the rain. Paul was able to get a room on the third floor and Maddy walked up with him...just to make sure he got inside safely. He put his bag on the floor next to the bed and looked at Maddy. In the light, she was even more beautiful than he had realized. There was no way he was going to score with this girl. Maddy sat down on the bed. "Maybe we can exchange phone numbers, Paul? I'd like to hear how the rest of your trip turned out once you get back home."

"S-s-s-sure," Paul stuttered. Maybe he was a little nervous. He scribbled his number on the pad that was lying on the nightstand and ripped the sheet off. He handed it to her, and as she slipped it into her pocket he asked, "How about your number?"

She took the pad and pen out of his hands and laid them back down on the nightstand. "Later," she replied. "Paul, I want to ask you something personal and you don't have to answer it if you don't want to."

He realized that his throat was dry and as he croaked out his "okay," his throat clicked from the dryness. She patted the bed to get him to sit down next to her. He did.

"Paul, I know you are young and boys your age like to lie about these things, but I need you to be honest with me. I promise I won't make fun of you, okay?"

"Okay." His mind began racing as he tried to figure out what she was about to ask him. In the light of the hotel room he was able to take a better look at her and she was flawless.

"Paul, are you a virgin?"

Paul wanted to lie to her and tell her he wasn't, but she had asked for the truth. As his cheeks turned red, he answered, "Yes, I am."

Maddy seemed happy with his answer. "Good. I have another question for you now."

"Okay."

"Do you want to lose your virginity?"

"To you?" His voice cracked as he raised his voice to form the word "you."

She scooted closer to him on the bed and placed her hand on his thigh. "Yes, to me."

"I mean, that would be every guy's dream...um...to, you know, lose it to someone as beautiful as you." He placed his hand on top of hers.

"That's very sweet of you to say, Paul." She kissed his cheek, which caused it to turn even redder.

"What's the catch?"

"There's no catch, sweetheart," she answered. "I'm just a girl who is looking for something, just like you are."

"You don't want anything in return?"

"Only that you keep this between you and I. You can't go back telling your little friends about this."

"I can do that," Paul said as he finally was able to look her in her eyes. Even though he was nervous to lose his virginity, the oddness of this situation didn't bother him at all. He was ready to do this.

"Good." She smiled. "Now, how about we get out of our wet clothes?"

With that, she undressed him first, and she seemed to be pleased with the size of his cock. Paul was even more embarrassed at how hard his penis already was before she even touched him. He looked away from her, hoping he wouldn't seem less manly to her. She grabbed his face and moved his head so that he was looking at her again. She smiled as she began stroking his penis, letting him know that it was okay. She then took all of her clothes off and placed his hands on her tits. "My body is yours to do as you please. Don't be shy, Paul."

With that, Paul "dove right in." As he lost his virginity, all Maddy was thinking about was that this was fate. She was ovulating and she was supposed to meet this clean boy. There was no protection used. It was never even mentioned. An hour later, Maddy was giving her goodbyes to Paul and he thought he had seen the last of her.

Fast-forward to two years later, Paul was in that very same hotel for training in the police academy. They sent them from Maryland to Missouri because there was a really good class held there on how to defend yourself. Paul was surprised when he ran into Maddy at a grocery store close to the hotel. He'd had no contact with her since they hooked up. She never did call him, and she never had given him her number. He had thought about her often, though. What was even more surprising about seeing her out of the blue was the little baby sitting in a car seat in the shopping cart. He looked just like Paul.

Maddy went on to tell him that he had given her a gift. She was in love with a man who couldn't give her the one thing that Paul could and had. She told him she didn't want anything from him, and that the baby had a father. Paul was still young, and at the end of the conversation, he had agreed to go on with his life as if this child never existed. He never made any attempts to find her again and he never told another living soul about it.

"Paul! Earth to Paul!?" The captain was shouting in his ear. "You all right?"

Paul snapped out of his memory. "Sorry, sir. I was just thinking."

"I can see that! Did you come up with something?"

"Maybe."

"Maybe? Do you care to elaborate on that?"

"Not yet. I need to process all my thoughts so they make sense. I'm going to call it a day for now. We'll get back to this tomorrow, bright and early."

"Okay, you're the boss applesauce," the captain laughed.

Paul drove to his "thinking spot." It was the Rocky Gorge Reservoir off of Route 29 in the Laurel area. Not many people came there, even in the spring and summer. It was usually quiet, and this evening was no different. He sat down on a bench in front of the water and let his mind process the new information. How in the hell was Maddy Eck connected to all of this? He thought about the boy, his boy. He would have been just a few years older than Krystal now. Was she coming after him for some reason? She told him to forget about her, and so he only did as he was told. He never thought much about her or his son because he got busy with his family and his career. He assumed it was all over and done with. Maybe this was all just a coincidence. That would be a pretty big coincidence, though. So Carl Eck was Maddy's cousin. Carl Eck was linked to this Thomas character, even though that wasn't his real name. Could this Thomas guy be an Eck too? He pulled out his notepad and looked over his notes. He realized that the old lady had mentioned the names Drew and Foster. Could Drew Foster be an actual name? Could Drew Foster be Thomas?

He had his laptop with him. He opened it up and signed on to the police database. He searched the name "Drew Foster." He got a hit within seconds and the mug shot, although more than fifteen years old, revealed that he was, in fact, Thomas Sharver. The old photo must be why it didn't pop up on the face recognition system. He knew that name was a phony. As he searched more, he didn't see any relation between Drew Foster and the Ecks. Maybe he was just a hired associate, but he could have been related to his son. "His son." He'd always wanted a boy, but Laura was happy with just one kid. And now he knew why he had starting thinking about his secret the other day and feeling an urge to tell Laura. He still hadn't told her, but now he knew he really had to.

It had been years, but it was time for him to find Maddy Eck. Maybe she could shed some light on this, or maybe it would make things worse, but there was only one way to find out. He did a search on Maddy Eck and was able to find a last known address in Missouri. He found the number for the address and gave it a call on his work cell phone. Someone picked up on the second ring. A man. "Hello?"

Paul hesitated. What if it was his son answering the phone? "Hello?"

Paul opened his mouth to speak but he choked.

"Hello?" the man shouted over the phone.

Paul took a deep breath. "Hello. I'm sorry about that. Um, I'm trying to reach Maddy Eck."

"Who is this?"

"Um, an old friend of hers. I was just calling to see how she's doing."

"An old friend? Do you have a name, old friend?"

"Jason." Paul lied without even thinking about it.

"Jason? I don't remember any friends of hers named Jason."

"Well, we went to school together, briefly."

"When was the last time you spoke to Maddy, Jason?"

"Oh, it's been well over twenty-five years if not longer. Is she there? I'd really like to talk to her."

There was silence on the other end.

"Hello?" It was Paul's turn.

"I'm sorry, but it's not possible for you to talk to Maddy. She passed away over twenty years ago."

Paul didn't know what to say. He stuttered the words, "Passed away? Um, how? She was so young, from what?"

Another pause of silence.

"Hello, sir?"

"I'm sorry. Even though it's been over twenty years, I still get choked up. I mean, she was my only sister and I miss her."

"I – I – I'm sorry. Really."

"It's okay. I'm still not used to it. She was actually murdered by her husband."

"What?"

"Yeah. He went off his crazy meds and, well, he went crazy."

Paul took a second to let it soak in as he realized that his son now had no parents. He started thinking back again to the night he

177

met Maddy. He somehow felt responsible for her murder. "Wow. I'm really sorry, I had no idea. Um, her husband? Where is he at? I mean, he's locked up now, right?"

"In a way, I suppose. He killed himself after he killed her. We're just lucky that their sons were in school at the time."

"Their sons?"

"Yeah. Sean and Toby. They were twins, actually. They had to deal with a lot before all that happened. I mean, there was so much abuse in their house. CPS wouldn't let any of us in the family even take legal custody of Sean and Toby. They both ended up in foster care. Sean won't speak to any of us now. It's really sad. What's even sadder is that Toby was killed about six months ago by a police officer after he broke into a house over in Maryland. He was on drugs real bad. I just feel like I should have…" The guy changed his trail of thought. "I'm sorry. You're not my therapist and I'm sure this is a lot for you to take in. I'm sorry I was babbling."

Paul was still in shock – twins?! – but held himself together. "No, it's okay. I'm really sorry for your loss and all that…well, that mess. I'm sorry for bothering you."

"No bother, none at all. You have a good one."

"Thank you," Paul responded. "You as well."

He hung up and started crying as he realized that the robber he had shot had been his very own son. He thought some small part of him knew but just never put it together. He remembered that day and seeing the guy's eyes and thinking they looked familiar. Now he knew why. They were his son's eyes, which meant they were his own eyes in a way.

Chapter 28

Krystal woke up the next morning in Brittany's apartment, on her pull-out couch. Brittany had actually crashed beside her. They fell asleep watching *Dirty Dancing* and scarfing down some Rocky Road ice cream. She was grateful that she wasn't at home. Her mom called her yesterday, yelling at her for going to Trent's house. It took a while to convince her mom that Trent didn't hit her. Then she had to put Brittany on the phone to reassure her mom that she was at Brittany's house. Then both her parents called her later in the evening. They wanted her to come home, pleaded with her to, but she told them no and that's when she turned her phone off.

She turned her phone back on and checked the time: 9:23. She had no messages from Trent. That should have been a relief but she felt sad because of it. She did have a couple from her parents and she knew she'd have to call them back soon, before they showed up at Brittany's doorstep. She sat up and realized that her head was throbbing as well as her bruised eye. She got up and took a look at herself in the bathroom mirror. It was bad. Her right eye was purple with a tint of green mixed in. She wasn't sure any makeup would cover it. She looked at herself in the mirror for a while as she contemplated what she should do. She really wanted to talk to Trent. Maybe he had calmed down since last night. She quietly came out of the bathroom, got her shoes on, wrote a quick thank-you note to Brittany and stuck it on her refrigerator by a magnet, and slipped quietly out the door.

Once she got inside her car she called her mom, who answered on the first ring. After reassuring her that she was okay she told her she'd be home soon. Then she called Trent. It went straight to voicemail. That was odd, but maybe he was just as mad at her as she was with him and kept his phone off. She drove over to his

179

apartment. She knew she should just go home but she felt bad about the fight they had the night before. She didn't like having things unsettled. In some small way, she felt like the fight was her fault. She should have listened to him and what he needed from her. She didn't stop to think that she was doing the very thing that Dr. Simms always warned her about. She was being destructive.

After not getting an answer at the door, she tried calling him again. Straight to voicemail again. She had a key to his apartment and let herself in. Her eyes immediately went to the wall with the two holes in it. "What in the world?" she said out loud. She then saw his cell phone on the floor. "No wonder he wasn't answering." She went to his bedroom to see if he was there. He wasn't. She began wondering where he could be when she heard the door to the apartment open. She jumped, clearly startled, and walked out of the bedroom door to come face-to-face with Trent. He looked like hell and smelled even worse.

"Krystal? What are you doing here?"

"I – I'm sorry, I let myself in with my key. I was hoping to talk to you, but you look like shit. Where were you?"

"None of your business," he answered as he walked by her to get to his bedroom.

"Well, what happened to your wall and why is your cell phone laying on the floor?"

Trent didn't answer her. He only undressed. Once he was totally naked, he walked to the bathroom and started the water in the tub. "If you'll excuse me, I need to get a shower."

Krystal looked at him dumbfounded. He didn't care that she was there. He didn't even seem like he was sorry for anything. Between the holes in the wall, the cell phone, and Trent looking like something a cat wouldn't even drag in, she was starting to get a little

180

frightened. But she pushed on anyway. "What in the hell is going on with you, Trent?"

He continued to ignore her as he stepped into the tub, closed the shower curtain, and started the shower. "You better not still be here when I'm finished," he called out over the sound of the running water.

She sat down on his couch and waited for him to finish his shower. She wasn't going anywhere.

Trent cleaned all the filth of last night off him – there was no way he'd be able to talk to her when he looked so rough and smelled like sex and alcohol. He knew she'd still be there when he got out of the shower. He gave himself a pep talk to remind himself to stay calm when he spoke to her. He had questioned Sean last night about him breaking into Krystal's room, but Sean only told him that it was none of his business why he did it. Trent told him what had happened between himself and Krystal, and Sean said he could use what Sean had done to her to his advantage. He now had a reason to comfort her. He got some good advice from Sean on how to handle Krystal and get back on her good side, and he was going to see to it that he did just that. He wasn't going to fuck this up. He thought Sean was going to be upset with him for hitting Krystal, but he was actually happy. He said it was good that he was losing that connection with Krystal, and it didn't matter if she forgave him or not, as this would all be over very soon. He said he hoped Krystal would let him back in but if she didn't, it wouldn't be a big deal. Trent read between the lines, though, and he knew he had to get back on Krystal's good side.

Krystal practiced in her head what she was going to say to Trent. She was not going to let him hit her again, for starters. She wanted to know what was wrong with him. She loved him too much to let this be the end of them. Besides, with everything that was going on, she needed him right now. She just ignored the warning that her mother gave her about Trent. She didn't want to believe it. She was in denial about it. Her phone beeped with a text message notification. It was from Brittany, asking her where she was. She texted back that she was at Trent's house, waiting for him to get out of the shower because she was going to talk to him.

Krystal! Have you lost your mind? Get out of there! Right now!

No! I need to speak to him...ask him what happened.

It's not safe! PLEASE LEAVE!

I'm sorry but I won't. <3

She then turned off her cell phone. She would not have any interruptions. This was going to happen even if Trent didn't like it.

He walked out of his bathroom buck naked and acted startled to see her still there, sitting on his couch. "I thought I told you to leave," he said as he walked in, still naked.

"I don't care what you told me. We need to talk, and we need to talk right now!"

He sat down next to her and looked her in the eyes. "Man. I really did a number on your beautiful face, didn't I?"

She looked away from him and down at her lap. "You did. It hurts."

"Krystal, I'm really sorry."

"Why did you do it, Trent? Why were you so mad at me? I've never seen you so mad before."

He grabbed her hand. He was going for an Oscar award now. "I, um...I used to have anger problems....Like really bad anger problems. I haven't told anyone, but for the past few months I've been getting help for it. When I met you, though, you actually helped me not want to be angry. You're so beautiful and you were so kind to me. I knew you were the one for me and I didn't want to do

182

anything to mess it up. I never once felt the need to even raise my voice at you all these months. You really did bring the best out of me and I kept my anger away from you. Plus, I didn't know how to handle the fact that some dude broke into your bedroom. I'm scared about this whole situation too. I guess what happened last night was...I guess it was like a relapse in a way. I think the beating I took woke my anger back up. I'm ashamed of myself."

Krystal looked at him, trying to figure out if he was being sincere. She wasn't sure but then he started crying.

He lowered his head and sobbed, "Oh god, Krystal. I am so sorry. I never meant to hurt you or for you to ever see that side of me." He looked up at her through his tears. He softly touched her face. "Your gorgeous face. I'm so sorry."

Krystal began crying. "I guess it kind of makes sense now....I mean, why you wanted to tie me up and stuff."

"I'm sorry about that. I guess after being so calm all this time, I was...getting antsy."

"I was so scared of you last night. How come you never told me about your anger issues?"

"I didn't want to scare you away, I guess."

"I'd rather know every rotten thing about you than not know. You wouldn't have scared me away."

"What about now? Have I scared you away now?"

Krystal thought about this for a second. She believed that he would not hurt her like that again. "No. I mean, it's going to be rough for a while but I'm not going anywhere unless you want me to."

"No!" he said as he pulled her in for a hug. "Please don't go anywhere! We can work on this and fix it. I'm certain we can!"

"I think we can too," Krystal said as she pulled out of the hug and kissed him.

He kissed her back and before she knew it, he was taking off her clothes.

"Can we go to your room?" she asked. "Do you still have the ropes on your bed?"

"They're still there, but…are you sure?"

"I am," she said as she stood up and walked with him to his bedroom. She allowed him to tie her up and do whatever he wanted to her. She would have done anything to get the trust back, and she figured this was the only way how.

Chapter 29

Now that Paul and Laura were on the same page concerning Krystal not seeing Trent anymore, Paul felt it was time to talk to his wife about his past. It had been eating him up. Since Dr. Simms was back at home, he asked if they could have a session with her at her house and she agreed to it.

Since Krystal was spending time with her friend Brittany, he thought this would be a good day to meet, and Dr. Simms agreed. Mimi had opened the door and let them in after they knocked. "It's nice to meet you two," Mimi said after introductions were made.

"You as well," Laura said. "Thank you for trying to help me that day I got attacked at the hospital."

"Oh, of course." Mimi smiled.

"Yes," Paul chimed in, "thank you."

"Mimi," Dr. Simms said, "do you mind giving us some privacy now? Maybe you can run to the grocery store for us?"

"Of course," Mimi responded. "It was really nice meeting you guys."

Once Mimi was out of the house, Dr. Simms began. "So, I understand that you have something you need to talk to Laura about?"

"Yes," Paul answered. "I'm just really nervous about it, so thank you for doing this for us."

"Of course. I'll let you start, Paul."

Paul turned to his wife. "Well, this is a conversation I've been putting off for a couple of weeks now, but I need to tell you. I need you to listen to me until I'm done and, more importantly, I need you to be understanding."

"This doesn't sound good."

"It's not horrible, but you are going to be shocked. I don't even know where to start."

"How about from the beginning?"

"That would be back when I was eighteen years old."

"What? What in the world are you talking about, Paul? Have you been keeping a lifelong secret from me?"

Paul looked down. "You could say that." He was talking to his lap, not to Laura.

"Paul," Dr. Simms interjected. "Can you look at your wife while you are speaking to her?"

Paul did as he was asked. Her eyes revealed that she looked really worried, and that broke his heart. He took a deep breath and started his story with the time he was hitchhiking and met Maddy. Laura had known about his hitchhiking days, but she didn't know anything about Maddy. He told her everything about the past and what had been going on recently.

"I'm concerned," he finished up, "that this all has something to do with everything that has happened. I just haven't been able to figure out how it all fits together yet. I needed to tell you so you are aware of what's going on. I have a feeling that none of it is over yet."

Laura stayed quiet the entire time as her husband let his skeletons fall out of his closet. He had asked her to listen to everything he had to say, so she did. Inside, she was confused and didn't know what to say.

"You're quiet. I just told you an earful and you're quiet. Are you okay?"

"Laura?" Dr. Simms asked. "Do you need a minute or are you okay to keep going?"

Laura opened her mouth to speak but promptly shut it. She didn't know what to say and she didn't want to say the wrong thing.

She wasn't sure if she really had a right to be mad, but she felt a little betrayed that he had kept such a huge secret from her.

"Honey," Paul said. "I'm really sorry that I never told you about any of this. It was never my intention to keep things from you."

"But you did." She was now looking down at her lap.

"Keep the eye contact," Dr. Simms told them.

"I know. I'm sorry for that. It's just that she told me to pretty much stay out of her life and I was really busy with the academy, meeting and falling in love with you, then starting our family. I honestly never gave it another thought."

"You knew you had another child out there and you never gave it another thought? How can you even do something like that? That's your own flesh and blood, Paul!"

"I know! I was young and didn't think I could really give the child any kind of life. Once I established a career, like I said, I was focused on you and Krystal."

"Krystal! Does she know she has a brother somewhere out there?"

"No. I don't plan on telling her any time soon." Paul grabbed her hand, which made the tears dump out of her eyes. "I'm sorry. I know I just unloaded a bunch of shit into your ears. Do you hate me?" He was starting to cry now.

"No. I could never hate you. I'm upset that you kept something so big from me. It makes me feel like you didn't trust me with the information. It makes me feel like you took your promise to Maddy, to not say anything, more seriously than the vows you made to me on our wedding day."

"Please, honey. It really wasn't like that. Not at all. I don't know why I never said anything to you about it. I really didn't think much about it as the years went on. I mean, I never saw or heard from her again so it was easy to let it slide out of my mind and into the universe. I never forgot that I had a son out there, but it was something that was like, I dunno, put in the back in my mind for a rainy day. I never spent any time thinking about him or wondering what he looked like or how he was doing. It was like it was a passing thought once in a blue moon that never had any credit in my life. Does that make me a horrible person?"

"No," she answered. "You didn't have the biological connection to him like a mother does so I can see it not really bothering you. I just wish you had told me."

"Me too. You know I love you."

"I do know that. I still love you too."

Paul smiled. "There is something else that is tearing me up inside."

Laura took a deep breath.

"Paul, can this wait for another session? I don't think we should pile too much on Laura right now," Dr. Simms warned.

"It really can't, and it's something that really only affects me."

"Laura, are you okay with him continuing?"

"Sure," Laura answered, but unsure herself.

"Well, through my investigation and finding out that my son is involved with this somehow, I also found out I actually had twins."

"So you have two sons?" Laura asked.

"I did."

"Did?"

"Do you remember that incident I had like six months ago where I ended up shooting a burglar in someone's house?"

"Sure, the one where the sixteen-year-old was?"

"Yes."

"What about it?"

"It turns out that the guy I shot, that was actually my son." Paul started crying harder.

"What?" Laura asked. "Well, are you sure?"

"Yes. It was just a pure, dumb coincidence but I'm sure."

Laura hugged Paul, thinking about how awful he must be feeling.

Paul was convinced at that moment that he had the most perfect wife in the entire world. She now knew everything, and he felt relieved that she did.

"Paul," Dr. Simms said, "you must be having a really hard time with this. If you'd like to have some one-on-one sessions with me, we can set that up."

"I'd like that," Paul answered.

PART TWO

Chapter 1

Krystal was currently in her car, windows down, music blaring, on her way to visit with Dr. Simms, who had called her that morning and told her she'd like to see her. She was still recovering at home but she said she would like to start having sessions again. Three weeks had gone by and things had been really quiet. There hadn't been any more instances with Thomas Sharver or the other mystery man. She didn't feel the need to see Dr. Simms, but the doctor insisted. She was still seeing Trent behind her parents' backs.

When she got to Dr. Simms's house, before she could even look for a doorbell or knock, the door slowly opened. There before her was a woman, probably in her mid-to-late forties. She had big poofy hair like girls used to wear in the eighties. She was wearing all black clothes. Her pants were tight, almost like skinny jeans, and over the bottom of them were big black boots that went up to just below her knees. Her low-cut shirt revealed a big bosom and the arms of the shirt were wide and loose. "You must be Krystal," the woman said to her.

"Yes. I'm here to see Dr. Simms."

"Of course you are. Please come in." She moved aside so Krystal could step in.

The doctor's house was modest at best. It was a small brick rancher style but the yard it was settled on appeared to be pretty big – at least an acre if not more. She walked farther in and saw Dr. Simms sitting in the living room off to her left.

"Krystal!" Dr. Simms said. "Please, come in and sit down with me. It's so nice to see you!"

Krystal walked over to her. The doctor had her left leg propped up on a footrest but she looked comfortable. "How are you feeling?" she asked as Krystal went in to give her a hug.

The hug was returned as she answered, "Physically, I still have a little bit of pain but it's not too bad. How have you been?"

"Pretty good, actually."

"That's good," Dr. Simms said. "I'd like you to meet my good friend Mimi."

Krystal turned around to the lady who had let her in. "You're the famous Mimi?!"

"The one and only!" Mimi answered.

Krystal gave her a hug. "My family owes you a huge thank-you. I don't know how you knew that guy was coming after my mom, but we greatly appreciate you trying to look out for us that day."

"No thanks are needed. It's just what I do." She motioned for Krystal to sit down on the couch next to Dr. Simms. Mimi sat down in the chair next to them.

"Is my mom working here today? Has she met you yet, Mimi?"

"We've met," Mimi answered.

"I gave her the day off today," Dr. Simms said. "I wanted to speak to you without her here."

"Oh. Okay. Well, you know I tell her everything, so…" Krystal said.

"You do?" Dr. Simms asked. "Before you answer that, do you mind if Mimi sits in with us today? She's got some things to go over with you."

"No, I don't mind at all," Krystal answered.

"Good," Dr. Simms said. "You say you tell your mom everything?"

"I usually do."

"Well, did you tell her or your father that you're still seeing Trent or that Trent hit you?" Dr. Simms asked her.

"What? Who told you that?" Krystal asked.

Dr. Simms looked toward Mimi as Mimi raised her hand. "I did," Mimi said with a proud tone to her voice.

Krystal didn't know what to say. She wasn't sure if she should deny it or admit it. She suddenly wanted to leave.

"Krystal," Dr. Simms began, "I need you to be honest with me. It's very important. There's a reason that Mimi waited a couple of weeks before coming here. Things have been quiet, have they not?"

"They have," Krystal answered. "And I've been feeling really great. I think it's all over with."

"It's not," Mimi warned.

"We can't figure out why things were so quiet for a couple of weeks, but we do know that things are not over with," Dr. Simms explained. "In fact, there are going to be some pretty bad things starting to happen, but we can do our best to fight them. Since we know they are coming, we have a better chance of fighting this."

"Fighting what, exactly?" Krystal asked.

Mimi answered, "This evil darkness that is lurking around you all."

Krystal gave her an unsure look.

Mimi said, "I know it sounds hokey or whatever but I was right about the attack on your mom, I was right about Trent hitting you, and I'm right about this too. That's why I'm here. My friend here is in trouble too. I'm here to kind of protect her. I won't let anything happen to her and I won't let anything happen to you and your family…regardless of what you believe."

"Well, if you're so great about seeing all of this, then why didn't you warn me about the guy who broke into my room a few weeks ago?" Krystal asked Mimi.

"Your father told us about that. I didn't sense that one, but it's probably because of one of two reasons. Either he decided to visit you spur of the moment, or my guard was down that day. I could have been sleeping or something. It does happen."

"Krystal, why did Trent hit you?" Dr. Simms asked.

Krystal looked down at her feet. She felt ashamed. The only person who knew about it was Brittany. "Does it really matter?" she mumbled.

"It does," Dr. Simms answered.

"I don't know. It's kind of embarrassing, but...he, well, he was upset with me because I wouldn't let him tie me up for sex. He was really weird that day. I mean, it wasn't him. It wasn't the guy I've known all this time. He was someone else. He had gotten robbed that morning and was beat up pretty bad. It was the same day that guy broke into my room, and we just started yelling at each other. When we both calmed down, for whatever reason, he was turned on. I was confused by that because he was clearly in pain. He told me he was in pain but the pain and anger turned him on. I had never heard him say anything like that before. He took me to his bedroom and he had a rope tied on the bed. He wanted to tie me up and I just wasn't feeling it. I was scared of him, I mean, really scared. I told him no and he didn't like that. He got angry and I attempted to get away from him but he slapped me a couple of times and then punched me. I was able to kick him in the crotch and get away from him."

"You're still with him?" Dr. Simms asked.

"I am. I went to his apartment the next morning and we talked about it. He told me he's been struggling with anger issues for years until he met me. He apologized and said it wouldn't happen again, and it hasn't."

"I know I had told you before to take things slow with him. Not because I knew anything about him, but because I know how you jump into things too quickly. How are things now?" Dr. Simms asked.

"Good...better than good. I've allowed him to start tying me up now. I even tie him up sometimes. Things have gotten interesting in that department. We're good, though."

"Why did you agree to let him tie you up now? You said you were scared the night he hit you, but now you're not?"

"I'm not scared. That night, he was in a weird place. I thought maybe the doctors had given him some sort of pain meds but he said they hadn't. He was really odd that night but he's been fine since then. We've been fine."

"Krystal, we've talked before about how you like to be in control of situations. Do you think that's why you forgave him and are letting him tie you up? So that you feel like you are in charge of the relationship?"

Krystal hadn't really thought of that. "I dunno. Maybe."

"And you trust him?" Dr. Simms questioned.

"I do. I mean, that was the main reason I let him start tying me up. I had to get the trust back and I thought that would be the fastest way to do it."

"Does hitting go with the whole tying up thing?" Dr. Simms asked.

"Not really. We do use a little whip but it's not that bad."

"Does he hit you hard with it?"

"Sometimes, when he's really into it. I can usually handle it, though."

"And the times you can't handle it? What do you do then?"

"Grin and bear it."

Dr. Simms studied Krystal for a minute. "Are you really okay with doing that with him? Or do you think maybe you feel like you are stuck? Or maybe it's more that you want to keep him close to you right now with everything that's been happening?"

Tears started to well up in Krystal's eyes and as much as she tried to keep them in, she couldn't. "I have to be okay with it. Otherwise, he might…"

"He might what?" Dr. Simms asked.

Mimi was sitting quietly and listening to them.

"I don't know. I think if I didn't do this with him, that he may hit me again. I'd rather let him tie me up and do whatever he wants than to punch me again. But it's not just that. I still love him. I'm still insanely attracted to him. That's why I'm still seeing him behind my parents' back."

Dr. Simms handed her a box of Kleenex. "What did you tell your parents about your bruise?"

"I told them that Trent and I had gotten into an argument and I turned around to leave and didn't realize how close I was to his bedroom door and ran into it."

"Did they believe you?"

"I'm not sure if they did or not but they didn't push the issue, so I'm assuming they did. Dad seems to think Trent is wrapped up in all of this somehow but I don't believe that." She wiped her tears.

"Listen to me," Dr. Simms said as she leaned closer to Krystal. "No one, and I mean no one, should ever make you do anything for any reason. While Trent isn't making you do these things with him, he's still controlling you. You have a fear that if you don't let him tie you up that he will hit you and that is a legit fear. Do you think him hitting you is okay?"

"No, of course not."

"Then why are you doing whatever you need to do to keep him from hitting you?"

"You want him to hit me?"

"No. But you said that if him tying you up keeps him from hitting you, then you'll do it."

"Right. It keeps whatever that urge is that he has under lock and key. I'm safer that way."

"Listen to yourself right now! You are subjecting yourself to something you don't really like to do to keep something bad from happening. You have to see that this behavior is not okay! I want you to think about this too – your dad warned you that Trent may be wrapped up in all the bad things that have been happening, but you chose to ignore that. Trent is abusive all of a sudden and for some reason, you don't make the connection between what your dad told you and the fact that Trent actually did hurt you."

Krystal began crying even harder. "I was having a good day. You are ruining it now."

Mimi finally stepped in. She got up and knelt down in front of Krystal. "I know you don't know me and I have no right to say anything here, but I need you to listen to me. Your dad is right. Trent is not a good person. His only mission is to hurt you. You need to cut things off with him and you need to do it right away."

Krystal looked at Mimi through her teary eyes. She looked into Mimi's bright green eyes and saw nothing but warmth, compassion, and honesty. She saw a woman that had a gift that most people didn't or at least didn't know how to use. While she felt like she should be beyond pissed off at this woman that she didn't even know, she found herself entranced and in tune with Mimi. Something was telling her that believing Mimi was okay. She felt safe. "We've been together for almost seven months. He's never been bad to me. He's been wonderful. I still love him."

"I know, honey, but it's all been an act. I can't figure out just what is going on but I do know that he's out to hurt you. I see him in my nightmares. I see him doing bad things."

"What am I supposed to do? If he's as bad as you are saying, don't you think breaking up with him will only anger him? Wouldn't I be putting myself into more danger?"

"You are in danger any way you look at it," Mimi answered.

"So I might as well stay on his good side," Krystal said, starting to cry even harder.

"It's your decision," Dr. Simms responded, "but whatever you decide, I just need you to be careful and be on guard. I don't think letting him tie you up is a thing you should allow to continue. He may not untie you one night."

"I still love him," Krystal sobbed.

Mimi rubbed Krystal's shoulders in an attempt to calm her down.

"How are your mom and dad doing?" Dr. Simms asked in an effort to change the subject. Mimi sat back down in her chair.

"They're okay, I guess. I need to get to my doctor's appointment," Krystal said, standing up. "I'm getting my cast off today! Trent is going to go with me and…"

"Just remember what we said," Dr. Simms cut in as Krystal let her words trail off. "Call me if you need me. I don't care what time of the day or night it is."

"Okay," Krystal replied, giving her a hug. "Thanks."

Not long after Krystal left, Mimi started to have a panic attack. She lay back on the couch and actually blacked out for a few minutes. She woke up to Dr. Simms shoving her and calling her name. "Mimi! Mimi, are you with me? Mimi?"

Mimi slowly opened her eyes and sat up. "Wow."

"Are you okay? You scared the crap out of me!"

197

"I am. I just had a premonition. I've never had one that powerful before."

"Is it bad?"

"It is. We're in danger. We have to get out of here, right now!"

"What? Wait a minute. What do you mean we're in danger?"

"I mean, whoever that guy was that tried to run you down, he's coming back tonight."

"Are you sure?"

"More than anything."

"Well, is he gonna come here? To my house?"

"I believe so."

"Well, okay. We're not leaving. I'm calling Lieutenant Jennings so we can have the police waiting for them."

Chapter 2

Trent had to call Krystal. She wasn't going to be happy but duty called.

"Hello?" Krystal said, while getting into her car after saying goodbye to Dr. Simms.

"Hey, hun."

"Hey! I was just on my way to your apartment! I'm so excited to get this cast off!" She was in acting mode now. Right now, her plan was to keep going on as if she knew nothing. She was afraid to upset him. She didn't care about the danger she could be in. She kind of welcomed it, as it excited her.

"That's why I'm calling. Something came up at work and they need me to come in right away."

"So you can't come with me?" She was upset but not really.

"No, I'm sorry. I'm sure your mom or dad can go with you to help you celebrate."

"I'm sure they can. I can also just go by myself. It's not really a big deal."

"Yes it is! You will finally have use of your arm! I can finally tie up both of those arms now."

That statement gave Krystal the chills. She faked a little laugh. "There's that! Well, I'm going to get on the road then. Can we get together later this evening?"

"Yes! I'd like that!"

"Great. I'll talk to you later."

"Okay. I love you."

"You too," Krystal said as she hung up her cell phone. She knew she was doing the wrong thing by still carrying on with him, but she pushed that thought out of her head. She felt like she needed to do this. Besides, it was too hard to just stop loving him.

199

Trent was glad that the conversation went so easily. He knew Krystal would be okay with it underneath it all. He knew that she was a really good woman who loved unconditionally. He also knew that he would be losing her soon. He still had mixed feelings about that, but he was fighting them because the money this job was going to pay him meant more to him than she did.

He pulled up to the warehouse. He sat there for a second, preparing himself for this meeting. He knew things were about to take a turn and he had to get himself in the right mindset for it. It was time to change gears and get down to business.

When he entered the clubhouse he saw Jack, Sean, and some guy he had never seen before.

"Finally! You got your ass here!" the stranger said to him.

"What?" Trent asked. He knew that voice but not that face.

Sean said, "Can we sit down and start this meeting, please? We got a lot to go over."

They all sat down in the makeshift living room. Trent was still looking at the stranger, trying to figure out who it was.

"Can you stand up, Drew?" Sean asked.

The stranger stood up.

"Whoa!" Trent and the douche bag said at the same time.

"Drew? Really?" Trent asked. "You look like a totally different person!"

"I feel like a totally different person too!" Drew laughed.

Drew had traded his brown hair in for blond hair. His cheeks were not as fat as they were before, his lips were fuller, and his eyebrows were lifted to reveal more of his eyes. Blue tinted contacts changed his eyes from brown to blue. He'd had a full facelift done. He had even lost some weight and toned up. He could have been a model.

"Because Drew's face was plastered all over the news, we had to change his looks up so he can carry out this job. That's why we've been laying low for the past couple of weeks. Well, between that and getting Trent back in line, we had to put things to the side. But it's finally time to carry out this job. At the end of it, you all will be rewarded very nicely. I'll even be giving you bonuses if there are no messes to clean up."

"That sounds great!" Douche Bag said.

"We start tonight with the doctor. I have been told that she was sent home from the hospital a couple of weeks ago. It's now time for us to take care of her. For good this time."

"Are we all on this tonight?" Drew asked.

"Yes," Sean answered. "Jack scoped the place out yesterday. She's got a nice little chunk of land. It's very private and there's not much traffic in the area. She lives alone as far as we can tell, but she may have a nurse with her or a family member or a friend, so we have to keep our eyes peeled. There's a good chance that Laura is her nurse, but we don't think she spends the night there. We will do this in the middle of the night to be safe. We don't know how many people will actually be in the house. Luckily, it's not a big house. It looks like it's only one floor, although it could have a basement." He passed a picture of her house over to Trent, who took a look at it and then passed it over to Drew. "She does have one cop sitting outside watching her house. You'll have to take care of him first if he's still there when you first arrive."

"Is this going to be a breaking and entering attempt?" Drew asked.

"Yes," Sean answered. "I want you all to steal whatever you can fit in your pockets. Money, jewelry, whatever, but don't waste your time on big things like a TV. That will only slow you down.

Whatever you take, you can keep or get rid of. I don't really give a shit. We just need to do this as swiftly as possible."

"Okay!" Drew said excitedly. "I'm ready to get back to work! What is the outlined game plan?"

"This is my idea, but I want you all to pipe in if anything I say doesn't make sense or could cause a problem. The more heads we have in this plan, the better we'll pull it off."

Drew loved that the boss allowed them to give input. He really was a good boss. He began daydreaming. *I wonder what he thinks of my new looks. I'm a lot hotter than I was before. He's got to be attracted to me now. Maybe when this job is over I will make a move on him just to see what happens....*

"Goddamn it, Drew!" Sean shouted, throwing an empty glass toward Drew's head but missing on purpose.

Drew jumped.

"I can't have you zoning out right now! Do you fucking hear me, you little shit?" Sean screamed.

"S-s-sorry, boss. I was just thinking about the kill. You know how I love it," Drew said while his newly modeled cheeks turned a bright shade of red.

"Then fucking pay attention! This job is important to me, the one I've been working up to my entire life. I really want it to go smoothly. We've had enough fuck-ups for one job. No more!"

"Yes, sir," Drew said with a bit of a defeated mumble.

"As I was saying, you three will be the main guys. I'll have Larry and Fritz outside as lookouts. I want you guys to get there around two in the morning. If you're swift, you can be in and out by no later than two thirty. When you get in there, you all need to go separate ways. It's a small house so you should be able to keep tabs on each other if you are listening to your surroundings. The goal is to find the doctor first, and anyone else who may be in there. Remain as quiet as possible. Make sure you have silencers on your guns. Getting her while she's sleeping will be the easiest way to do this job. I want it over as quickly as possible. No torture bullshit and no acting like you are God. Do you all understand that?"

"Yes, sir," Drew said.

"Yes, sir," Jack replied.

"Yes," Trent said. He was not about to call him sir.

"Good. The doctor has done nothing wrong to me but she has made this her business and that's why we have to off her. I just want it over as quickly as possible. You guys don't need to go in there and put the fear of death in her before you do your thing. Trust me, I'll let you guys have that kind of fun later on."

Trent wondered if Krystal would be involved in that "fun."

"Once you've gone through all the rooms and made sure that you got all the occupants taken care of, you can then root through her shit and take things, make a mess, make it look like it was just a robbery. Make sure you all are wearing gloves, though. I can't have any of this coming back to any of you. I need you all for the next part of this job. Don't take too long making the mess. Five to ten minutes tops and then get the hell outta there! Remember to be quiet the entire time," Sean ordered.

"Do we know if the doctor has a dog or any other pets?" Trent asked.

"Good question," Jack answered. "I watched her house for damn near twelve hours yesterday. Not once did I see her come outside to walk any dogs. I was positioned where I could see the front and the back of the house and there were no dogs outside at any time, front or back. So, I'm going to say no, she doesn't have any dogs. Any other animals will be no big deal."

Sean said, "Thank you, Jack."

Drew didn't like that Douche Bag just got praise from the boss. He thought he'd take his shot too. "Boss, what about my failed attack on the doctor? Don't you think they will think it's me again?"

"Of course, but that's why we are stealing things as well. This way they will think it's just a normal breaking and entering."

"But we're killing her while she's sleeping. There will be no signs of a struggle. Why would a robber kill someone who doesn't even come after him?"

"Drew!" Sean said with authority. "I told you, there will be no torture."

"I heard that, boss," Drew said. "But like I said, it won't make sense if we kill her while she's sleeping. Most robbers don't do that unless the homeowner is up and in their way."

"Well, what do you suggest we do?" Sean asked him.

"What if we break into some neighbors' houses too? Steal their shit and off them as well?" Drew suggested with hopes that the boss would praise him for the idea.

"Absolutely not!" Sean answered. "That would only cause more problems for us if we get caught. Do you hear me? Do *not* do that."

"Of course, it's not your ass that's on the line," Trent said before thinking about what was coming out of his mouth.

"What is that supposed to mean?" Sean asked Trent with a little bit of anger in his voice.

"I just mean that Drew's face was plastered all over the fucking place and even though he's got a new mug, he's going to be the first person they think of. I mean, what are the odds that someone tried to take the doctor out in a car and now breaks into her house and kills her and makes it look like a robbery? This is just a bad idea. I thought you were smarter than this."

The room fell silent. No one ever got away with talking to the boss like that.

It took a few seconds for Sean to respond. He was walking on the edge of either backhanding Trent or giving him a hug for being so mean. He decided to do neither. "A simple mind would think that this is a bad idea, but if you really stop to think about it, it's not. Even if they do figure it's the same guy, they still won't find Drew. Why? Because not only is the face that they have plastered all over the news not his anymore, they are putting out his false name as well. They don't even know who he is. They will never find him."

"You're wrong," Trent told him quickly. "Evidently, you haven't been keeping up with the news. They reported a few days ago that the name they originally gave was found to be a false name. They actually stated that his name was Drew Foster. They know who he is now."

"That's not true, is it?" Drew asked the boss, now really worried about his future.

"It's true," Jack answered. "I saw it earlier this morning."

Sean knew about it but he was hoping they wouldn't have heard.

"It still doesn't matter," Sean replied. "They will never find him because his face is different and we're giving him new IDs. He's no longer Drew or Thomas or whoever they think his name is. He's now Shane Murphy."

"I am?" Drew asked, shocked.

Sean pulled an ID out of his front pocket and handed it to Drew. "In the flesh!"

"Shane, huh? I always have liked the name Shane. Thanks, boss!"

"Can I just ask," Trent continued, "why it's so damn important that we off the doctor? I don't like her myself but I don't understand why she has to go."

"All I'm going to say is that this doctor of theirs knows more than she should. She puts good thoughts in their minds and I need to get rid of that. She helps that family way too much and she'll get in the way, I think," Sean answered. "Unless you have another way of doing this, then we do it my way."

The room fell silent again.

"It's going to be okay," Drew finally said. "I think I will be okay, guys. If not, once this job is done, I can run away and go into hiding somewhere. I will never be found unless I want to."

Trent rolled his eyes at Drew. It was Drew's ass on the line so why did he care? He didn't even like Drew all that much anyway.

"Thank you, Drew, for having my back," Sean said.

Drew smiled, glad that he finally got his praise from the boss.

"I still think it's a bad idea," Trent said again, "but you're the boss so whatever!"

"Well, unless you can come up with a better idea, this is how it goes down," Sean said.

"I just came up with something," Drew said excitedly. "What if we go in, off her and anyone else in the house, and then start a fire, but make it look like an electrical fire or something. The dead body will burn in the fire and no one will even know the body was shot first!"

Sean looked at Drew as his mind began reeling. "That may not be a bad idea, Drew. It will be the middle of the night so any neighbors will be sleeping. By the time a neighbor wakes up and calls 9-1-1, the house should be fully engulfed. You'd have to start the fire in whatever room the doctor is in so her body burns fast."

Drew was really proud of himself now. "Do any of us know about electrical fires?" Drew asked.

"I do," Jack answered. "I used to work with my dad when he owned an apartment complex. You wouldn't believe all the codes and regulations he had to stay on top of. I can figure something out when we get in there, no problem at all!"

"I think that's a better answer than robbing and running," Trent said, finally satisfied.

"Great!" Sean said. "You all are awesome. You'll be even more awesome and richer if you pull this off tonight. Be careful and be sober! We party after the job is done!"

Chapter 3

"Is she okay?" Laura asked Paul, who had just gotten off the phone with Dr. Simms.

"No. Mimi had a vision and they are pretty sure that the guy is coming after her tonight. I knew this wasn't over. We need to be ready for this guy."

"Are you seriously going to go over there and wait for him?"

"As long as the captain approves it, we are…and I think he'll approve it."

"Please, can't someone else do this job? Why do you have to be in there?"

Paul looked at Laura and saw the worry on her face. "I'll see what I can do but I'm not making any promises. To be honest with you, I want to be there to help nab this bastard."

"I can understand that, but I'll be worried about you all night if you're over there. Please don't go there. Please?" She had started crying.

"Okay. Let me call Captain Zitzer real quick."

Before he could even think about pulling the captain's number up in his phone, his cell phone rang. It was the captain himself.

"Are you psychic? I was just about to call you!" Paul exclaimed.

"Maybe I am. I was just checking in with you. What's up?"

Paul told him what he had just learned. "Do you think my idea is good?"

"It's a great idea, except for one part of it."

"Which part?"

"I don't want you anywhere near the place."

"What!? No, I have to be there!"

"I understand that, Paul, but you're way too close to this case and this situation. I can't have you there and have you make a fatal mistake. Besides, if we nab him, you'll have all the time in the world with him while he's locked up."

"Well," Paul sighed, "you just made my wife very happy."

"Good! Speaking of your wife, did you tell her about Maddy Eck and your sons?"

"I did. She knows everything now."

"Excellent!"

"How about I be the one to drive you and the rest of the guys to Dr. Simms's place?"

"I can allow that much. Meet us at the office in one hour."

As he hung up, Krystal walked in the door. "Hey, guys!" she said as she walked into the kitchen. "Guess what it's almost time for!"

Paul and Laura exchanged looks.

Krystal saw that something was wrong, and her shoulders drooped. "What's going on?"

Laura tried to change the subject. "Hey! It's just about time to get that cast off, right?"

"Yeah. I was wondering if you guys wanted to come with me? We could go out for dinner afterward to celebrate!" Krystal said, even though she knew something was up.

"Well," Paul said, "I can't because something has come up and I have to get to the office, but I'm sure Mom can go. She can also fill you in with what's going on."

"Yes," Laura said. "I'm more than happy to go with you. I wanted to go with you anyways! We can still celebrate with dinner though. Dad should be home by then, right, honey?"

"I'm not sure," Paul answered. "I'll see how things go." With that, he kissed them both goodbye and was out the door.

209

"What's going on?" Krystal asked her mother.

"I'll tell you on the way to the doctor's office. Let's go, I'll drive."

As they pulled down the driveway, Laura asked Krystal, "So you had a session with Dr. Simms, right? How did it go?"

Krystal didn't want to talk about it with her mother but she swallowed her pride. "Not good."

"Why's that?"

"Dr. Simms, you know I love her, but..."

"But what?"

"I just...For the first time ever, I'm not so sure I agree with her."

"On what?"

"Well...Mom, I need to tell you something."

"This doesn't sound good."

"Promise me you won't get mad?"

"I can't promise you that, but I'll try not to get mad."

Krystal took a deep breath. "Well, I know you and Dad told me not to see Trent anymore but the truth is, I've been seeing him."

Laura slammed on the brakes before thinking about what she was doing. Luckily, there was no one behind her. She pulled into a nearby gas station. "You what? Why in the hell are you still seeing him?"

Krystal began crying. "I'm sorry. I still love him and I couldn't just stop seeing him."

"Your father is going to kill you – well, unless I do first."

"Please, Mom, can you just stop. I'm sorry for lying to you guys. I just thought it would be okay, and it has been."

Laura sighed. "What did Dr. Simms do that upset you?"

"Well, Mimi was sitting in on our session, which I was fine with, but they both were telling me that Trent was bad news and I needed to stay away from him."

"Why were they saying that? Did something happen?"

"Mimi said she was having nightmares about Trent and he wasn't a good person and that I need to stay away from him."

"You think he is a good person, then?"

Krystal was silent.

"Has Trent ever done anything to you to hurt you?"

Krystal remained silent.

"Krystal, I know you've been with Trent for a while and he's a huge part of your life. I know you love him, but if something is going on with him and you, you have to let me know."

Krystal sighed as more tears started coming. "I can't tell you," she sobbed.

"I need you to tell me everything. It's very important."

Krystal saw fear in her mother's eyes and knew that she was being serious. "Mom…" She didn't know where to start.

"Is he the one who bruised your eye up a few weeks ago?"

Krystal started crying harder. "It was the first time he's ever put a hand on me and he hasn't done it since!"

Laura closed her eyes as anger flowed through her. The thought of anyone hurting her child was enraging. "Why? Why did he hit you?"

"Mom! Please! I don't want to talk about that part. He slapped me a couple of times and then punched me. I kicked him in the crotch and then got out of there. I saw him the next morning and we talked. He explained things to me and said he'd never do it again…and he hasn't."

Laura knew that Trent would hurt her again. She felt it. "Honey, someone like that, they don't just hit once and are finished. He's going to do it again. You need to listen to Dr. Simms."

"I know, Mom, but I love him."

"I know you do, I believe you do, but you have to listen to your instincts here and the voices of reason. Listen, there's something I need to tell you about Trent. Something that I thought was no big deal but now I'm not so sure."

"What?" She was looking at her mom through blurry teared eyes.

"Do you remember that night at the house when your father asked Trent to leave?"

"Yes. I was really confused about that."

"Well, when Trent went upstairs to talk to your father, he made a pit stop in your room. Your father came out and walked by to see Trent sniffing a pair of your dirty underwear."

"What?!" Krystal shouted. "You guys didn't tell me?"

"I'm sorry. Your father wanted to but I told him not to. I mean, he was sniffing his girlfriend's underwear, that's not all that weird. If he had been sniffing mine or someone else's, then sure, it would be weird."

Krystal calmed down. "You still should have told me."

"I'm sorry," Laura said. "You should have told us that he hit you, as well."

"I know. I'm just scared, is all."

"Why are you still with him?"

"I told you, I still love him. He was kind of out of it that day because he had been mugged and beat up. He said the doctors didn't put him on pain meds but I think they did. He was just not acting like himself. He's still not totally himself but I was feeling better about things, for the most part, until I talked to Dr. Simms this morning."

"Well, there's something else you need to know."

Krystal sighed. "Please, Mom. I don't think I can handle much more right now."

"I'm sorry, but there are a couple more things I need to tell you."

"Fine." Krystal sat back in her seat and closed her eyes.

"Well, the night that Trent hit you, I don't think he was mugged that morning."

"Why?" Krystal still had her eyes closed.

"Your father has been investigating everything and Trent came up in the middle of it. He was involved with some bad people. The GPS in the stolen car led your father to a warehouse in Jessup. He saw Trent coming out of that warehouse that day, blacked and bruised. Someone that he's involved with did that to him, we think. We also think he's involved with all this craziness that's going on."

"No," Krystal sobbed. "That can't be true. He loves me. I know he does."

Laura turned toward her daughter. She pushed her hair behind her ear as if she were a child. "He may love you but he's bad news, honey. His love is probably not the same as yours, and I think you know that."

"I'm just scared to end things with him. What if he comes after me?"

"Your father and I will not let that happen. We'll keep you safe, and you know that too."

"What else is going on?"

"Dr. Simms called your father a little while ago. It must have been right after you left. Mimi had a pretty strong vision that the asshole that hit Dr. Simms is coming back for her tonight. Your father and his guys are getting her and Mimi out of her house and are going to be there waiting for them."

213

"You know what? Trent was supposed to go with me to get my cast off. He called me at the last minute and said something came up at work and he couldn't go. That's too much of a coincidence. It's all starting again, isn't it? It was so quiet for a while. What in the hell happened?"

"I don't know," Laura said while trying to push back her own tears. "Um, we better get to your doctor's appointment before you're late and have to wear that thing for another week."

Chapter 4

Drew locked himself in the bathroom at the warehouse office with one of the whores. He dropped his pants and said, "It's not going to suck itself." As the whore went to work, he closed his eyes and tilted his head back. This was how he got ready for a big job like this one. Trent was pacing back and forth as Candy tried to get him to clear his mind. "Trent, baby! Stressing before a job is not going to do you any good. Why don't you sit down and let me give you a shoulder massage?" she had offered.

"No," he simply replied. He wasn't stressing out like she thought he was. He was psyching himself up. He had to get his adrenaline moving. He had to talk himself into believing that what he was doing was a good idea and it had to be done and it was going to work out perfectly. He also knew that Krystal was going to be devastated, and that if she found out he had played a part in it, she would never forgive him. He also never mentioned to anyone that a cop was following him around. He was hoping he wouldn't have one trailing him tonight, since they would be leaving out the back and he wouldn't be in his car. He'd only ever seen the cop in the main parking lot, so he was hoping that would be the case tonight as well. He was putting positive vibes out into the universe because what you put out is what comes back to you. Candy sensed that she should just leave him alone.

Ten minutes later, Sean called for them all to round up in the makeshift living room. The only one missing was Drew. They could hear moans and bangs coming from the bathroom. Sean looked at his watch. It was one thirty in the morning. "Will one of you please go get that numbskull?" he asked Trent and Jack.

"I'm on it," Jack said, jumping up. He went over to the bathroom door and began banging on it. "Hey, Drew! It's time to get going. C'mon, man!"

"Just a second!" Drew shouted through grunts.

"We don't have a second!" Jack shouted back. He banged on the door again.

"Aaaaarrrrggggh!" Drew moaned from the bathroom.

A second later, a flushed-faced Drew opened the bathroom door. "Let's do this, then," he said, zipping up his pants.

They went back to the living room and sat down.

"It's so nice of you to join us, Drew," Sean said, half amused and half pissed off.

"I just had to get myself ready." Drew smirked.

Sean rolled his eyes. "Anyway," he started, "Larry and Fritz are already over there and they said that everything looks good. It's quiet and all the lights are out in the house and they said there are no cops outside. It's time for you all to head out. Be careful, be quick, and get the job done!"

"Yes, sir," Drew and Jack said in unison.

"Yup," Trent said on his own.

"Trent," Sean said, "I need you to make sure that you are wearing a full-faced mask. If something goes wrong, we don't want the doctor to be able to identify you."

"I already thought of that," Trent said as he pulled his mask out of his back pocket. "Mama didn't raise no fool." He and Sean exchanged looks, as they both knew that Trent never really had a "Mama."

Sean watched his men head out, then went to his office and turned on the police scanner. It really was a pretty quiet night, it seemed.

Drew, Trent, and Jack arrived at Dr. Simms's house twenty minutes later. Trent looked behind them often as they were driving and was relieved to see that there weren't any cops following them. As they pulled into the driveway they waved to Larry and Fritz, who gave them the "all okay" sign, and very quietly exited the vehicle. They pulled their masks down over their faces, locked and loaded their guns, and made their way to the front door. Drew tried the doorknob. Of course, it was locked.

Inside, Captain Zitzer and his men had been there for hours waiting. They had all doors and windows covered. They heard the rattling of the doorknob and knew it was time. Captain Zitzer gave the "Ssssh" signal to his boys and motioned for them all to stay low. The signal passed down from one to the other.

Drew let his lock-picking skills go to work and he had the door open in less than a minute. He stood back and let Jack enter first, then Trent, then himself. He always brought up the rear for more than one reason. He wanted his boys to think that he had their back but he really just didn't want to be the first in – just in case they were walking into danger. Speaking of danger, something didn't feel right. He suddenly had a really bad feeling. He pushed Trent out of the way and grabbed Jack just as he was about to take his second step into the house. He pulled the door closed.

"What the fuck are you doing?" Jack shouted in a whisper.

"I have a bad feeling, man," Drew answered.

"Are you fucking kidding me?" Trent asked him. "Larry and Fritz have been here for a while. They say everything is okay."

"No!" Drew debated. "Something isn't right. Look, all the lights were off, even the outside light. I got that door unlocked way too easily. And why is there no cop on watch?"

"Okay," Jack said. "Well, then you can call the boss and tell him we aren't doing the job."

"No," Drew said. He didn't want to let the boss down, and how lame would it have sounded if he told the boss they didn't do it because he had a "bad feeling?" "We are doing this. Just be careful, okay?"

"Duh," Jack responded as he faced the door and opened it once again.

As Jack entered, Drew pulled Trent back. "Wait a second," he whispered to Trent.

Captain Zitzer and his boys were on high alert after the door unexpectedly closed. They remained still and quiet and waited. They were smart to do that. As Jack entered the door, they were not stirring nor speaking. It was pitch black.

Captain Zitzer, who was standing by the light switch, flipped on the light and shouted, "Police! Freeze!"

As his eyes adjusted to the new light, he was face-to-face with a masked man and had his gun aimed right at his nose. The masked man also had a gun on him.

Without even thinking about it, Captain Zitzer pulled his trigger.

Startled to see a cop, Jack pulled his trigger at the same exact time.

They both went down.

Trent and Drew had taken off running when they heard the word "Police!" They were already in their car when the shots were fired. By the time the other troopers were able to come to terms with what had just happened, Trent and Drew were squealing tires. Larry and Fritz were right behind them. They were both out of sight within seconds.

Sean was listening to the police scanner, wondering what in the hell just happened.

Jack was dead.

Captain Zitzer was alive thanks to his bulletproof vest. He only had the wind knocked out of him. His men helped him to his feet. "Shit!" he shouted. "We should have let them all get inside first. Goddamn it!"

"Fuck, fuck, fuck," Drew was saying over and over again as he was doing well near a hundred miles an hour. They were already out of the neighborhood.

"Fuck!" Trent shot back. He looked behind him through the rear window. "I think we got out okay. I don't see anyone behind us."

"The boss is going to be so pissed," Drew said as he started to slow the car down. "Was Douche Bag dead?"

"I'm not sure. It's hard to say," Trent answered.

"Oh fuck!" Drew said as he saw police lights approaching from behind. By that time, he was doing the speed limit.

"Pull over," Trent said.

"What? Are you crazy?"

"No. Pull over. I don't think he's after us. How could he know we were at that house? No one was around when we pulled out. There's no way the officers got a good look at our car. Trust me. Move over. I bet he goes around."

Drew hesitantly pulled over.

Trent kept his hand on the pistol that was strapped to his side but out of sight.

Drew looked in the rearview mirror, certain the police car was going to pull up behind him.

Trent and Drew exchanged looks as Drew grabbed his gun and placed it on his lap, ready to use it the second the police car stopped behind them.

Drew took a deep breath and held it.

The police car zoomed past them.

Drew and Trent sighed. "Thank god," Drew said. "Good call, buddy," he said to Trent.

"Good call for knowing something was up," Trent said to him. "Otherwise, we'd either be dead or in handcuffs."

They slowly pulled back out onto the roadway and headed back to the warehouse.

"Captain, are you okay?" Sergeant Hill asked Zitzer as he led him to a chair.

"I'm okay," the captain answered. "That shot knocked me over and it hurts but I'm alive. Any word on the other ones who took off?"

"They haven't been found yet," Sergeant Hill answered.

"Shit," Captain Zitzer said, lowering his head. "Mission failed," he mumbled as he looked over at the body lying on the floor.

Chapter 5

Drew and Trent had just walked into the warehouse. Sean had called them a couple of times but they didn't answer. They didn't want to try to explain anything over the phone.

"What the fuck happened?" Sean shouted at them as they came through the door. "Where's Jack?"

Drew and Trent exchanged looks – neither of them wanting to answer the boss.

Trent sat down, refusing to speak. Drew sighed and began, "He's still at the house. He was shot. I think he may be dead."

"How in the hell did that even happen?" Sean was furious.

"Sir, the cops were there waiting for us. The second we walked in, we were ambushed by them."

"How did you two get away, then?"

"I had a bad feeling," Drew answered. "I actually stopped us from going in at first but I ignored it and allowed us to continue."

"How many times have I told you to never deny your instincts?" Sean asked him, calming down now.

"I know, but I didn't think coming back here and telling you that we didn't do the job because I had a feeling would've had positive results," Drew said as he hung his head.

"I would've gotten over it," Sean replied.

"Anyways, after Jack walked in, I pulled Trent back and told him to wait a second. The second we heard someone yell 'police' we high-tailed it out of there. We heard gunshots, got in the car, and took off. I'm sorry we didn't stick around to check on Jack but there were cops in there. I could hear them yelling. If we stayed, they would've gotten us."

"Where were Larry and Fritz? Where are they now?"

"That's a good question," Drew answered. "We saw them when we got there and they gave us the okay sign to go in. I'm pretty sure they took off when we did. They should be here by now."

"The pussies are probably too scared to come here," Trent finally said.

"How in the hell did the cops know we were coming?" Sean asked.

Silence.

Sean looked at Trent.

"It wasn't me!" Trent said defensively.

"Well, you're the only one with connections to her that knew what we were doing tonight. You called in that tip to the cops before! What am I to think?" Sean asked.

"It wasn't me, Sean!" Trent said again.

"Sean?" Drew asked. "Why did you call him Sean?"

"Because he's an idiot!" Sean answered.

"I mean Doyle," Trent said. "You remind me of an old boss I used to have who was named Sean." This was why Trent didn't have a fake name for himself. He was no good with keeping fake names straight.

"Well, how do you suppose they knew we were coming then, if you didn't tell them?" Sean asked.

"I don't know, but why would I tell them and then put myself in the position to be there? Why would I put any of us in that position?" Trent asked with not much worry in his voice.

"Oh, I don't know, maybe you are on Krystal's side now? Maybe I do need to be worried about you," Sean answered.

"I don't know, boss," Drew chimed in. "I don't think he tipped them off. He was as surprised as I was."

"Well, then what in the hell happened?" Sean asked.

"I'll talk to Krystal about it tomorrow. Maybe her father will tell her," Trent responded.

Chapter 6

Around the time that Jack was getting shot, Krystal was tossing and turning in her sleep. Before she knew it, she woke up screaming. Paul and Laura came running into her room to make sure she was okay. Paul flipped on the light. He had his service pistol in his hand. "Krystal?" Paul asked as his eyes focused on his trembling daughter.

Laura pushed past him. "Krystal, what's wrong?"

Krystal was shaking and crying. "I had a dream that the weird guy was back."

Laura put an arm around Krystal as she sat down next to her. "No one is here. Just us."

"Don't forget that we got the new alarm system put in and there are still some of my guys sitting outside on watch."

"Is Trent wrapped up in all of this?" Krystal asked through her sobs.

"We're not sure just yet," Paul answered.

"Dad, I have to tell you something. I told Mom earlier but I don't think she's told you."

"I haven't told him yet, honey," Laura said. She looked nervously at Paul, hoping he wouldn't get mad at her for not saying anything.

"Tell me what?" Paul asked, looking from his daughter to his wife and back to his daughter again.

"That black eye that I had a few weeks ago…"

"Trent did it, didn't he?"

"It was the only time and the last time he ever hit me. I swear! He was a different person that night, one I had never seen before. It scared me but we got past it."

"What do ya mean you got past it?"

224

Krystal looked at her mom to try to find some strength and then said, "I've still been seeing Trent behind your and Mom's backs."

"What? Didn't we tell you that you were not to see him anymore?" Paul asked, trying to not sound as outraged as he was.

"Yes, I just couldn't stay away from him. I don't know. He said he'd never do it again and I'm…well…I'm kind of afraid of him now. I'm afraid if I leave him, he'll hit me again or maybe something worse. It's like I've been trying to trust him again and I have to a point, I guess, but it's still not there one hundred percent. Now, I just don't know. Dr. Simms told me I needed to stay away from him because he's bad news. Her friend Mimi told me the same thing."

"Then I think you should," Paul said to her. "For real this time! You know me and my guys will protect you."

Krystal nodded. "Yes. I know that. I'm still scared though."

"I'd think something was wrong with you if you weren't," Paul said as he hugged her. "You need to promise me that you will not see him anymore."

"I can't promise that, Dad."

"Do it anyways!" Paul said angrily. "He is bad news and he's not the guy you think he is. We're going to be bringing him in for questioning very soon. I can't have you being wrapped up with him anymore. I'm not asking you to stay away from him. I'm telling you to!"

"I want to but I can't. There's a huge part of me that still loves him. More than that, I want to stay with him so I can keep tabs on him. I didn't realize that until after talking to Dr. Simms and Mimi, but if I keep seeing him, I can know if he's up to no good. Like today. He was supposed to go with me to get my cast off. He told me at the last minute that he was needed at work and wouldn't

225

be able to go with me. I haven't heard from him since then. Do you think he was involved with the break-in?"

"I think it's a good bet," Paul answered. "I don't want you staying with him just so you can find out, though. I really think you should stay away from him."

"I agree with your father," Laura said.

"It puts you at risk more than you already are," Paul said. "Maybe you can just stay in touch with him by phone and tell him for right now, you are staying home with us where it's safe."

"Well, it's my decision, and right now I'm not going to make it. I need to think about this some more and I really want to see what happened tonight. He could be in jail right now for all we know."

"There's only one way to find out," Paul said. "I'm going to go call the duty officer and see if he's heard anything."

Five minutes later, Paul's face looked flushed. "Well," he sighed, "there was a break-in. The first guy came in and they flipped on the light and the guy had a gun. Him and the captain shot at each other at the same time. The other guys took off almost immediately."

"What?" Laura asked. "Is Captain Zitzer okay?"

"He is," Paul answered. "He was wearing his vest so he only got knocked out of it for a second. The guy he shot didn't survive. The good news is that it wasn't Trent. The bad news is that the other two guys got away, so we have no idea who they were."

"Shit!" Krystal said. She was getting more upset by the second. "I mean fuck!" she shouted. She stood up and started pacing in her bedroom. "How did they get away? Didn't you have guys outside too?"

"No," Paul answered. "We couldn't risk them being seen. We figured they would all come inside and then we'd nab them. We didn't know how many there would be, either. The other ones must have sensed something for them to have taken off so quickly. I don't think they even entered the house."

"They just left their friend there to die?" Laura asked disgustedly.

"I guess so," Paul answered. "They're working on IDing the guy, but as of right now we don't know who he is. He doesn't look familiar to any of us."

"That settles it, then," Krystal said. "I'm staying with Trent for the time being. I need to be able to know what's going on with him. Like today, how he just blew me off for work! I knew something was up! I'd be willing to hurt my wrist again if I was wrong about him being a part of the break-in tonight."

"You don't need to stay with him, though," Paul told her. "We already have eyes on him."

"What?" Krystal asked. "Since when?"

"A few weeks now. He's been spending a hell of a lot of time at some warehouse down in Jessup. Any idea what he'd be doing there?"

"Mom told me about that," Krystal replied. "I don't think he's ever mentioned going to Jessup before."

"We tried to get a search warrant but the judge denied us. There are a lot of different businesses in there. We don't know which one he's going to. It's also the same warehouse that the GPS from the stolen vehicle took us to. He's connected to all of them somehow. That's why we're bringing him in for questioning."

Krystal sat back down on her bed and sighed. "Well, if you guys are following him, didn't you follow him tonight?"

"No," Paul answered. "When we left him this afternoon, he was at his apartment. We needed the guy watching him for the job tonight. Maybe we should have kept some eyes on him."

"You think?" Krystal asked sarcastically.

"There's no need to get nasty," Laura told Krystal. "I'm sure your father and his guys are doing the best they can."

"We are," Paul chimed in. "We almost had them tonight. We'll get them because we're sure they're gonna try to finish the job. This is the second time they've come after her. They want her dead for some reason and I don't think they're going to stop until they do it."

"That doesn't make me feel any better," Krystal said.

"Me neither," Laura said, looking at her husband for answers.

"I think we should all try to get at least a few hours of sleep," Paul said. "We know we're at least safe for now so let's take advantage of that and get some shut-eye."

Chapter 7

The next afternoon, Krystal woke up around one o'clock. She walked downstairs to find her mom sitting at the kitchen table, looking like she hadn't slept a wink. "Hey, Mom. Did you get any sleep?"

"None at all. Your dad went to work and I feel like a prisoner with two patrol cars sitting outside. I walked out to get the paper and one of them jumped out of the car to make sure I was okay."

"This sucks the big one, that's for sure. But you know what, Mom? I'm ready to fight."

"Don't get too cocky."

"I'm not, but I refuse to sit around and be scared. I'm going to keep living my life and I'm not going to let anyone have me walking on eggshells."

"You still need to be careful."

"I will, Mom. I noticed that I had a missed call from Trent. He called me about an hour ago."

"Did you call him back?"

"Not yet. I've been contemplating on if I should or not."

"I agree with your father, you need to be done with him – but between you and me, I kind of understand what you were saying last night."

Krystal smiled at her mom. "Good. At least I'm not crazy for thinking that way."

"Oh no, you're definitely crazy for thinking that way, but I guess that makes me crazy too because I'd probably do the same thing."

"Okay, then," Krystal said. "I'm going to go call him right now."

She got up and ran back up to her bedroom. She picked up her phone just as it started ringing. It was Trent again. She picked it up immediately. "Hey, babe!" She thought it sounded real enough.

"Hey." He sounded down.

"I was just getting ready to call you. I got worried when I didn't hear any more from you yesterday."

"Well, it was a long day at work. I didn't get home until early this morning."

"Wow! That must have been a long day for you. I just got out of bed myself."

"Sleep in, did we?"

"Yeah, well, I didn't sleep well last night. I woke up screaming at one point because I thought that guy was back in my room. Things are pretty hectic here. Someone tried to break into Dr. Simms's house last night so my dad has been going a little nuts with that."

"Really?"

Krystal thought that sounded like a fake "really." *Am I being paranoid?* Krystal wondered. *The way he said that almost sounds like he already knew about it. Either I'm being paranoid or I'm starting to really pay attention to him and notice things that I just didn't notice before.*

"Yeah. One dead body, evidently."

"Who was he?"

"I didn't say it was a he," Krystal said.

"No, I just mean, who was the dead body?"

"They don't know yet. Some guy. There were other guys, evidently, but they got away."

"How did the cops get the one guy but not the others?"

"My dad and his guys knew they were coming for Dr. Simms. They were inside waiting for them. Dr. Simms wasn't even there."

"How did your dad know they were coming?"

"Well," Krystal began, but then stopped herself. She wasn't sure if she should tell Trent about Mimi knowing it was going to happen. He knew that Mimi was the one who tried to help when her mom was attacked at the hospital, but he must not have put two and two together. "I, um…I'm not really sure. My dad wasn't too clear on that part."

"Huh," Trent said, sounding interested and stumped. "Well, is Dr. Simms okay?"

"Yeah, as far as I know. Like I said, they weren't there last night so they were safe."

"They who?"

"Oh!" Krystal said, trying to scramble for an answer. "Her, um, her and her brother. He's visiting with her from Virginia."

Trent knew she was lying, and he was pretty sure he had just figured out how the cops knew to be at Dr. Simms's house. "Listen, I have to go. Maybe we can get together later for dinner?" he asked her.

"S-s-sure. Is everything okay? You have today off, don't you?"

"I do, but I have to go help my cousin with something for a few hours."

"Okay. I might be busy tonight. Brittany and I were talking about getting together. She may just come over and watch a movie or something."

"I'd really like to see you tonight."

"Maybe. Can I let you know later?"

231

Trent sounded a little annoyed as he asked, "I'll call you in a little while?"

"Okay."

He hung up without saying goodbye.

Chapter 8

Trent came barreling through the warehouse doors and startled Sean and Drew, who were sitting in the makeshift living room. "I figured it out!" Trent shouted. "I know how the police knew we were gonna be there last night."

"Well, please," Sean said, "enlighten us."

Trent paced back and forth like a madman. His words were fast and hysterical. "I was talking to Krystal, you know? Just a bit ago and we were talking about last night. She told me the cops knew we were gonna be there. I asked her how they knew and she started to answer me and then stopped. She then told me, you know, that she didn't know." He was still pacing and was flailing his arms around as he spoke. "I then asked her if the doctor was okay. She told me that as far as she knew, *they* were okay. I asked her who *they* were and she stumbled on her words. I know the bitch was lying to me. She said it was the doctor and her brother who was visiting from Virginia but she was lying. She's never lied to me before, but I know she was lying just then because she was stumbling all over her words and that's when it hit me." He made an explosion motion with both his hands above his head.

"What?" Drew asked him excitedly.

"I bet that fucking psycho bitch friend of hers is with her."

"What psycho?" Drew asked.

"Umm, do you mean psychic?" Sean asked.

"Yeah, what the fuck ever," Trent answered. "That little cunt who tried to save Laura in the hospital that one day. Her! Mimi! I bet she's here. She can sense things. She must have known we were coming."

Drew and Sean contemplated what Trent had just told them.

"Oh give me a break!" Drew said with a smirk. "There's no way someone can see things like that. I think you're making it up to save your own ass!"

"Actually, it does makes sense," Sean said. "I think he may be on to something."

Drew looked at Doyle as if he must be crazy.

"Aaaarrgh!" Trent screamed right before he threw his fist through the wall.

"You're gonna pay for that," Sean said. He wasn't surprised or mad. He wanted that anger from Trent. It worked out in his favor.

Trent gave him no answer.

"So, we need to get this Mimi chick then? Is that what you're saying? If so, let's go do it now. I mean, they can't move faster than us if we weren't even planning on going. I bet they're back in their home now. Let's go off them," Drew added.

"In broad daylight?" Sean asked him.

"Well, how else are we supposed to do this? You want us to off the doctor first, right? How can we do that if there is some weirdo telling her when we're coming? Not to mention if we don't, she may know when we are going after the others."

"I got a plan," the boss said. He pulled out his cell phone and called someone. "Can you stop by?" he said into his phone. After a second pause, he said, "Great. See you in a bit."

"Who was that?" Trent asked, a bit more calm now.

"A good friend, who actually is in the same line of work as Mimi. He's actually been helping a bit with this case. That's why I believe what Trent is saying. It's also why I've been wanting to take care of the doctor first. My friend warned me that this could happen." Sean smirked.

Chapter 9

Dr. Simms and Mimi had just gotten back to Dr. Simms's house. "Well," Mimi sighed, "I hope they did a good job of cleaning up."

They walked through the front door, Mimi behind Dr. Simms. Dr. Simms walked all the way through the door but Mimi stopped at the door jamb. She froze.

"What's wrong?" Dr. Simms asked her.

"I, um...I just have a weird feeling is all. I think this is where the guy was shot."

"Well, I don't see any mess on the carpet. They did a great job of making it look like nothing happened."

"Maybe on the outside it looks good, but on the inside, my inside, I can feel it." She dropped to her knees and started rocking back and forth. "Oh, god!" She sobbed. "The guy didn't even want to be here. He had no choice. He has a sick mother and needed the money to help her pay doctor bills. This is going to kill his mother."

"Come on," Dr. Simms said, grabbing Mimi's left arm. "My guess is that his mom knew what he was like. She's probably better off in the long run. Come sit down and get yourself together."

They sat down on the sofa in the living room.

"I wanted to thank you for being here, Mimi. If it weren't for you, I'd probably be dead right now."

"You don't need to thank me. That's what friends are for. You'd do the same for me."

"You know it! I just worry now that they'll be back."

"That's why we have to stay together. We'll be ready for them if they do try to come back. I..." Mimi yawned. "Wow,

235

excuse me. I guess I'm more tired than I thought." Her words started dragging toward the end. Within a second she was fast asleep.

"Mimi?"

No answer.

"Wow," Dr. Simms whispered. She moved over to the recliner chair, kicked it back so she could elevate her leg, and turned on the television, hoping to find a good movie.

Mimi twitched in her sleep. She wasn't really asleep, although that's how it appeared. She was actually in a forced meditation and there was no waking her up out of it. Her mind wandered as she saw herself on a sunny beach, sipping a cool frozen margarita, with a handsome man sitting next to her. She had never seen this man before, but he was extremely good-looking and had the same abilities as she did. In another life, he would have been her soul mate. In this life, though, he was her enemy. She felt it but she couldn't do anything to stop it. He was much stronger than she was. She sipped on her drink as she gazed at him in a lovesick kind of way. "Where did you come from?" she asked the mystery man.

He smiled at her and caressed her face. He kissed her softly on her lips and pulled back. "I came from your dreams, Mimi. I'm here to make you feel good."

Mimi heard him say "to make you feel good" but she also heard his voice say "to distract you." It was as if he had the ability to say two sentences at once. She tried to focus on the one that sounded more like a warning, but the other voice was much stronger. It was much more intriguing. She smiled at the mystery man as she took another sip of her drink and let his soothing voice enter her thoughts.

"It's lovely here, isn't it?" he asked her. "No humidity, no rain, no clouds, no wind, just quiet and warm stillness. It almost feels like heaven. Can you feel it? Can you feel it taking over? Like a warm liquid running through your veins? Can you feel it?"

Mimi was feeling something. It did feel like something running through her veins. Something was wrong…

Chapter 10

"She's out now," Trent said into his cell phone. He was standing over Mimi and had just taken a needle out of her arm.

"Good," Sean said into his ear. "Remember, she needs to come back with you guys, alive!"

"Understood," Trent said before hanging up.

Dr. Simms watched in horror while another man held her back. Everything had happened so fast that she had no time to react. Mimi dozed off, she sat down to watch some TV and dozed off herself. She woke up to someone breaking down her back door. She couldn't jump up because of her leg. Before she knew what was going on, two guys were in her house, in ski masks. One went to her and the other injected Mimi with something. She was wondering what happened to the cop outside. "Let's get this over with quickly," Trent said to Drew.

"Nope. The boss is pissed now. He wants us to put this doctor bitch in her place!" Drew said. "He said that we have a thirty-minute window before the new cop arrives outside for her protection. I can't believe they leave the house unattended when they change shifts. What idiots!"

"Who are you and why are you doing this to me?" Dr. Simms asked.

"Oh, you know me," Trent said as he pulled off his ski mask.

"Trent? What are you doing?" Dr. Simms asked even though she wasn't really surprised.

"You know me too," Drew said without taking off his ski mask.

"Your voice sounds very familiar. You are one of my patients, aren't you?"

"I was. You didn't do shit for me!"

238

"Is that why you're doing this?"

Drew laughed. "No! We're doing this because you're getting in the boss's way."

"Boss? Who's the boss?" Dr. Simms asked. She wanted to keep them talking.

"You ask too many questions!" Trent shouted at her as he got in her face. "You know? I never did like you. You've always tried to change Krystal even though she's perfect just the way she is." Trent kicked her hard in her broken leg.

Dr. Simms screamed in pain.

"Hey!" Drew shouted at Trent. "Let me do the honors! We owe her...for Jack!"

"We both can do it!" Trent said. "This witch doctor of hers is knocked out and will be for a while. We don't need to watch her."

"Where should we start?" Drew asked, licking his lips and looking at Dr. Simms.

Trent whipped out his pocketknife and smirked as he moved closer to Dr. Simms.

"Please stop!" Dr. Simms pleaded. "What are you doing?"

Drew ignored her question as he got in her face and said, "Shhhh."

"No!" Dr. Simms cried. "We can talk about this. I'll do whatever you want!"

"Shut up!" Trent shouted as he slashed the blade of his knife across her face.

Her cheek immediately began bleeding. Drew laughed.

Dr. Simms screamed out in pain.

"I told you to be quiet," Drew said to her. He opened his pocketknife while keeping his eye on her, enjoying the fear in her eyes. He put the knife up to her throat.

"Please stop!" she cried.

239

Drew just laughed as he started using the knife to cut off all of her clothes. He then took off his mask. "Do you like my new look, Doc?"

Through her tears, Dr. Simms looked at Drew. That voice. She knew it. "Thomas?"

Drew laughed. "Yeah, it's me. I'm back to finish the job! But I think I need to take a little keepsake." He laughed as his gaze fell down to her breasts. "You know, I had no idea you were packing such a nice set!"

He told Trent to hold her down. Trent did as he was told and Drew began sawing away at one of her nipples.

Dr. Simms squirmed and screamed.

Drew finished sawing off her nipple and held it between his finger and thumb. He held it up to examine it. There was some blood dripping from it. He licked the nipple and made a moaning noise. He moved his tongue over the nipple as if he were pleasuring it orally. He chuckled as he put the nipple in his shirt pocket.

Trent rolled his eyes, trying not to look too closely at what Drew was doing. He knew he himself wasn't right in the head, but he thought Drew was beyond psycho. He couldn't understand why Drew was like that.

"Let me do just one more thing," Drew said.

Trent did not understand how Drew got off on all this torture. He understood wanting to kill somebody, but he thought doing it fast was best. "Okay, but I get to off her!" Trent demanded.

"Sure, fine, whatever."

There was blood gushing out from the newly formed hole on Dr. Simms's breast. Drew smeared the blood around her chest. He then dropped his pants and began jerking off. He was already hard. It only took him a minute to cum. He made sure to aim his cum on her chest. He then smeared the cum around with the blood. "It's a work of art!" he shouted as he stood back to admire his work. He took out his cell phone and took a picture.

He laughed as Trent just continued to roll his eyes. "Are you done yet?" Trent asked him, clearly annoyed with his lunatic partner.

"Just one more thing," Drew replied.

Before Trent even saw it coming, Drew quickly pulled his gun out of the back of his waistband and blew a hole through Dr. Simms's head. She was dead instantly. He had a silencer on his gun so Trent wasn't sure he actually shot her until he saw all the blood.

"Asshole!" Trent said to Drew.

"You'll get over it. Now help me get the other one out to the car and into the trunk."

When they got back to the warehouse, getting Mimi in proved to be a bit more difficult. There were too many people coming and going.

"Drive the car around back," Sean said into Drew's cell phone earpiece. "We'll meet you back there."

Drew drove the car to the back of the warehouse. There was almost no one out there. Only a tractor-trailer truck that was getting ready to drive off. When the truck was out of sight, Sean and his buddy Byron opened a door from the inside of the warehouse. "Get her in here quick. Hurry up while there's no one in the hall. We only have to get her in the elevator now," Sean ordered.

Byron, Drew, and Trent quickly pulled Mimi out of the trunk of the car and into the warehouse. They were in the elevator within a few seconds. No one saw them. The elevator opened up into their office warehouse and they were home free. It was a good thing, too, because Mimi was now starting to wake up. They put tape over her mouth so she couldn't speak or scream. They sat her on the couch and surrounded her, standing over her, looking down at her. She looked from one guy to the other, scared and confused. Her eyes stopped on Byron. It was the handsome guy from her meditation trip. He was a real person after all, but he didn't look nice like he did in the daze and haze. "Hello, sweetheart," Byron said to her. "We meet again."

She looked at him with eyes that asked who he was.

Byron smiled at her. "You're not the only one with special abilities, but it seems as though I'm more powerful than you. You gave me a run for my money though, didn't you? I felt you trying to fight me but you just weren't strong enough. Your strength is impressive though. Imagine the damage we could cause if we were working together." He laughed as he looked over at Sean. "Thank you, Doyle, for finding this powerful woman for me. Her and I, we're gonna move mountains."

"Not until you've fulfilled your services for me," Sean said to him. "You better be sure about this. If not, you're both dead – and you won't see it coming, either!"

Byron looked at him and laughed in his face. There was no way Doyle could overpower him, especially now that he had Mimi, but he would let Doyle keep thinking he could. He had no problem helping out Doyle. They were buddies and he owed him one anyway. "I'm sure about this," Byron told Doyle. "You'll see. We're your lucky charms but together, we're your golden horseshoe. You're gonna be amazed at what we can do together."

Byron caressed Mimi's face.

Mimi pulled back from his hand.

Byron laughed before he lightly slapped her across the face. "Don't fight me! You'll be sorry if you do."

Mimi kept her eyes focused on Byron's forehead instead of looking directly at him. She had never been one to back down from a fight and she wasn't going to start now. She could feel him crawling around in her mind. It took all her strength but she kept her mind a blank slate. There was no way she was going to let him read her thoughts. No way!

"Okay," Byron said out loud. "You are more powerful than I thought. Since you aren't going to let me read your mind, I'm going to take the tape off your mouth so you can speak." He quickly pulled the gray tape off her mouth. Her first instinct was to throw her hand over her mouth, as if that would stop the sting, but her hands were tied behind her back.

"I know that hurt," Byron said as she flinched back. He rubbed her lips. She didn't dare move. "Where's Janet?" she asked as she backed her head away from his hand.

"Oh, we killed that bitch!" Trent said proudly.

"What?" Mimi asked, even though she had already known her friend was gone. She felt it. "Why didn't you kill me too?"

"Have you not been listening?" Byron asked as he sat down next to her. "I'm going to untie you. You can't go anywhere since we have you surrounded. If you try anything, you'll be sorry. Okay?"

She only looked at Byron without answering him. He untied her hands and she slowly pulled them in front of her. Byron grabbed her hands and held them between his. He was smiling. She was trembling. She could feel his power and he could feel hers, and he was right – the power flowing between them was very strong. This could be bad.

"I'm not going to do anything you ask," Mimi told him, not even paying attention to the other guys in the room.

"Oh, but I think you will." Byron smirked. "You see, I got a guy out in LA, and he has your daughter. What's her name? Jennifer? Yes, I think that was it."

"You liar," she said, still keeping her eyes on his forehead.

243

"Nope. Our guy went to her dorm room and took her. See?" He pulled out his cell phone and showed her a picture of her daughter, tied up and in a very dark-looking room.

Mimi was angry and began breathing harder. She said nothing.

"So, either you do as we ask you, or she's dead," Byron said.

Mimi still said nothing.

Drew approached her from behind and got in her face. "Hey, lady!" he said up close and personal. "The man asked you a question. Answer him!" he shouted.

She broke her gaze with Byron and peered into Drew's eyes. Even though they appeared to be blue, she knew they were brown and beady underneath. There was a devil dancing in his eyes and it looked like he had lost his soul. She shivered. "What was the question?" she asked Drew, staring him down.

"Are you going to do as we ask?" Drew responded.

"Depends on what you ask," Mimi answered coldly. "I'm not afraid of you assholes."

"Oh, is that so?" Drew asked as he straddled her and sat on her lap. He pushed her back onto the couch and leaned on her and into her face. "Because I think we can be pretty persuasive." He began rubbing his crotch on hers. "I think I can make you do anything I want you to do." He placed his right hand around her neck. "Do you like how this feels?"

Mimi didn't answer. She turned her eyes away from him.

"That's enough!" Byron shouted to Drew as he shoved him off of Mimi. "She's mine!"

He grabbed Mimi's hands and forced her to her feet. He led her to the nook. There was no door but he knew that none of the guys would bother him. The room smelled of old sex, warm beer, and stale cigarettes. The bed was a mess. The sheet was rumpled, the blankets were half on the bed and half on the floor, and there were used condoms all over the floor, as well as a pair of fuzzy handcuffs and women's underwear. He forced Mimi to sit on the bed but did it in a caring way. "I'm sorry about the mess," he said to her. "This isn't my place. My place is much nicer than this, but you'll soon get to see that for yourself."

Mimi didn't say anything. She only looked forward at the wall.

Byron sat down next to her and placed his hand on the top of her thigh. "Look, I know you don't want to be here, but it's because of me that those guys didn't kill you, so you owe me one. So just look at me, okay?"

Mimi shifted her eyes to Byron but didn't really look at him, more like past him. She had to at least humor him in order to keep her daughter safe.

"No," he said, squeezing her cheeks with his other hand. "Look at me, for real. Look at me, not through me!" He moved his head until his eyes were even with hers. He got close enough to her that she couldn't see anything but him.

She fought looking into his eyes. She knew what kind of power that could drum up between them. She also knew it would be hard to fight. When she was being controlled in the beach setting, she was intrigued by this man. Not just because of his good looks but because of his powers. They were so much like hers that it frightened her but also interested her. She also wasn't sure if her powers were strong enough to fight him off. Against her better judgment, she slowly looked at his eyes but only for a second. That was all it took for their power to connect. She immediately felt electric jolts run through her. It was like an instant orgasm but she felt it through her entire body. She quickly looked away.

"See that!" Byron said excitedly. "I know you felt that too. It felt good, didn't it? Made you feel powerful, right? That's how it made me feel. Now look at me again."

"No." Her voice was calm and trance-like. She was trying to keep herself contained.

"Don't tell me no," he said, squeezing her face a bit harder. "Look at me!"

"No," she said again in the same manner.

Byron pushed her so she was lying on her back, and crawled on top of her. He held her arms down so she couldn't move. He laid himself on top of her and was once again in her face. "I told you to look at me, now do it!"

Mimi felt tears starting to well up and she did her best to fight them, but they slowly started pouring out of her eyes. "No," she said through her quiet tears. She closed her eyes.

"I know you're thinking about your daughter. My friends won't think twice about offing her. You need to do this for your daughter."

He was right, but Mimi didn't respond. She tried pushing him off of her but he was too strong. She finally gave up and closed her eyes.

"Okay, then. Just lie there, I'll take control of this situation." With that, he lowered his lips onto hers and began kissing her.

She moved her head back and forth to try to stop him but he put one hand around her neck. He reached his fingers up and grabbed onto her cheeks to keep her from moving her face. "Don't fight it!" he said as he began kissing her again. Surprisingly, it wasn't a hard kiss. It was gentle – or as gentle as he could be in that position.

She fought it for a few seconds…

She tried to keep fighting it…

She could no longer fight it.

The power flowing between them was more powerful than both of them. Neither of them could have controlled what happened in that moment.

She began kissing him back.

Chapter 11

Later that afternoon, Krystal and her mother were having lunch at home when they got a call from Paul. He told them that the new trooper that was sent to the doctor's house for the rest of the day had knocked on her door to let her know he was there. When he didn't get an answer, he became worried and walked around the house and saw the back door busted in. He discovered Dr. Simms's body and realized Mimi was nowhere to be found. Paul instructed Krystal and Laura to make sure the doors were locked and not to open them for anyone. Right after he hung up, Krystal's cell phone started ringing. It was Trent.

"Answer it," Laura told Krystal.

"Hello?" Krystal said into her cell phone.

"Hey, babe. I'm all done helping my cousin if you still want to get together."

"I, um…I don't know if I'm up for it tonight. It's been a really bad day."

"What's wrong?"

"Um…Dr. Simms has been shot. She's dead."

"What!? I'm sorry to hear that. When did it happen? Do they know who did it?"

"I don't know any of the details. We just found out."

"Damn. Are you okay?"

"Not really." She started crying. "Where were you today?"

"I told you, I was helping my cousin with some things."

"Like what?"

"What's with all the questions? He needed some help with his car and some small repairs around his house. Listen, I'm going to come over, okay?"

"Um, I don't think that's a good idea. I'm not going to be any fun and me and my mom aren't really up for company, I don't think."

Laura shook her head no. She whispered, "Don't let him come here. Your father will kill him!"

"I don't care if you're not any fun. I want to be there for you and for your family," Trent said while trying to keep a straight face.

"I appreciate that, really, but it's not necessary."

"I'm not taking no for an answer. I'm coming over."

"No," Krystal repeated.

Trent hung up.

"He just hung up on me. What should we do?"

"I'm calling your father," Laura said as she picked up her cell phone and quickly called her husband.

"What's wrong?" Paul asked as soon as he answered his phone. He knew something must be wrong since he had just gotten off the phone with her.

"Trent just called Krystal. He said he's coming over even after she told him not to."

"Shit! Lock the doors and make sure the alarm is set! I'm going to call Sergeant Hill and make sure he is still on Trent. I'm coming home so just stay put!"

Paul called Hill, who told him that Trent was just now coming out of his apartment and walking to his car. "I'm not gonna let him anywhere near Krystal," the sergeant told him. "I'll follow him and let you know if he is headed in that direction."

He watched Trent pull out, and slowly followed behind him. Trent wasn't headed toward Krystal's house, though. He drove back to the warehouse.

Hill was able to park far enough away from Trent so that he couldn't be seen. He watched Trent get out of his car and walk into the building. Very quickly, Hill got out of his car and followed behind Trent. He saw Trent get on the elevator and watched as the number flashed on three and stopped. "Third floor," he said out loud. He pushed the button so that the elevator would come back down to him. When it did and he stepped in, he saw there was no button for the third floor. "What in the world?" he said out loud again. The doors closed and he stood there, trying to figure out what to do. He pressed the button for the fourth floor and put his hand on his gun as the elevator started moving up. When it stopped and the doors opened up, he was in fact on the fourth floor. "How did I pass the third floor like that?" He stepped out and saw that he was in an open room that appeared to be a warehouse for making windows and doors. A man came running up to him. "Officer? No one is supposed to be up here without a hard hat. Is everything okay? No one said you were coming up."

"Sorry about that, sir. I'm Sergeant Hill and I'm not really sure how I ended up here. I was trying to get to the third floor."

"The third floor?" the man in the hard hat asked. "I'm afraid that's not possible."

"I saw that there is no button for it. Why is that?"

The man began fidgeting. "Um, well, it's kind of off-limits to the general public."

"Why?"

"Do you have a warrant to be here?"

"I don't need a warrant to ask you some basic questions. However, if you keep acting strangely, I will obtain a warrant."

"I'm sorry. It's just that, well, the person that owns the third floor is some big shot businessman and he likes his privacy. We've all been told to stay away from him and that he's not very friendly."

"Who is he?"

"I don't know. Honestly, I don't, and I prefer not to know who it is."

"Well, how do I get onto the third floor?"

"I don't even know."

The man was lying. Hill could tell.

"Well, you've been no help to me. Thanks for nothing."

Hill turned around and got back on the elevator.

The man in the hard hat pulled out his cell phone and called down to the secretary who then called Sean.

Trent had been looking for Candy when Sean approached him. "Well, Trent! It seems that you have a trooper following you around."

"Excuse me?"

"You just came in, right? A trooper was right behind you. He ended up on the fourth floor and was asking how to get onto the third floor."

"I didn't see any trooper following me," Trent said, playing dumb. He was still mad.

"Well, there is one following you, so maybe you should be more observant! We don't need that kind of attention around here. Got it?"

"Sure," Trent said, rolling his eyes. "Where's Candy?"

"She should be the least of your worries right now, Trent! This is a problem! The cops now know where we are!"

"I'll find her myself then," Trent said as he walked away from Sean. "Don't worry about the cop following me. I got it all under control!"

"Trent! Goddamn it! Get back here!"

Trent continued to ignore him until he found Candy as she was coming out of the bathroom. He grabbed her without even saying hello and pulled her into the nook. Mimi and Byron were in there, naked, having sex like a couple of teenagers. Trent didn't care, though. He threw Candy on the floor and took out his frustrations on her pussy. Once he was finished with her, he planned to slip out and head to Krystal's house.

Chapter 12

Paul sped home and ran into his house to find Laura and Krystal sitting in the kitchen. "Has he shown up yet?"

"No, not yet," Laura answered.

"Good. I'm gonna call Sergeant Hill and see if he's still on Trent."

Paul walked upstairs to the office and called Hill. He answered right away. "Hey, boss. I was just about to call you."

"What's up? Are you on Trent?"

"Yes, sir. I thought he was gonna go to your house but he didn't."

"Let me guess, he's at that warehouse again."

"You got it, but there's something weird here."

"What do you mean?"

"I mean, I followed him inside and watched him get on the elevator. The light said it stopped on the third floor."

"Okay."

"I got in the elevator to follow him, but there's no button for the third floor."

"What do you mean there wasn't a button? That doesn't make any sense."

"Who are you telling? It went from one to two to four."

"So what did you do?"

"I hit the button for the fourth floor and it opened up into an open room. It looked like they were making windows and doors, you know, that type of thing. Some man came running up to me to tell me I wasn't supposed to be up there. I didn't catch his name but when I asked him about the third floor, he started acting nervous. He told me that it was owned by some big businessperson and no one is allowed to go down there. When I asked him how you even get to the third floor, he told me he didn't know but I'm pretty sure he was lying."

"That's really bizarre. You're still there, right?"

"Yes, sir."

"Okay. Stay put unless he comes out. I'm gonna come over there and take a look around. I'll see if the captain will come as well."

"Ten-four."

Thirty minutes later, Paul and the captain were meeting with Hill in the parking lot. "Let's go get on this mysterious elevator," Paul said.

"I should stay out here in case Trent comes back out," Hill said, "but good luck. Maybe you can find the third floor."

With that, Paul and the captain went inside the building. It was the first time Paul had been inside other than going into the main office and talking with that little bitch at the desk. He hadn't thought about just exploring the halls. He was a trooper, after all, and he was allowed to walk around, right? There were no signs about trespassing or being a private facility. The elevator was on their immediate right as they walked in. There was a directory next to it. They studied the directory and realized that there was no mention of the third floor. "This is really odd," the captain said.

"Yup," Paul replied as he took a second to look around. There were offices on this first floor. There was an insurance office, a lawyer's office, and what appeared to be a temp agency. "This floor looks pretty normal."

He looked at the directory for the second floor. According to the sign, the second floor was an open warehouse for art exhibits. "Let's see where we can end up, shall we?" the captain said as he pushed the "up arrow" button. The elevator doors swung open. There stood Trent, looking disheveled and drunk on fury.

"Trent?" Paul exclaimed. "What in the world are you doing here?" Might as well play stupid.

"Mr. J.? I could ask you the same thing."

"We're just looking around," the captain answered. "Are you all right, son? You look like you were in a fight or something."

"Yeah, I was just, um, working out," Trent said quickly.

"Working out?" Paul asked him. "Where?"

"In the gym upstairs," Trent answered.

"Gym?" the captain questioned. "And what floor is this gym on?"

"The third," Trent replied.

"Oh okay," the captain said. "Maybe I'll check it out real quick. I've been looking for a new gym."

"Oh, you can't," Trent said.

"Why not?" The captain was curious.

Paul didn't say anything as he studied Trent's face and his eyes to see if Trent was lying or not.

"Well, it's a private club and it's by invitation only." His eyes shifted to the right as he scratched his ear.

"Okay," the captain said, playing along. "How do I get an invitation?"

"It has to come from a member," Trent answered.

"Well, can't you give me one?" the captain asked.

"No. I'm a new member and I'm not allowed to do that yet." Trent looked over at Paul, wondering if Paul was believing him.

"Well maybe when you are allowed to give me one, you will?" the captain asked.

"S-s-sure," Trent answered. "So, what are you guys doing here?"

"Just looking around," Paul finally said. "Listen, Trent, we need to bring you in for questioning."

"Questioning? Why? I haven't done anything."

"Well, for starters, you're lying about what you're doing here. We know you come here often," Paul replied.

"Yeah, to work out, like I said."

Paul ignored him and said, "I also know you hit my daughter a few weeks ago and I have a big problem with that. You're lucky she didn't want to press charges against you."

"What? We worked that out. We are fine. I was just on my way to go see her, in fact."

"Wrong. You're on your way to the barrack with us so we can question you about some things," Paul said, taking a step closer to Trent.

"I'm not going." Trent took a step back.

Captain Zitzer stepped in. "Either you come with us now or we get a warrant for your arrest. It's up to you."

"So I'm not under arrest then?"

"Not yet." Paul smirked. "But if you don't come with us, then you will be."

"Fine, I'll come but I'm going to call my lawyer and have him meet me there."

"Fine by us," Paul replied. He then called Sergeant Hill and asked him to come in, get Trent, and take him to the barrack.

Trent went willingly enough.

"Let's see if we can check out that gym," the captain said after Sergeant Hill and Trent were out of sight.

The doors opened and they stepped in. Just as Sergeant Hill had said, there was no floor three. The doors shut. "Do you think there's a hidden button somewhere?" Paul wondered out loud.

"I don't know," the captain said as he began sliding his hands across the walls. "Hill said he saw the light go to the third floor so there's got to be a way."

They both spent the next few minutes casing every inch of the elevator but they came up empty-handed. "The only thing I can think of maybe before they go up, they call up there and someone up there presses a button to send the elevator to the third floor," Paul said.

"That would have to be what's going on, but why? What's up there on the third floor?"

"I don't know. I really wish we had gotten that search warrant."

"You and me both. Maybe we can now, now that we know there is something fishy going on here. I wonder if there's steps. There would have to be, right?"

"Yes!" Paul said with some hope. "There has to be a stairwell. Let's go find it!"

They spent the next fifteen minutes wandering around on the first floor looking for a stairwell entrance. They finally found it on the far end of the building. The captain pulled on the door. It was locked.

"Of course," Paul said, defeated.

"Well, fuck."

Chapter 13

By the time Paul and Captain Zitzer made it back to the barrack, Trent already had a lawyer there waiting with him. They were sitting in one of the questioning rooms.

"Sorry to have kept you waiting," Paul lied as they sat across from Trent and his lawyer.

Trent just gave him a dead stare. He was clearly not happy. "Mr. J., I know you don't like me all that much…"

Paul put up his hand and cut off Trent. "In here, it's Lieutenant Jennings."

"Fine! Lieutenant Jennings, I know you don't like me all that much, but there's no reason to have me in here. I've done nothing wrong!"

"We'll be the judges of that," Paul replied.

Trent wasn't feeling too worried. He was pretty sure they didn't have anything on him, at least no solid proof of anything. He was more annoyed that they were wasting his time. Not to mention, when he called Sean to get the lawyer, Sean went through the roof. "Whatever," Trent mumbled.

Paul pulled out the picture of Drew Foster from his notebook and smacked it down onto the table. "This is Drew Foster or Thomas Sharver, depending on who you ask. Do you know him?"

"Nope."

"Is Trent Carson your real name?"

Trent rolled his eyes. "It's the one my parents gave me."

"Where are your parents?"

"Your guess is as good as mine. What does that have to do with anything?"

"Oh, you know, I've never really heard much about your family."

"Again, what does that have to do with anything?"

Paul didn't respond to his question. "We've been following you for weeks, Trent. You've been at that Jessup warehouse multiple times. What do you do when you go there?"

"I already told you that I use the gym there."

"See, that's the odd part. We tried to get up to that third floor and we couldn't. We've been told that it belongs to some big shot businessman and he doesn't want anyone up there. So why are you allowed up there?"

"I don't know what you're talking about. I only use the gym."

"So how do you get up there?"

"Um, the elevator?" Trent said before rolling his eyes.

"But how? There's no button for the third floor."

"Yes there is. It's right between the two and four buttons." Trent smirked.

Paul was getting pissed off. "Don't get smart with me!" Paul said, raising his voice, before he slammed his hands down on the table.

Captain Zitzer placed his hand in front of Paul in attempt to calm him down. "Let me give this a shot," he said.

"Trent, let me back up a little bit. You know that Dr. Simms was hit in her car, right?"

Trent nodded, shrugging as if it was no big deal.

"Good. It just so happens that the car that was used in that attack had a GPS system in it. The GPS led us straight to that warehouse where you've been going. So you're telling me it's just, I dunno, a coincidence that you happen to be going to the same place as where Drew Foster goes?"

Trent shrugged again. "It's a small world, sir."

"So you're telling me that you have nothing to do with this Drew Foster guy. It just so happens that you two both hang out on the third floor of this warehouse?"

Trent looked over at his lawyer. The lawyer nodded as if to say it was okay to answer.

"That's what I'm tellin' ya."

"Hmm. Well, explain this one to me. We have a solid witness who can place you at the same house in Laurel as Drew Foster."

Trent's lawyer said, "Where is this so-called witness of yours?"

"She's not here but we could bring her in to testify when all of this goes to court."

The lawyer was not impressed. "Don't answer that question, Trent. They don't have anything."

Now Paul was furious. He stood up and slammed his hands down on the table again. He leaned into Trent's face and said, "How about you tell me why you hit my daughter?"

"I don't know, Mr. J. What did she tell you?" Trent was just as cool as could be. He wasn't worried about anything, it seemed. This just made Paul even more manic.

"She told me you're an asshole!"

"She didn't say that." Trent smirked. "She still loves me, and I love her more than anything." He knew that would get under Paul's skin.

Paul was standing in front of his chair, and he grabbed it and threw it back behind him in a rage that he was finding hard to contain. "You want to know what else?" Paul said through his clenched teeth.

"No, but I bet you're gonna tell me anyway." Trent smirked.

"I saw you sniffing my daughter's underwear in my house a few weeks back, you sick bastard!"

Trent smiled at Paul. "Yeah. Her used underwear smells so good to me. It brings so many memories to my mind."

Trent's lawyer gave him a disapproving look right before Paul really lost his shit. He reached across the table and grabbed hold of Trent's shirt. He pulled Trent toward him and Captain Zitzer pulled Paul away from Trent.

"All right, all right!" Captain Zitzer said as he pushed Paul out the door. He came back in and said, "Trent, we're holding you for forty-eight hours so you might as well get comfortable."

"They can't do that, can they?" Trent asked his lawyer.

"Unfortunately, they can. But they have to let you go after that as long as they don't have anything on you."

"Or," Captain Zitzer said, "we'll give you this one opportunity to tell us who these guys are and where they're at, and then you'll be free to go."

Trent knew he wouldn't really be free if he turned in Sean and Drew. It was tempting though. It would be the best way to show Krystal that he didn't want to hurt her and how much he really did love her. But one look at his lawyer's face told him to keep his mouth shut. He was really Sean's lawyer, and Trent knew he'd tell Sean everything that happened. So he said, "Are you going to show me to my room, then?"

Chapter 14

Mimi and Byron had no idea that Trent had been in the room with Candy. They never saw him come and they never saw him go. They were having sex when Trent got there and were still having sex when Trent left. When they first started kissing, Mimi tried to fight the power even though her entire body was intrigued. Her mind was no longer working right, and with each second of them kissing she lost a little more control of her mind. When the clothes started coming off, she lost all ability to even remember Janet Simms's name, and when the intercourse began, she didn't even know who she was anymore. She was still in there, though, somewhere. Her characteristics, her mannerisms, her morals – they were all still a part of her, she just had to reach for them and hold on to them or she would be totally lost from who she had been and still was.

When their sex was finally over, they fell back onto their backs, side by side. They both were breathing heavily and had new power running all throughout their bodies, veins, and minds. "That…was…a…maz…ing," Mimi panted.

Byron laughed. "Yes, it was! The best I've ever had!"

"I feel different. Do you?"

"I do too. It feels awesome, doesn't it?"

"I never knew I could feel this way just from sex."

Byron rolled over onto his side to look at Mimi. "It's because you and I are special. I've been searching for someone like you for a long time. I knew if I could find someone with the same abilities as me that if we combined ourselves with each other, we could be powerful. I can hear your thoughts right now. I know you can hear mine too."

"I can. It's weird to hear another voice inside my head."
Mimi also turned on her side to face Byron. "It's an added plus that
you are so handsome."

"And you are beautiful," Byron said, giving her a kiss on the
lips.

"Where do we go from here?"

"You know where we go from here. We got a job to do for
Doyle." *A job I'm not looking forward to.*

"Did you say that out loud?" Mimi asked.

"Which part?"

"A job I'm not looking forward to. Did you say that out
loud?"

"I didn't," Byron answered.

"See, I'm not even going to think anything because that
would just ruin our verbal communication. We have to help Doyle
kill someone, don't we?"

"Yes."

"Have you ever done anything like that before?"

"No. Never."

"You don't want to do it?"

"No. I mean, I'm not a saint in any way, shape, or form, but
my game is usually robbing banks, ripping people off, not murder. I
don't think anyone should take the life of another person."

"I agree with you," Mimi said. "Why are we doing it, then?"

"I owe him. He helped me find you."

"My friend, the doctor – he killed her, didn't he?"

"You remember?"

"I remember bits. They also kidnapped me and brought me to
you."

"I requested that part. I also requested that they keep you
alive."

"I do remember that she and I were close. I still feel that connection with her. I don't want to help this guy kill anyone else. I don't think I want to be anywhere near this guy."

"Me neither, love," Byron said. "But I owe him, which now means that you owe him too. We don't have a choice."

"Don't we, though? I mean, neither of us want to do it, so why don't we just walk out of here? We're not tied up or being held hostage."

"I know this guy. He's dangerous. He's bad news. He'd only come after us."

"So? You know as well as I do that he'd never be able to find us. We'd always be one step ahead of him. We'll know where he is at all times and we'll know when he's getting close."

"True, and he will know that, which is why he wouldn't come after us himself. He'd send someone we don't know."

"We'd still sense them, I think."

"Perhaps."

"So do you want to blow this pop stand or what?"

"Mimi, think about what you're saying. You're talking about a life on the run. This guy will not let us get away with screwing him over. We'll always be looking over our shoulders."

"I think as long as we have each other, we'll be okay. I feel that. Don't you?"

"I'm feeling a lot right now," Byron said before giving her another kiss.

"Run away with me then! We can both start a new life, together. We can run scams and never get caught. We can do it until we have enough money to live on some island somewhere and live each day as if we were on vacation. I want to live that dream you made me have. Sitting on a beach, sipping a fruity drink, you kissing me all over. We can get there! I know we can. I feel it."

"You're a dreamer!" Byron smiled. "I've always been more of a fly-by-the-seat-of-my-pants-and-see-what-happens type of guy. I never made plans before. I just floated."

"Well, what do you think of my plan? My dream?"

"I think it sounds like heaven."

"So. When do we take off?"

"We need to tell Doyle something. If we just walk out of here without telling him where we're going, he's gonna know something's up."

"Okay. How about we tell him our new power has us so revved up that we need to go see if it's actually working. Test it out. We can say we're gonna go see if Krystal is where we think she is and report back to him."

"That might work. It's worth a shot."

Mimi smiled. "One other thing?"

"What?"

"I remember my daughter. Can you let her go or is she being held by Doyle's guys?"

"No, it's a friend of mine that's with her. I will call him right now to tell him to let her go." He called his friend by video chat and Mimi was able to talk to her daughter to see that she was okay, and she watched as the man untied her and let her leave.

"Thank you," Mimi said. "Are you ready to do this?"

Byron thought about what he was about to do. Doyle did get him out of a bad situation once – his vision told him one thing but he wrote the wrong thing down, and he lost a lot of money on a horse race. He had met Doyle during the race and they had become fast friends. When Doyle found out that Byron was in trouble, he paid his debt for him and told him he'd cash in on his favor one day. He had watched Byron win a few races back-to-back, and thought he was maybe telling the truth about his psychic abilities. When Byron

265

insisted that he could win the money back on his own, Doyle patted him on the back and said, "Let me take care of my new friend." He realized now that Doyle had just forced him into owing him a favor. But the more he thought about it, the more he felt like he had already helped Doyle out enough with the Jenningses and Dr. Simms, so he didn't owe him anymore.

They found Doyle and told him about their plan to scope out Krystal. Doyle agreed to let them go chase their vision, thinking they would be back later that night.

Chapter 15

"FUCK!" Sean screamed out loud after throwing his cell phone down on his desk. Not only did he have to find a new office location and get moved as quickly as possible, but three days had gone by since Byron and Mimi left, saying they were going to go see if they could find Krystal. Three days had gone by since he had last spoken to them. "Those little bastards took off on me!" he said out loud to no one. Byron was not answering his calls. In fact, the phone was going straight to voicemail for the first two days. The call he had just made to the cell phone told him that the number was no longer in service. He picked up his phone and made a call.

"Phil? It's Doyle. I have a job for you and this one is gonna pay big bucks."

"Go on," said the man on the other end of the phone.

"I need you to find someone for me. Two someones. They took off on me before they did the job I hired them for. I've already wired ten grand into your account to help you get started. I've emailed you all the details. Once you find them, I'll give you a final payment of fifty grand. I need these two found. I need them to be sent back to me, alive and unharmed. Do you understand?"

"Yes, sir! I'm on it."

Sean hung up and then called a meeting with his men. It was time to start moving forward. They all met in the makeshift living room. "This place is a fucking pigsty!" Sean shouted, kicking a bra out of the space where he was resting his feet. "Why the fuck can't you people clean up after yourselves? I give you a place to stay, to play, to enjoy yourselves, and this is the thanks I get?"

No one said anything. They looked down at their shoes, except for Trent. He was still pissed off about the situation with Krystal and being questioned by Paul and locked up for forty-eight hours. Luckily, they let him go, but told him not to leave town. He hadn't seen or spoken to Krystal in days and he was getting madder each day. "With all due respect, Doyle," Trent began, "I'm pretty sure you didn't bring us here to yell at us about the mess."

Sean looked at Trent. Some days he just wanted to knock him in the corner. He couldn't stand his disrespectful mouth. He needed him, though. Now more than ever. "Shut your fucking mouth!" Sean told him. "It's time for us to move forward. I want this job over and finished with. We do it tonight!"

"So what's the plan?" Drew asked with a smile on his face. "I've been ready for this!"

"We got three people to take care of – Krystal, her mother, and her father. I want the mother to go first, then Krystal. They need to be killed in front of Paul. I want him to watch his wife and daughter die!"

"Damn, boss, what did this guy do to you?" Drew asked.

"How many fucking times do I have to tell you that my business with Paul is none of your business?"

Drew lowered his head. He was only trying to bond with him. He hated it when the boss yelled at him in front of the other guys. Today it was him, Trent, and three other men that Sean trusted enough: Brett, Brandon, and Snake. Drew and Trent were his key players, though. Trent, because he knew the family and the house, and Drew, because he was just as bloodthirsty as him. Drew didn't need a reason to be so thirsty, though, he just was.

"I think the best place to take them down is in their house, in the middle of the night, so we can catch them off guard. Trent, that is where you're gonna be very much needed. I need to know, though, that you are not going to pussy out on me because you are in love with this girl."

"Love? I ain't got shit for that girl," Trent said with a stone-cold face. Although inside he wasn't so sure he meant that. He was mad at her but he also still felt a lot of love for her and he wasn't sure he'd be able to do this. "Besides, if I was gonna pussy out, I would've when I was locked up."

"Good point," Sean said, though still not sure if he should believe him. "Now, my weapons took off on me so we're left to do the job on our own without their help."

"Where the fuck did Byron go?" Drew asked. He didn't like that someone backstabbed his boss.

"I don't know, but I got someone looking for them. I'll deal with them when they are found. In the meantime, we need to stay focused on this job. I can't let anything go wrong. I want it done and over with swiftly, especially since the cops are now sniffing around Trent and I have no idea where Byron and Mimi went. So let's put this job to bed so we can all leave once it's done. We all need to move on, alone, once it's all said and done. Is that understood?"

"We got it, boss," Drew answered. "But, how in the hell are we gonna do this now? They have police protection outside of their house all the time. There is no way we are going to get in there without being caught."

"We will have to take care of the officers sitting outside. How many is it? One? Two? I think we can handle it."

"They were keeping two out there," Trent answered.

"Great," Sean said. "I'm sure you guys can handle them before we go in. Then all we'll have to worry about is how to get in the house. Do they have an alarm?"

"They do," Trent answered. "I know the code unless they changed it."

"If they did, I can crack those things," Brett replied. "I can do it within a second. It's a piece of cake."

"Good!" Sean smiled. "And I know Drew can pick a lock so you all should be able to get inside."

"We don't need to pick any locks." Trent smirked. "Krystal told me a long time ago, she keeps a spare key in a magnetic box on the bottom of her car. She probably doesn't even remember telling me that."

"Once we get inside," Brandon said, "what do we do? How do you want this job done?"

"I was just getting to that. I want this night to feel like a nightmare to all of them. I want them to suffer. I want you all to torture them in the evilest ways you can think of. Have fun with it."

Drew liked the sound of that. His mouth turned into an evil grin and his mind began wandering to the things he could do to these people.

"Once you've gotten all of them detained, before you kill anyone, I want you to give me a call. I want to be there for the killing of all of them."

"I get to off Krystal, right?" Trent said. "You told me I could."

"I know what I told you," Sean answered. "You will get your chance, once I'm done with what I need to do. When I get there, you all will give me some privacy with all three of them. I have things I need to say to them that I'd like to keep between me and them. Once I'm done, you'll kill Laura first in front of Krystal and in front of her father. Then you will kill Krystal. Then Paul. I want him to watch his wife and daughter be tortured and then murdered. I want his death to be the worst, though. I want him to die very slowly and very painfully. I will not help in the torture or the killing. I will be there, though, to watch it for myself. Once you guys are done, we clean up anything that could leave a trace of any of our DNAs and then we all go our separate ways. I have a couple of buddies parking cars around the neighborhood now and your payout will be in your car. You all will get your own car and you'll leave separately, and alone. Is all this clear?"

"So, after the job is done, we won't see you anymore?" Drew asked with a little bit of sadness in his voice.

"Not for a while at least. I may be in touch with some of you if I need to hire you for another job, but we need to all be smart about this and live as if we don't know each other. If one of us gets caught, we will not confess anything. If any of you do, I'll have you killed in jail. If you get caught, I'll have a lawyer for you but you won't see me anywhere near you. I think you can all understand that."

"We aren't going to get caught!" Drew said. "We got this."

"There's only one more problem," Trent said softly.

"What?" Sean asked getting annoyed.

"I still have a trooper tailing me. I made sure to lose him so he wouldn't know where we are now, but he'll catch up to me. He always shows back up at my apartment."

"Should he pop up before we take off to do this job, I can take care of him," Snake said with a smirk.

Chapter 16

Krystal and her parents had just arrived home from Dr. Simms's funeral service. "Well, I guess that's that. I still wonder what happened to Mimi," Krystal said, grabbing a glass of water.

"I have the guys looking for her," Paul stated. "They haven't had any luck, though. It's as if she fell off the face of the earth."

"She must have, to not even come to the funeral today," Laura agreed.

"I just hope she's okay," Krystal said.

"I'm sure she is. She was smart," Paul replied.

"Well," Laura said, "I know this is bad timing, but how about some dinner? It's been a while since we've all been home at the same time to enjoy a dinner together."

"I think I'd like that." Krystal smiled.

She hadn't seen or heard anything from Trent in a couple of days now. She wasn't sure how she felt about it. She knew she needed to stay away from him, but there was a small part of her that missed him and what they had when it was good. She had to stop herself a couple of times from calling him, thinking he must be going through something to be acting the way he had been. She was never able to complete the call. She still wondered, though, what had happened to him, what was wrong with him, and if he still loved her. She still had some love for him. She figured that was normal, maybe. They had spent a lot of time together and they were good times. She couldn't believe how much he had changed over the past few weeks. She missed what they'd had. Her heart missed his love, her body missed his touch, and her eyes missed his smile. She wished Dr. Simms was still around so she could talk to her. She always had a way of helping Krystal make sense of her thoughts and feelings.

Chapter 17

Sean was sitting in his car a block away from Krystal and her parents' house. This was the night he had been waiting for, for years. Everything he had ever worked on and for was leading to this very moment. Soon, he'd finally get his chance to meet the man he had wanted to meet his entire life. He was about to get his revenge for himself, for his brother, for his shitty life. Nothing in his life mattered except for this moment that he was about to embark on. It was one in the morning and the lights had gone off in the Jennings household two hours ago. It was time. He picked up his phone and texted the word "NOW!" to Drew.

Drew, Trent, and the other three men were five houses down and were ready to go. Brandon got out of the car and ran up to the police car, making sure to work himself out of breath in the process. Trooper Marx was awake and alert and heard Brandon's footsteps before he saw them, since he had his window down. He shined his spotlight out in front of him and saw a man running toward him. The man stopped at his window and was out breath. He looked and sounded frantic. "Officer, thank god you're right here!"

"What's wrong, son?" Trooper Marx asked, not feeling too worried.

"I, um…listen…I, well, I hit someone with my car just right down the street."

Trooper Marx stepped out of his car. He didn't stop to think that this could be a setup. He didn't stop to wonder how this guy even knew he was sitting there. All he thought about was that someone was hurt right down the street and he needed to help them. Not to mention, he had been bored the last few nights sitting outside a house where nothing was going on. He was ready for some sort of action.

273

"Okay. Calm down. Are you sure you hit someone?"

"Yes! It was some dude on a bicycle. I didn't see him because it was dark and he didn't have any lights on his bike. I think he's really hurt. My cell phone is dead so I just started running, hoping I'd run into a passing car or something. Please, you've got to help. I think I really hurt the guy!" Brandon was still frantic and breathing heavily. He was very convincing.

"Okay. Let's get back there."

Trooper Marx took off running with the guy. He was about to grab his radio so he could radio in what was occurring but before he could, out of nowhere, three men came out of the bush on the right. They knocked him down and then shot him in the head two times. He was dead after the first bullet. The neighbors didn't hear anything, as the guns they were using all had silencers. He had been the only cop on watch at that time, with another one scheduled to come in a couple of hours.

Krystal was asleep in her bed when Trooper Marx was murdered, but was tossing and turning. Surprisingly, Paul and Laura were asleep in each other's arms. The house was quiet and dark.

Trent, Drew, Brett, Brandon, and Snake quietly dragged Trooper Marx's body back to his car and propped him back up in the driver's seat. Then they walked up the driveway. There weren't any cars going by, which was not surprising since it was a Wednesday night. As Trent walked by Krystal's car, he felt around the bottom for the key box. He knew it would be there, knowing that Krystal probably forgot she even told him about it. He was pondering on if he should pretend like it wasn't there so that it would be harder for them to get into the house. He was still having some doubts about killing Krystal. He eventually found it on the opposite side from where he started. He let his reflexes control him instead of his thoughts. "Bingo!" he whispered to his coworkers.

They walked up to the door and Trent quietly slid the key into the keyhole. He turned the key and then turned the knob. They opened the door to the sound of three beeps coming from the alarm.

Krystal heard the beeps and sat straight up in bed. She got up and walked over to her door. She listened for a second to see if she heard anything else.

Trent entered the code that he knew but it didn't work. He pointed to Brett to tell him his assistance was needed. Brett quickly went over to the keypad and punched in a series of numbers. It wasn't the actual code for the alarm but he knew how to deactivate alarms based on the brand. The alarm beeped one final time as it was disarmed.

Krystal locked her bedroom door. Someone was in the house. She grabbed her phone and texted her mom and dad. Neither of them answered. They were both still fast asleep. Before she could hit the 9 on her phone to call 9-1-1, her doorknob began jiggling. Someone was trying to get in. She backed away from the door and as she tried to compose herself to hit the 9 on her phone, she heard someone picking the lock and within a second, her door came open. She screamed as she saw Trent coming through the door. He was by himself. The other four men went to gather Paul and Laura.

Paul jumped when he heard his daughter scream but it was too late, there were four men surrounding his bed. Laura jumped at the sound of Paul struggling to get to his pistol.

"What are you doing here?" Krystal shouted at Trent. "You need to leave."

"I'm sorry, sweetheart, but I can't do that," he said as he cornered her against a wall in her bedroom. "I'm here for work, not play."

"What does that mean?" she asked him before he threw his hand over her mouth.

"Shhh…you don't get to ask the questions today."

Krystal tried to remember her self-defense tactics but it was useless. He was ready for her this time, and his grip was just too strong. Tears began rolling down her cheeks as Trent led her downstairs to the living room. He threw her on the couch. He opened the duffle bag that he came in with and grabbed the duct tape. As he was doing that, Krystal jumped up and tried to kick him in the crotch as he came toward her. He was too quick for her and was able to push her away from him before her foot made contact. Krystal screamed and charged toward him again but Trent was able to push her back on the couch and sat down on top of her, straddling her. "Listen to me. I need you to calm down." He kissed her as she shook her head, trying to get him to stop. He slapped her across the face. "Don't fight me!" he ordered. "I just want one last kiss before I put this tape over your mouth." Again, he took a kiss from her before he pulled off a piece of the tape. He grabbed his pocketknife out of the front pocket of his jeans and cut the tape off. He placed it over her mouth. She screamed through the tape.

Trent was shaking with fright and excitement. He couldn't wait to torture her but there was still the side of him that wanted to let her go. He still felt some love for her. He didn't want to hurt her but he did. If the angel and devil sitting on your shoulders was a real thing, he would have had that going on in that very moment. He grabbed the rope he had brought and used it to tie up her arms and then her legs, all the while fighting with himself inside.

She's really scared right now. I don't think I've ever seen her cry this much. I used to love her so much. Why did she have to turn crazy on me? Or was I the one who went crazy? I just wish I knew what she and her family did to Sean. That would make this so much easier. Am I really going to go through with this? I've never hurt someone that I actually loved before…but then again, I've never loved someone before like I've loved her. I've already hurt her, so why stop now? I should stop because she doesn't deserve this. Neither does her family, even though I don't like them much. They are really good people. I need to do this though. The payout is going to be killer. I can retire at my young age. It will be great. Let me just get this over with…

Back upstairs, the four other men were having no problems at all. They were able to get to Paul before he was able to get to his gun. Two of them took down Paul while the other two took down Laura. They forced them down the steps, where they met up with Krystal and Trent. When Paul saw Trent, he lost it, screaming, "You little piece of shit! I knew you were a part of this. When I get my hands on you…"

Trent shut him up with a slap across the face while Brandon and Snake held on to him. "It's not me doing this, Daddy," Trent said with a smirk. "I'm just following orders. Maybe you should've kept me locked up."

Laura only cried as Brett and Drew held her back.

Trent looked over at Krystal after he said those words. Krystal began crying even harder after seeing her parents. "Oh, honey," Trent said walking back over to her on the couch. He wiped away her tears. "You were only a job at first but I really did fall in love with you…until you ruined it by not giving me what I wanted. If you had only given me what I wanted, we'd still be happy and in love right now. It's your fault this is happening. I could've saved you and your stupid-ass parents." He kissed one of her tears, licked it off his lips, and then went back toward Laura. He tied up her arms while she was being held, and put tape over her mouth. He then did the same with Paul. He shoved them onto the couch with Krystal and then pulled out his cell phone. He texted to Sean, "We're ready for you."

Sean came through the door a minute later and told them all to wait outside in the backyard and to not get themselves seen. They did as they were told. Once they were out of sight, Sean approached Krystal first. She was still crying. He looked at her with a sort of fascination, as if he had never seen a female before. He wiped her tears away like a father does for his daughter. "You are so beautiful. It's a shame that you have an asshole for a father. You and I probably would have been pretty close if he had only given us a chance."

Krystal was beyond confused and she couldn't say anything with the tape on her mouth.

Paul was even more confused. He knew this man, but he wasn't sure just yet from where. The man then turned his attention on Paul. "Well, if it isn't Daddy Dearest here!" he said. He looked Paul in the eyes and Paul looked him over. He tried speaking but he couldn't. Sean pulled the tape off of his mouth. "What's that, Daddy?"

"I know you, don't I? Where do I know you from? Have I arrested you before?"

Sean laughed. "Ha! You wish! I'm too good to get caught." He then punched Paul in the face.

Krystal and Laura screamed through their tape.

"Look at me!" Sean shouted at Paul. "Look at me real close! Think really hard!"

Paul did as he was told even though his face was stinging from the punch. He knew this guy, and after looking in his eyes he figured it out. "Wait...what...you...you...you're dead. I killed you."

"Oh, so you remember me now?" Sean asked.

"You're the one who broke into that home and shot that sixteen-year-old..." Everything came together in Paul's mind as he finally realized that this was Sean.

"Ah, you do remember. Only, you didn't kill me because it wasn't me that you shot."

"I know…"

Sean laughed before he shouted, "It was my twin brother! You killed him!"

"I…I was just doing my job," Paul said nervously. "If I hadn't killed him, he would've killed me first."

"Maybe, but I guess we'll never know, now will we?"

"Please, this is between you and me. Please just let my family go?" Paul pleaded.

"See, no…I can't do that. We're not done talking, Daddy."

Krystal and Laura were still crying – silently, but still crying.

"Your poor wife and daughter have no idea what you really are. You're not just a cop that killed someone, are you? Oh no, you're a sorry excuse for a father as well."

"That's not true," Paul mumbled.

Sean punched him again.

Paul's head flew back with the punch and he had to shake his head to keep from passing out.

Krystal and Laura tried to scream again.

"I wonder, Daddy, if your wife and daughter here know about your other children? Do they?"

Paul looked over at Laura. It killed him to see her so scared. Krystal too. He didn't even bother to answer Sean.

"What? The cat got your tongue now?" Sean asked him. "Or did you forget about your other family?"

"I…I don't know…" Paul stopped himself because he did know.

"Oh, you know, but I'm guessing the little wifey here doesn't, and if she doesn't, then neither does your daughter, right?"

"Please," Paul pleaded. "They are innocent in all of this, please let them go."

"I can't do that. You see, what goes around comes around, but first I want them to know. I want you to tell them your big secret. I want you to face them, look them in the eyes, and tell them!" He pushed Paul off the couch and made him face his wife and daughter while on his knees. "You tell them, right now!"

Paul held back tears as he choked on his words. "My wife already knows."

"Well then tell your daughter! I bet she doesn't know, does she?"

"I...um...well, I told you about that little trip I took right after high school, right?"

Krystal nodded yes.

"Well, there was something I didn't tell you about that trip. I was, um...well, I was young, you know. I met this woman, this really pretty woman who picked me up one night. One thing led to another and," Paul began crying. "Oh god, I never meant to keep this from you. It just kind of happened. Time goes by so very fast and things have a way of getting away from you." He took a minute to get some tears out and then continued. "I had to go to Missouri for training and I was in the grocery store and I saw that woman there. She had a baby in the cart, probably about a year old. It didn't take a genius to figure out that it was my child. She told me that I gave her the one thing that her husband couldn't. She said she didn't want anything from me and to just forget about her and the baby. I never saw or spoke to her again." He began crying harder.

"And of course Daddy Dearest here was okay with that," Sean said. "Weren't you? You didn't have to take care of your child. You got to have your fun and walk away from it." He yanked Paul up and threw him back on the couch.

Krystal felt sad that she had brothers that she hadn't even known about. She had always wanted a sibling.

"There's more to this story," Sean said. "More that I guess you don't even know about. You see, that guy that you shot in the house burglary...that was your son."

"I've figured that out..."

"That's right!" Sean said, ignoring what Paul just said. "I'm your fucking son too! It just so happened that Toby – that was his name if you even care – was coming back here to look for you. Our mother told us on her deathbed that our father wasn't our real father, and then she told us about you. He was always getting himself in trouble and he had just gotten out of jail and decided he needed a dad because the one we got was a piece of shit. He used to beat us and rape us and lock us in a dark closet. All Toby wanted was to find a man he could call Dad. I, on the other hand, never wanted to meet you, but I let him go. He needed money so he was robbing that house, and as small as this world is, wouldn't you know that you were the officer to show up?"

Paul said nothing, he just cried.

"You killed your very own son! How does that make you feel?"

"Like shit, okay? It makes me feel like shit. I didn't know. I should have tried to find you when you were younger but I didn't. I'm sorry about that, more than you'll ever know. I made a lot of mistakes. If you just let us go, you and I can talk about this. I can make it right. We can fix it. I assure you we can, but you have to let my family go."

"I'm your family too, you know! I'm not letting any of you go. I've been waiting a long time for this!"

Paul said nothing to that, and cried as he looked through blurry eyes at his wife and daughter. "I'm sorry," he said to them.

"Oh, you're sorry to them?" Sean shouted. "What about me and my brother? We went through so much abuse from our father until he killed our mother and then himself! We were only seven, so we were put in foster care where we were just abused even more! It's all your fault! You abandoned us and then went on to start a family of your own as if we never existed! Do you really think I'm going to let you get away with this?" Sean shouted. "Everything! Every shitty thing that has happened in my life is because of you! Now I'm going to make you pay! First, though, I'm going to take away your family just like you took away mine!"

"Please," Paul pleaded again through tears. "Just let them go. This is between you and me."

"Oh, it is? Because I'm pretty sure that's my sister sitting over there." He walked over to Krystal, who was crying hysterically, and took the tape off her mouth. "Hey, sis. So how does it make you feel, knowing that you had two brothers and didn't know anything about them?"

"Is it true, Dad?" Krystal asked through her sobs.

"Me having twin sons is true, but whether this is one of them, I just don't know for sure, honey."

"Oh it's true and I'm one of them!" Sean said. He wiped more tears off of Krystal's face. "I promise you it's true. I only wish we could've been close like normal brothers and sisters."

"We still can," Krystal pleaded. "It's not too late."

"It is. You see, I'm here for justice. For my brother, for my mother, and for me. You all are gonna be dead very soon and that is all I need to be able to move on from this nightmare. Daddy here gets to watch you two die first before he goes, though, because I want him to suffer just as much as I have. I'm sorry, sis. You really are a beautiful young lady and I'm sorry you got caught in the middle of this. I'm sorry you're gonna be dying because of me, but death is not a terrible thing. It's really a gift if you think about it. We'll see each other in the afterlife, I'm sure of it. You'll finally be free of everything. I'm glad to be the one to give you the gift of death."

"I've seen you before," she sobbed. "You're that guy that broke into my room last month."

Sean smiled lovingly at Krystal. "You remember? You were so hopped up on those pills that day, I thought maybe you wouldn't remember me. How sweet!" He kissed Krystal on the cheek and then put the tape back over her mouth.

Laura screamed and cried.

Sean didn't even look at her. He walked back in front of Paul and said, "Everything that is about to happen is your fault. Remember that, Dad."

Sean walked to the back door and called his men in. He pulled a chair from the kitchen table and placed it on the other side of the living room and had a seat. It was time for him to enjoy the show. Even though he felt like doing the torturing himself, he knew he'd enjoy it more if he were able to sit back and really watch the horror on Paul's face. He wanted to keep yelling at him and he wanted to hit him a few more times, but he also knew he needed to make sure that this was completed as quickly as possible.

Chapter 18

"Remember what I said," Sean said to his men. "Laura first, then Krystal, then Paul."

"You got it, boss," Drew said as he was the first to approach Laura.

Krystal and Paul screamed through their taped mouths.

"Now what should we do with this pretty lady right here?" Drew said while very slowly pulling the tape off her mouth.

"I think we should have some fun," Trent said as he stood next to Drew. "I always wondered what it would be like to kiss the mother of my girlfriend." He took over with pulling the tape off and pulled it off quickly. He then threw himself on top of Laura and began kissing her, using his tongue.

Paul watched as Laura tried to squirm him off of her, but he was too strong and she was too tied up. Paul began yelling muffled screams through the tape and tried to use his body to push Trent off of Laura. With that, Brandon and Snake grabbed him and threw him on the recliner away from them. They made sure he was watching.

"Now, now," Drew said to Trent. "You get Krystal, so you need to let the rest of us have some fun."

Trent agreed with this statement so he sat down in between Krystal and Laura. He wanted to be close to Krystal.

Drew untied Laura, stood her up, and he and Snake took off all her clothes. Again, Paul watched helplessly as Laura tried to squirm free from them but all four men were surrounding her. She was blocked.

"Wow, I see where Krystal gets her tight body from," Trent said with a smirk.

Paul began shaking and trying to break his arms free from the tape. He heard Krystal sobbing.

"How should we do this, boys?" Drew asked his coworkers.

"The way I see it," Snake answered, "there's four of us and she's got three holes and a nice pair of knockers."

"Gang bang!" Brett yelled. "Me first!"

Laura tried to get away again but they were all still surrounding her and they were too strong for her. Brett threw her on the floor and got on top of her. He was already hard. He began raping her while holding her arms down. She screamed and cried, which just turned him on even more. It only took him a minute before he came. He pulled out and let his spluge go all over her face. Then he rubbed it in. He laughed as he got up and allowed Drew to have a turn. Drew wasn't hard yet so he decided to shove his cock in Laura's mouth. He began humping her face as she choked and cried. Without even thinking about it, Laura bit down on the limp penis that was invading her mouth. Drew yelled out in pain as he pulled his dick out of her mouth and slapped her, hard, across the face. "You bitch! You're gonna pay for that!"

"Please, just stop!" Laura pleaded through sobs. "Stop!"

Drew laughed. "Hold her down," he told the other two men.

Drew got his switchblade out of his bag and walked over to Laura. "I'm tired of hearing your mouth," he said. With that, he forced his hand inside her mouth and even though she closed down on it, he was still able to grab her tongue. It kept slipping out of his gloved hand but eventually, he was able to get a good grip on it and pull it out of her mouth as far as he could. He then began sawing away at it with the switchblade. She screamed at the pain of losing her tongue. Blood was gushing out of her mouth. Drew held up the tip of the tongue that he managed to cut completely off. He licked it and the other men laughed at this gesture.

Paul was still struggling to try to get free but he knew it didn't matter because the other guys were watching him like a hawk. So was Sean. He looked over at Sean and saw that he was smirking as if he were watching a comedy show. He couldn't believe the sick fuck was actually enjoying this. Paul just wanted to scream.

Sean smirked and enjoyed the show as he kept his eyes on Paul.

Drew shoved the tip of her tongue in the front pocket of his pants and then told the other men to stand back.

Laura was done fighting. The pain from her tongue being cut off was enough to make her almost pass out. She was now just silently lying there with blood flowing out of her mouth. She was in shock and was unable to process anything that was going on now. That was probably a good thing considering what was about to happen.

Drew grabbed his gun. It was a .38 pistol with a 6.5-inch barrel. "I've been saving this one for a special occasion," he chuckled as he screwed the silencer onto the gun.

Paul was screaming through his tape, trying anything to get them to stop. Krystal was crying, frozen with fear.

Drew glanced over at Sean and saw that he was enjoying the show. Good. Drew then spread open Laura's legs. He licked her pussy and said, "Sorry, but that's all the foreplay you get."

Drew then shoved the barrel of his pistol into Laura's vagina. "I'm sure that it's harder than I will ever be and I'm sure it's a little cold. Sorry about that. It's about to get a little warmer for you, though, in just one second. Don't take this personally, hun. You are just a paycheck, money in my pocket. Killing you is just a bonus for me."

Drew looked over at Paul and asked, "Any last words?"
Paul screamed again.

"Oh, that's right!" Drew laughed. "You can't say shit! Too bad."

Paul closed his eyes. Brandon ran over to him and slapped him across the face. "You keep your eyes open and you watch this!"

Paul cried, which was a blessing as it blurred his vision.

Drew looked over at Sean, who gave him a nod as if to say, "Continue."

Drew looked up at Laura. She was still just lying there, not even screaming. He felt chills run up the back of his neck as the adrenaline took over. He had never tried this one before. "I'll give you a countdown."

The other guys stood back.

"One, two…" Drew started.

Krystal closed her eyes as she finally found herself unable to scream.

"Three!"

Drew pulled the trigger.

The muffled gunshot was music to Drew's ears. He backed away from Laura and they all looked at the mess it had made. The bullet never made an exit. It was as if it just exploded inside her body and pieces of her flesh and intestines blew all over the living room. Surprisingly, she was still squirming. Snake walked up to her and put a bullet in her head. It made an even bigger mess. She was dead, though.

Krystal and Paul were both screaming and sobbing. Paul stood up, not sure of what he was going to do, but felt like he needed to try something. Drew turned around and punched him in the face. He fell back down into the chair.

"Oh shut up!" Drew shouted as he glanced over at his boss. Sean had a huge smile on his face which made Drew very happy. He turned his attention back to Paul and Krystal. "This is gonna happen

287

no matter how much you try to scream, so you might as well just calm your tits."

Krystal looked over at her father, wishing he'd do something to make this stop.

Drew looked over at Trent, who was still sitting next to Krystal wiping her tears away. "You're up, buddy."

Trent gently pulled the tape off of Krystal's mouth. She immediately began screaming. "What the fuck is wrong with you guys? Leave us alone!"

Drew walked over and slapped her across the face. "Shut up, you bitch!"

This enraged Trent. He stood up and pushed Drew. "You don't fucking touch her, man!"

"Oh get over yourself!" Drew said to Trent. "You better not fuck this up. If you're going to do this, then me hitting her is not a big deal!"

"It is a big deal!" Trent screamed in Drew's face. "She has to be done the way I want! So you better not fuck this up for me!"

"You are so fucking mental!" Drew said, taking a step back.

"And you're not?" Trent asked as he turned away from him and went back to Krystal.

He wiped her tears and said to her very softly and calmly, "I really did love you at one point but I have to do this now. I worked so hard to keep my anger in check, but my surroundings, my boss, and my friends want me to be this angry person and to be honest with you, it feels good. I like being angry. I like hurting people. It's the only way I know how to be."

"Please, Trent. I still love you, you know? If you really ever did love me, then you won't do this. Listen to me, not them!" she cried.

"I wish I could, but I can't. Do you know how much this job is paying me? I'll never have to work again if I don't want to. The money is worth more to me than you and your family. That sounds horrible, I know, but this is who I am. Who I really am. No fucking cunt will ever change that. Now I want you to lie down on the floor."

"No," Krystal said.

"You don't have a choice," Trent said as he grabbed her arm and got Snake to help him move her onto the floor. They laid her on her back.

Trent sat on top of her and untied her legs. He left her arms tied up. "I finally get to do to you what I've always wanted to do with you. I'm going to kill you once I'm finished, but this is going to feel so good for me, you know why?"

Krystal didn't respond.

"Because," Trent answered, "I've never been able to do this to someone that I actually had feelings for. This is going to be amazing for me. I can't think of anyone else I'd rather do this with. I'll forever be grateful for you, Krystal."

Paul started screaming through his tape again and was trying to get up.

"Oh no, you don't," Drew said. "You sit there and you watch this!"

Trent got his pocketknife and cut Krystal's shirt off and then removed her bra. "Look at this, Mr. J.," he said to Paul. "I bet you never knew your daughter has such a nice pair of knockers, huh?"

Paul closed his eyes. "I told you to watch, asshole!" Drew shouted at him before slapping him across the face. Paul opened his eyes and was once again thankful for the tears blurring his vision.

"Now," Trent said to Krystal, "I'm going to keep your arms tied up because that turns me on. I had to untie your legs, though, so I can get to the goods."

"Please just stop." Krystal cried softly.

Trent threw the rope to the side and positioned himself on top of Krystal. "Oh, keep crying, honey. It turns me on even more." He kissed her just like he used to kiss her when things were good with them. It brought back the feeling of the love he knew he still had for her, and it was at that moment that he knew he needed to do what he was planning. He only hoped it worked.

She didn't kiss back but didn't fight him, either. His lips were all too familiar. Even through her tears and fright, she still felt the love she once had for him. She'd had no idea she was in love with a monster. She opened her eyes as he was kissing her. Looking at him so close up gave her chills.

He slid himself down her body and undid her pants. He pulled her pants and panties down and pulled them over her feet. He threw them over to Paul, who used his body to throw them off of himself. Krystal was now totally naked, in front of her father and these six men. She silently cried, knowing there was nothing she could do. Even if she were able to fight off Trent, there was no way she could fight off five more men.

"Please," she said again. "Please just stop this. I know there has to be a part of you that still loves me and doesn't want to do this. Please, Trent."

Trent looked up at her. He looked in her eyes and all the fun times he had with her came flooding back. All the concerts, the times spent with friends, the family dinners, the romantic nights, the sex, the boring lovemaking, and the connection he felt with her – it was all there in his memory. It was front and center in his mind and he began to feel a moment of weakness. *She's messing with your mind, Trent. You know she no longer loves you. What you had with her is gone. You need to do this or these guys will kill you too, and you know it. Sean would never let these guys kill me. I'm like a*

290

brother to him. He'd be pissed, sure, but he wouldn't kill me. I could just take her and have a life with her. Just her and me with no one to bother us. We could be happy again. Maybe. I really have been looking forward to this night though. All the shit that I've been handed. Someone has to pay for it and it should be someone sweet like Krystal too because that's just how life is. It's fucked up.

"I'm sorry," Trent whispered in her ear. And all of a sudden it felt like it was just him and her in the room.

He kissed her on her lips and then worked his way to her neck, down to her chest, her nipples…those perky nipples that he loved so much. He took his time kissing and biting them, then worked his way down her stomach and down to her pussy. He licked her clit a few times and was upset to find that she was not even wet. He raised himself back up to her face and kissed her as he used his fingers to fuck her.

Krystal cried.

Paul cried harder, blurring his vision even more. He cried out in disgust and discomfort.

Trent then undid his pants and pushed them down to his ankles. He slipped his member inside of her and began pumping in and out of her – hard. He fucked her as if he was never going to have sex again. All the rage and anger he had ever felt in his life was put into those thrusts. He placed his right hand around Krystal's throat and used his left hand to help hold himself up. He tightened his grip around her neck as he continued to thrust inside of her. He pushed harder and harder and with each push, he squeezed a little more on her neck.

"Oh yeah, baby," he said in delight. "Let yourself go."

Paul screamed through his tape.

"Please!" Krystal managed to push out of her mouth. "I love you, Trent." It was getting harder for her to talk so her voice was almost at a whisper. "Let me go and I can help you take these guys down. We can fight them, I know we can. Then we can be free!"

Trent said nothing as he squeezed harder and watched as Krystal's eyes began to roll up and backward and she began gasping for air. He squeezed harder and pumped even harder.

Just as she passed out, he came inside of her. He had never felt so good in his entire life. "Aaaaahhhh," he screamed as he released himself. He got up and looked over at Drew. "I'll finish her off," he said as he pulled up his pants.

Trent fired two shots into Krystal, who just lay there lifelessly.

Paul screamed and cried.

Sean smiled. His plan was going perfectly.

As far as Trent was concerned, his job here was finished, but he knew he had to stick around until the end. He quickly grabbed the blanket that was lying on the back of the couch and placed it over Krystal's body. He didn't want anyone to see what he had done.

"Now," Drew said, turning his attention to Paul, "it's all you now, Pops! We saved the best for last. We got big plans for you."

"Yeah," Snake joined in. "You see, we've been ordered to torture you and we're really good at doing that."

Drew slowly pulled the tape off Paul's mouth. "Any last words?"

"You pieces of shit!" Paul shouted. "You all are gonna rot in hell!" He spit in Drew's face.

Drew cocked his arm back and punched him.

"Yup, we're looking forward to hell!" Drew laughed.

Knowing he now had nothing to lose, Paul decided to try to fight them. He shook off the new punch to the face and stood back up. He ran head first into Drew who was the closest to him. He didn't really stop to think that it would be an unfair fight with six against one.

Drew stumbled a little bit at the shove he got but it wasn't enough to do anything. He just laughed. "Really?" he asked Paul.

"Why don't you untie me and make this a fair fight, you little fuckin' pussy!" Paul said.

Sean stood up before any of them were able to say or do anything else. "You know what? He's right. Untie the bastard!"

"What?" Drew asked. "Seriously?"

"He wants to fight like a man so we should let him. But to make it fair it will be one on one. Just him and me."

"Boss, I thought you weren't going to be a part of this?" Drew asked.

"Things change. Now untie him."

Drew did as he was told, and then he and Trent held on to Paul.

"Come on, then," Sean said to Paul.

Trent and Drew let go of Paul and backed up just a tad.

"I don't want to fight you. You're my son. Let me fight your men. One at a time."

"No. You either fight me or we tie you back up."

At that moment, it felt to Paul as if it were only him and Sean in the room. He knew this was his only chance at maybe getting free so he decided to go for it. He took off running toward Sean, who was still on the other side of the room. He was going to headbutt him but decided at the last second to get a good punch in and Sean allowed him to do it.

Sean stumbled backward as he realized that Paul was stronger than he thought. He wiped the blood from his nose and said, "Not bad. Who knew you could actually fight?"

Paul went to take another swing, but Sean's fist connected with his face before he could. Paul stumbled backward but stayed up. The next thing he knew they were on each other, throwing punches and trying to get the upper hand from each other. The problem was, Sean didn't fight fair. He had a knife that he was able to get to quickly from his waistband and he stabbed it into Paul's stomach. Paul keeled over in pain. He placed his hand on his wound and pulled it away to see blood, too much blood.

"You asshole!" Paul said faintly before he passed out from the sight of his own blood and the trauma he had already witnessed.

A few minutes later he came to and found himself tied up again and back on the sofa.

"Welcome back," Sean taunted him. Then to Drew he said, "We may have to make this a little bit quicker than we originally planned. Keep that in mind."

"Will do," Drew responded.

Brett pulled out a hatchet from the bag that he had carried in with him. It looked brand new and extremely sharp. Paul's eyes got big and wide. "Now," Brett said, "we figured we'd start off small. Maybe take one finger off at a time, then we'd move to your toes and maybe we'd butt fuck you while all this is going on. Drew loves a good tight ass."

Drew laughed. "Yeah, but I don't want his ass. He's a pig."

Brett laughed. "Let me start, guys. Help our friend here put out his pointer finger."

Drew and Snake untied Paul and forced Paul's index finger on his left hand open.

"Now hold still," Brett told him as he raised the hatchet above his head. "I'm not sure how my aim will be with this big thing and your little finger, but I'm going to do my best."

Paul's hand was resting on the arm of the couch. His palm was facing up with all his fingers curled in except for his index finger. He closed his eyes as he heard Brett bring the hatchet down. Brett slammed the hatchet down on his index finger which went flying across the room. He also cut up Paul's knuckles.

"Whoooah!" all the guys yelled as the finger went flying.

Paul screamed in pain as everything went black again but only for a split second.

"That was killer!" Brett laughed.

"Yeah, but you hit his other fingers in the process," Drew pointed out. "Let's use this, instead." He flicked open his switchblade. "I'll go next. I'll do the middle finger." The other guys forced Paul to lay out his middle finger only and Drew bent down and began sawing back and forth on the middle finger. Paul screamed again in pain. This one was much worse because it wasn't as fast.

Sean was watching this and enjoying the show when his text message alert sounded on his phone. He checked the message.

"The cops are on to you. They've just been dispatched to the residence. You guys have to get out of there!"

Sean jumped up. "Enough!" he shouted.

"What?" Drew asked. "We've only just begun. You said to torture him."

"I know what I said, but the cops have been dispatched and are on their way. We've got to get out of here, now finish the job!"

Drew picked up his gun and shot at Paul once before grabbing his bags and running out of the house. The other men scanned the room, making sure they left nothing behind that could tie things back to them, and then took off running.

They ran out into the dark early morning, each going a different direction to their assigned cars. Sean was already gone, as he'd had his driver waiting for him in front of the house. There were no neighbors or other cars in sight. They all were gone within a minute.

Paul sat on the couch, in pain and gasping for air. The bullet had struck him in the chest, just inches from his heart. He was still alive but felt like things were about to go dark, then he heard his front door being pushed open right before he heard Krystal say, "Dad?"

"Police!" someone shouted.

Paul let out the best moan he could muster with the last breath he could afford. He saw the captain standing in front of him before he blacked out.

Chapter 19

Paul woke up in the hospital. His hand was throbbing and his chest and stomach felt like they had a thousand pounds each resting on top of them. He looked around the room and then down at himself and saw that his hand was bandaged up. Everything came back to him as he remembered the torture, the death, the blood, the… "Laura!" he sobbed out loud. "Krystal!"

The captain ran into the room. "Hey, Paul," he said softly. "I'm glad you are awake. How are you feeling?"

"Horrible. I'm in a lot of pain."

"I'm so sorry, Paul."

"I… Krystal? I…I heard her say my name right before I blacked out. I swear I did."

"You did," the captain responded. "She's okay. We have her in a safe house."

"How… I watched Trent choke her and then fire two shots into her."

"No. You watched him choke her and then fire two blank shots into her. Did you not notice that there was no blood?"

"I…I guess I didn't. So she's okay?"

"She's alive. Is she okay? I'm not so sure she is okay mentally."

"Please tell me you got the guys who did this. Please tell me you got them?"

"I'm sorry, Paul. By the time we got there and got the roadblocks set up, they were gone. Who was it? Who did this?"

"The only one I really knew was Trent."

"I knew we should have locked him up."

"It wouldn't have mattered. He was just doing a job that he was hired for. He had been playing Krystal from day one. Even if we locked him up, this still would have happened."

"Was it Sean?"

Paul very slowly, through sobs, told his boss the entire story. The captain took notes, wrote down names, and asked questions. "Do you think you can give an accurate description to our sketch artist of these guys?"

"I think so. I caught all their first names too. Of course the last name of my...my...son is the same as the guy I shot. Craw. How did you guys know to come to the house?"

"The duty officer had been trying to get in touch with Trooper Marx because he had missed his check-in. When they didn't get a response, we knew something was wrong. We got a lot to do and a lot to go on, Paul. I want you to rest and get better. Let me and our guys handle this. We're going to get them, Paul."

"This guy is going to come after me. He's not going to stop until I'm dead. He wants me dead. The only reason I'm still alive is because they got spooked because somehow they knew the cops were coming. They were moving quickly and just shot me as fast as they could before they ran out."

"No one knows you're here, Paul, other than us. We put out word that you died too. They won't come looking for someone who is dead. We're gonna keep you safe."

"What about Krystal? Won't they come after her too?"

"We are still trying to figure that part out. We don't know if not killing her was part of the plan or if Trent just fooled everyone into thinking he killed her. So, we reported that she is dead as well. Just in case."

"I want to see her."

"Not right now. Just know that she is safe and we're taking really good care of her. You need to focus on getting better yourself for right now."

Paul gave no response as the captain got up and left. Paul lay in the hospital bed, alone and angry. He began sobbing. Paul thought about all the things in life that bring you joy and can make you feel great: family, friends, sex, music, the beach. They all bring a certain kind of euphoria into your life to raise you up. Paul didn't think he'd ever feel any of that ever again. He was staring at the things in life that bring you pain and despair: death, deceit, lies, anger, and murder. He wondered how long he would feel the emptiness that he felt. He was missing the only two things in his life that meant the most. His wife was dead and his daughter was somewhere alone and probably scared and it was his fault for the most part.

Paul sat up in bed. His head felt like it was rolling around on his neck uncontrollably. He thought the dizziness would make him pass out, but he just ignored the feeling. He made a fist with his good hand until his fingers and his hand turned white. He squeezed as hard as he could, feeling the pain in his mind seep through his muscles. The regret he was feeling in that moment was almost too much to handle. He didn't want the world to think he was dead. He wanted this guy to come back after him. He wanted to face him one more time before putting cuffs on him. He knew he'd never get that chance, though. He never would have thought that an encounter that happened when he was only eighteen would come back to haunt him like this. It was his fault that his wife was dead. His secrets caused so much pain to her and Krystal. They brought pain to him as well. He thought lying there in the misery inside his head was much worse than the torture. He thought he'd rather be dead and with Laura than lying there and feeling guilt and sadness. He was the one that should have died. He was the one that should have paid. Now he'd be paying for the rest of his life. For the rest of his life, he'd carry the death of his wife on his own shoulders. For the rest of his life, he'd miss Laura.

Paul wiped his eyes with his good hand and then let out a scream that started out as a grumble from the pit of his stomach. It hurt his head to scream like that, but he had to release the anger and rage that he was feeling. He had to do something before he burst into a thousand pieces. He had to feel like he was in control of something, even if that something was only his anger and sadness. A nurse came rushing in to check on him. "Sir? Are you okay?"

"Get me the hell out of here!" Paul shouted as he began to swipe things off of the stand next to his bed. His food and water went soaring through the air and fell onto the floor with a thump and splatter. He kicked his legs and tried to rip out his IV. The nurse yelled for help as three more nurses and a doctor came running in. They held him down and put bed restraints on his ankles and wrists.

"Goddamn it!" Paul shouted, feeling like he was back in his home and being attacked. He felt himself losing control again.

"Sorry," the doctor said, "but this is for your own good."

The doctor had a needle and injected Paul with it. "This will help you calm down and rest."

Paul began to tell him to go fuck himself, but before he could even get the word "go" out of his mouth, he went into a deep sleep.

Chapter 20

Sean was sitting alone in his office. He had just got there and needed a moment alone before he started clearing things out of the office. He sat back in his chair and focused his eyes where the wall met the ceiling. Memories of his childhood came flooding back. He did what he had done for so many years, and ran different scenarios through his head. He dreamed of his real father showing up at his foster home when he was ten and taking him away. He dreamed of having a perfect little life with his real father and his new mother. He dreamed of his father taking him out to his baseball game and cheering for him as he hit a home run. He pictured his father throwing him on top of his shoulders to celebrate the win of another game. He smiled as his sister came over and gave him a high-five, followed by his twin brother. He closed his eyes as he could almost smell the fresh cut grass and the leather baseball gloves. This was his defense mechanism to get out the ugly thoughts in his head. It only worked temporarily, of course. It only took a minute or so for him to snap out of his daydream and come back to reality.

Only, tonight was different. When he snapped back to reality, he didn't have the anger or the rage that he usually did. He had peace. He felt calm. All the years of abuse that he and his brother went through, as well as their mother, was finally dealt with accordingly. It was finally finished. He had made everyone pay, from the foster parents to his real father and his family. He felt vindicated. He had been afraid that even after it was all over he'd still feel his anger and rage, but he was pleased to see that wasn't the case. His mom didn't die in vain now. His brother didn't die in vain now. He made it all right again. Not only that, but he also helped out his sister that he never really got to know.

He pulled out a picture from the top drawer of his desk. It was a framed photo of Krystal. He had printed the picture off of her Facebook page and put it in a frame. None of this was her fault, but he knew he couldn't leave her be. He knew after he killed their father, she would feel pain and sadness for the rest of her life. He didn't want to leave his innocent sister like that. He lightly touched the picture of Krystal and ran his fingers over her face. "Hey, sis," he said out loud to no one. "I hope you understand why I did this. I know that you are in a better place now. I know you feel no pain, no sadness, and no emptiness. It's because of me that you're able to be with your mother and father, something that I will never be able to have anytime soon. I wish I could have gotten to know you, but Trent thought the world of you. He really did. If that guy could fall in love with someone, well, then that someone must be pretty amazing. I bet you were amazing. He only killed you because he had no other choice. I know he loved you, but I had to bring him back to his job at hand. If I didn't interfere, he probably would've tried to save you. You must believe that. I hope that wherever you are right now, that you are appreciating the gift I gave you. The gift of death. Death is better than sex, though. With death, the emptiness feeling will fade and you will float into the heavens and live in eternity with the people you care about. I truly believe that. Death isn't so bad unless you go down to hell. I won't be going to hell, so I'll be with you someday. Then we can be a real family. You'll forgive me, because in heaven you have to forgive. I bet you are feeling no pain right now. That must be a wonderful feeling. I did this for you too, sis. Until we meet again…" He kissed the glass of the photo frame and then threw the picture into a box that was sitting on the floor next to his desk. He felt good.

He turned on his iPod and began blaring some metal music. He turned it up loud, then got up and began taking folders and files out of his desk and file cabinet and putting them in the cardboard box. Within an hour, his office was empty. He only had two more things to do before he got the hell out of dodge to begin his new life. He had turned his cell phone off and knew it was time to turn it back on. He was sure all the guys had been calling and leaving text messages and voicemails. He didn't put the money in their cars like he was supposed to. He wasn't a stupid man. He wasn't going to leave money in their cars before he knew if they finished the job or not.

He was right, there were a ton of text messages waiting from him. He didn't even bother reading any of them. There were a few voicemails but he didn't listen to any of them. He called Drew. "Doyle?" Drew shouted as he picked up his phone.

"The one and only," Sean answered with a chuckle.

"Where the fuck is my money? I've talked to the other guys and they didn't get paid either!"

"Didn't I tell you guys to have no contact with each other after the job was done?" He wasn't mad. In fact, he was close to laughing.

"You also told us we'd be getting paid!"

"And you will! I want you to meet me at the office. I'm going to have your money for you. I want to explain things to you now that it's all over with."

"What about the other guys? They deserve to be paid too."

"They're all getting paid right now!" Sean laughed again. He was laughing because their payment was a bullet to the head. He had no intention of paying them, let alone leaving so many people behind that could turn him in if they got caught. Drew was a different story, though. "Will you come here now?"

"Yes," Drew answered. He sounded calmer. "I'll be there in five minutes."

"Great. Be sure you come alone too."

"Of course, boss." Drew made sure his gun was loaded and went on his way. He wasn't sure if the boss was really going to pay him and let him go now.

Chapter 21

Trent had run to his car as fast as he could after they left. His heart was beating a mile a minute. This wasn't the first time he killed someone, but this was the first time he tried to kill someone that he once loved. He got in his car and took off, but remembered to drive the speed limit. He knew he couldn't bring any attention to himself, even if the world was sleeping at that moment. He began driving, not really sure where he was going, just driving, when he started to cry uncontrollably. "I'm never going to see her again," he said out loud to himself. "Either way, she's gone." The tears came faster now. He could barely see the road through his tears, so he pulled over into a truck stop. "Oh god!" he said through sobs. "I love her! I really loved her…" He coughed as he began choking up on the tears. "I loved her and I probably killed her. What the fuck is wrong with me?" He pounded on the top of the steering wheel with his hands. "Stupid! Stupid! Stupid!" he shouted with each hit. "Ugh! Aaaah!"

He knew how lucky he was that no one, not even Sean, noticed that when he shot his gun at Krystal, no blood came. He put the blanks in when he was by himself before they left to do the job. He knew Drew would take care of killing everyone, so there was no point in worrying about needing real bullets. He also knew that he'd never be able to pull the trigger while pointing his gun at Krystal. He wouldn't be able to let any of the other guys shoot her either. But what he didn't know was if his choking her was too much. He knew she passed out from it, but had he killed her? He wasn't sure, but the fact that she never woke up made him believe that she was dead. He did murder her. He felt horrible.

He rested his hands on the steering wheel and then rested his head on top of his hands. He breathed heavily as he tried to calm himself down. *I had to do it,* he said to himself. *If not, they would've*

killed me. Besides, the money was too good to pass up… The money!
In his freaking out, he had forgotten all about the money. It was
supposed to be in the car already. He opened the glove box and
swiped everything out of it. No money. He opened the center
console and dug through it. No money. He looked under the
passenger seat. No money. He got out of the car and looked under
the driver seat. No money. He crawled into the backseat and looked
everywhere in the back. No money. He opened the trunk. No money.

"Fuck!" he shouted out loud into the night sky. He got back
in the car and tried to call Sean. No answer. He left a voicemail
asking where his money was and then hung up. He called the other
guys, only to find out none of them got paid either. *Would he really
do this to me? He's paid me for the other jobs. What in the world is
going on?* His cell phone beeped at that moment to let him know that
he had a new text message. He eagerly looked at it. It was from Carl,
Sean's accountant:

**"I have your money. Meet me at the park on Centennial
Lane. Make sure no one is following you."**

Trent felt some relief as he put on his seat belt and started the
car back up. He thought this could be some sort of trap and that he
maybe wouldn't be getting paid, but he went anyway. He had no
choice because he had nowhere he could go without money. The
park was about twenty minutes away. When he got there, the park
was, of course, closed, but they had frequently met in this park late
at night. They had found an entrance on the east end that was always
open. He drove the car into the park and parked it out of sight of the
main road. He got out and walked toward their meeting spot in the
woods, using his cell phone as a flashlight so he could see. He found
Carl standing there waiting for him with another guy that he didn't
recognize. "Hey, Carl. I was getting mad when I saw the money
wasn't in my car like it was supposed to be."

Carl smiled. It was obviously a fake smile. "Trent, Doyle wanted to make sure the job was done before any money was given out. Surely you can understand that."

"Ssssuuure," Trent said slowly, uncertain if this was a setup of some sort. "So just give me the money so I can get on with my life."

"I'm afraid I can't do that."

"What? Why not? I did what I was supposed to do." He was wondering if Sean knew the truth, though, about Krystal.

"Indeed you did, and Doyle wanted me to thank you for him. He was very grateful that you didn't turn your back on him."

"His gratitude is noted but it won't help me survive."

"Surviving won't be a problem for you, Trent."

"What the fuck does that mean?"

Carl nodded to the man who was standing next to him. The man had been holding a gun behind his back. He was now holding it in front of him and pointing it right at Trent's forehead.

"What's going on?" Trent asked with terror in his voice.

"The boss doesn't want any witnesses." He popped the trunk of his car to show Trent that the other men had already been murdered.

"What's going on?" Trent asked again.

Carl answered, "I just wanted to show you where you could end up. Doyle ordered us to kill all of them but to spare you and Drew. He trusted only you two, but if you speak a word to anyone about this, or if you get picked up by the cops and squeal, this is what will happen to you."

"No. I won't say anything. I plan to leave the country altogether – if I get paid, that is."

Carl pulled a briefcase out of the trunk and handed it to Trent. "It's all there plus an extra fifty thousand. Take it and get out of here!"

Trent grabbed the briefcase, muttered a thank-you, and took off as quickly as possible.

Chapter 22

Drew couldn't believe the money wasn't in his car like it was supposed to be, and he was wondering if he was even going to get paid at this point. He was confused as to why he was meeting with Doyle. He wasn't supposed to have contact with the boss once the job was finished, so what was going on? He made sure his gun was loaded, just in case the boss had plans of ending him. He didn't like the tone in his voice when he spoke to him on the phone. He sounded different.

He slowly walked toward Doyle's office. His door was open but the music was so loud there was no way Doyle heard him come in. He walked in to find Doyle taping up a box. "Hey!" Drew shouted loudly.

Sean didn't even jump or seem startled. He turned down the music. "Drew!" He put out his hand to shake it.

Drew studied Doyle. He even looked different. He looked like he was ten years younger. He looked happy, genuinely happy. He didn't even have the stress lines going across his forehead like he usually did. In fact, he looked like he had just spent a week at the spa. This just made him even more attractive to Drew and in that moment, he would have done anything for Doyle. Drew slowly put out his hand and took Doyle's in it.

"What's going on? Why are we here?"

"Have a seat!" Sean said as he himself sat down.

"You're not going to pay me, are you?" Drew asked as he slowly sat down.

Sean laughed. He reached below his desk and came up with a briefcase. He sat it down in front of Drew and opened it up. "It's all there. Three million big ones, just like we agreed upon. You can count it if you want."

Drew's eyes expanded. He picked up the bills and flipped through each stack, making sure there weren't fake bills underneath the ones on top.

"I promise you, it's all there and yours to keep, no matter what you decide."

"Decide? What are you talking about?" Drew asked as he closed the briefcase and placed it on the floor by his feet.

"Well," Sean began, "I know that I said this was the last of the job and you did great. You did everything I asked of you and you got it done. I saw the news online and it said that Mr. Jennings was pronounced dead at the hospital. We accomplished what we intended to do. However, there was one person in our entourage who didn't do what they were supposed to do."

"Are you talking about Byron?"

"Of course I am. I can't have him out there. He's too dangerous to me and could help the cops find me if he wanted. The way he took off on me was very disrespectful and you know I don't let anyone treat me like that and get away with it."

"I do know that. So what are you thinking?"

"Well, now that you got all this money, you are free to tell me no and I'll be okay with it. I would like for you to find Byron and bring him to me. You don't even have to kill him. I'll take care of him once he's in my hands."

Drew thought about it. He was rich now and didn't need to do this job or any other jobs. "I don't know, sir. I kind of feel like I should get out while I'm ahead of the game. I mean, a cat only has nine lives. What about the other guys? I bet Trent would be up for it considering the circumstances."

Sean sighed. "I did put Phil on the job but I haven't heard from him in a few days. Either he gave up and doesn't want to tell me, or Byron got him." Sean paused before he spoke again. "Drew, I

310

might as well tell you because you'll figure it out sooner or later. The other guys are all dead...except for Trent."

"What!?" Drew felt his heart leap up into his throat. He didn't care much for the other guys, but they were his family in a sense.

Sean held up his hands as if doing that would calm Drew down. "Hear me out. The other guys did what they were supposed to and they were great, but they were nowhere near as good as you and Trent. I couldn't have all these people knowing what we did. If even one of them were to get caught somehow and they started talking, you and I would be done for."

"Why didn't you off me, then?"

"Because you are my right-hand man besides Carl. I know I can trust you. I know if you were to get caught you'd keep my name out of things. I wasn't so sure of that with the other guys."

"And Trent?"

"Trent and I actually have a past. He got paid, and from what Carl has told me, he has already taken off to leave the country. I don't want to keep using him on my jobs. I want him to have a happy and stress-free life."

"And if I say no to this job? Are you going to off me then?"

Sean chuckled. "No, sir."

Drew liked Doyle calling him sir. He started to drift off into one of his fairy tales with the boss but stopped himself. He knew he needed to stay focused. "With all due respect, boss, even with Byron taking off on you, we were still able to get the job done, right? Why not just let it go and move on? We have a good chance of getting away with this."

"I can't do that. Mainly for the same reasons that I offed the other guys. Byron is much more dangerous though. He can figure out where I'm at any minute if he wants to. That's why I can't go after him myself. If he decides to tell the authorities what he knows, you and I are going to be locked up for life. You know that. To sweeten the deal for you, I'm willing to pay you another one million dollars."

Drew's ears perked up. "Another million? Just to find this guy and bring him to you?"

"Yes. That's all you have to do and I promise you that you can go into retirement afterward. I wouldn't ask if it wasn't important to me." He smiled at Drew.

The smile all but melted Drew. He couldn't say no to that smile. "Well, I guess if it's going to be the last job, then yes. I'll do it, but only under one circumstance."

"Which is?"

"You tell me why in the hell killing the Jenningses was so damn important."

Sean sighed and told Drew the whole story. There was no harm in telling him now why he did what he did. Afterward, Drew hugged Sean and told him he'd find Byron so he could finally end this chapter of his life. Drew thought this was one of the easiest jobs he had ever put him on, but he knew he'd do more for Doyle if he asked. He didn't like hearing all that Doyle had been through and how Paul was okay with not having his own son in his life. He'd do anything for Doyle now. He was off to start his next assignment.

Epilogue
Eight Months Later

Paul woke up with a groggy head and watery eyes. As he lay in his unfamiliar bed and tried to remember where he was and what was going on, a single tear ran down his cheek. Waking up was the hardest part of his new life. When he first awoke in the morning, there were a few single seconds when his mind hadn't started working yet and he had no worries in the world. His mind would go back to his old life. He'd tell himself that he had to get up and get ready to head to the barrack. Then he'd remember that he wasn't going anywhere. Then he'd remember why. Then the tears would start. Every day was the same routine. He'd wake up feeling okay, then remember, then cry. He'd look around at his private room with the white walls and the positive quotes hanging on them. He'd try to give himself a pep talk in hopes of being able to get himself out of the looney bin that he was being held at. That lasted for about five minutes before he gave up and told himself there was no point. It was useless. Then the nurse would come in and give him breakfast and ask him how he was feeling that day. "Shitty" was always his answer. The nurse would give him a smile that screamed pity and tell him to try to think positive.

He would try to eat, but after only a few bites he couldn't stomach it anymore. He had lost weight – a lot. The doctors started feeding him through an IV to keep him alive and nourished. He couldn't fight that. He figured he should consider himself lucky. They first moved him to Sheppard Pratt, and after the captain came to visit him, he got Paul out of there as quickly as possible. The agency moved him to a much nicer facility and paid for everything. An all-expenses-paid trip to the most top-notch loony bin. It really was much nicer than Sheppard Pratt, though. He was thankful for that but it really didn't matter. He had no desire to fight anymore.

It was a strange feeling to wake up in a world where everyone thought you were dead. You didn't even exist anymore. Even the doctors and nurses had no idea who he was. He had his name changed after the state held a fake funeral in his honor. They even placed a dummy in the coffin that looked just like Paul. He saw pictures and the video that was on the news. It was eerie. He also got to see who attended his funeral – lucky him. He was surprised at some of the people that he saw. He paused the video feed so he could take a better look. The church was full of people. His fellow officers, officers from neighboring states that he didn't even know (it's a brotherhood, after all), friends, neighbors, and even that old lady that helped him during his investigation. He saw some coworkers that he didn't even get along with there as well. People were weird when someone dies.

Paul would lie in that room all day. He'd try to do things to keep his mind busy like read or work a puzzle, but it never lasted. His mind always went back to what happened, he'd lose his temper, and then they'd poke him with a needle to knock him out for a few hours. He wanted to get out of that place so that he could help with the search for his estranged son. They still hadn't found him and he didn't think they would. He knew he'd be the only one to find him, but he just couldn't get his mind to work right anymore. He was stuck. He contemplated suicide many times, thinking that being dead would finally reunite him with his wife. He never found the balls to go through with it, though. He wasn't even allowed to see Krystal. The captain thought it would be better to keep them apart, since the world thought they were both dead and it would be too much of a risk for them if they were seen together. He was just starting to accept that this was his life now. He no longer had a wife, a daughter, or a career. His life was to lie there and be sad and angry and be force-fed food and medication. And he was okay with that. Until the day came that everything changed for him. Captain Zitzer stopped in one afternoon as he usually did. "Hey, buddy. How are you doing today?" he asked Paul as he sat down next to him.

"The usual," Paul answered. "Have you spoken to Krystal? How is she?"

"She's doing really good. I think she is one of the strongest people I have ever met in my life."

"I guess I just need to take your word on that since you won't let me see her."

"Actually," the captain responded, "you can see for yourself." He got up and opened the door. "Come on in, hun."

Paul sat up in his bed as he saw Krystal walk in. It was like a ray of sunshine. She looked the same but she did look strong. What was really shocking was that she was wearing a trooper uniform.

"Hi, Dad!" she said as she ran up to him. She fell on top of him and hugged him as hard as she could. They both started crying.

I owe a lot of thanks:

First, my husband, David, who allowed me to bounce ideas off him, who offered some great ideas, and for putting up with me when the only thing I wanted to talk about was my book(s).

Second, my early beta readers who encouraged me to keep going after completing the first draft (which changed drastically): Celeste Gebler, Joe Iacia, Joy Clarkson, Amanda Smith. Without your positive words and love for the book, I may not have kept going.

Third, to Celeste Gebler again just for being you and being, I think, my number one supporter. Also, for giving me some great ideas along the way…especially with the dreaded book blurb!

Fourth, to the staff of The Artful Editor: Naomi Eagleson, Ernesto Mestre, Robin Samuels, and Christina Palaia.

Fifth, to the book designers at 100 Covers.

And last but not least, to you, the reader, for taking the time to read a book by an unknown author just starting out!

About the Author

Joyce Elaine grew up in Clarksville, Maryland, in a big house with a big yard that allowed her to hide away from her five siblings and write feverishly in a spiral-bound notebook or on her typewriter. None of those stories and poems will ever see the light of day, but that passion for writing never left her. Unfortunately, she did what so many other people do and put her passion to the side to live a life she really didn't like. After getting an associate's degree in psychology at the late age of thirty-five, she decided to quit college and go back to the one thing that made her happy when she was younger – writing. When Joyce isn't working at her full-time job, you'll find her reading or writing, banging her head at a rock concert, sitting by the water somewhere and spacing out, spending time with family and friends, or exploring a new state or country she's never been to before. Joyce still lives in Maryland with her husband.

Made in the USA
Middletown, DE
17 August 2022

70553381R00191